MEANT TO BE

TIFFANY PATTERSON

A special thank you to There For You (thereforyou.melissa@gmail.com) for editing.

PROLOGUE

*B*rutus

I'd never seen him like this before. The cold, calculating, and *murderous* intent in his green eyes shone clear as day, as he crouched low in front of the guy in the chair.

"Wake the fuck up!" he growled, slapping the worthless soul that sat hunched over in the wooden chair, hands tied behind his back.

We were in the middle of one of Joshua's underground fighting rings just outside of Portland. Technically, Connor owned the ring, but Joshua was more of the silent partner.

"Brutus! Wake him up!" Joshua ordered.

I peered over at the look of sheer hatred on Josh's face as he kept his eye trained on the piece of shit still tied up in the chair. I shook my head slightly. Not because I felt sorry for the guy. He deserved exactly what he was getting. No. I shook my head because I hated the idea of getting blood on my suit. Nevertheless, as head of security for Townsend Industries and the Townsend family, I often found myself in these less than stellar situations. I didn't regret it at all, I just wished I'd worn a different fucking suit. This particular Armani was my favorite.

I grunted as I retrieved the smelling salts from my left pocket and broke it open. "Wakey, wakey, scumbag," I taunted as I waved the package a half an inch below the man's nostrils.

Within seconds the guy's eyelids were fluttering open. Well, open as much as they could seeing as how they were halfway swollen shut due to the beating Joshua had put on this guy not too long ago.

"Wha-what's happening?" his frightened voice called out.

Joshua stood to his full six foot one inch height, towering over the man in the chair. "Memory lapse so soon?" His voice was eerily light, as if he were greeting an old friend. But the undercurrent of rage was there. Joshua couldn't hide it even if he'd wanted to.

"Let me remind you of where you are, Mike. I can call you Mike, right?" Josh didn't wait for a response. "As I was saying, Mike. Look at me!" he growled, slapping him across the face when his head fell, likely due to exhaustion and pain.

Michael Stephens. That's who Joshua Townsend had tied up in the middle of the basement dwelling of this—from the outside—abandoned building.

"W-why am I here? Let me go!" Stephens demanded, earning him another vicious blow to his ribs. Joshua hit him so hard that the chair he was sitting in swayed and rocked, almost tipping completely over. It was only Joshua's grasping Stephens by his hair and tugging that prevented him from falling over.

"You don't make the fucking demands here." Joshua took a step back, his bare chest heaving and soaked in sweat. He had indeed put a workout in on this guy. "An hour ago you were on a bus to the state penitentiary. Unfortunately, that bus got a flat tire. And in the midst of waiting for the next bus to pick the prisoners up, you, Michael Stephens, escaped."

"What? No, no! That's not how it happened!" Stephens shouted.

"Oh, so you do remember?" Josh questioned, again taunting his prisoner. "Good. Well, that may not be *exactly* how it happened, but that's what the police and the marshals that are now hunting you will think. Don't worry though. They'll eventually find your lifeless body, eaten by the elements. Determine the cause of death was a wild animal attack. You know these woods are full of animals."

He paused again, a dark look covering his face.

"I was going to let you live." Josh made a disbelieving sound with his mouth as if he couldn't believe his own words. "I was. I promised …" He trailed off. "I was going to leave you to the fucking courts to decide your fate. And they did. Seventy-plus years in jail. You would've never seen the outside of the prison walls before taking your last breath. I could've lived with that. I could have. It would've been hard as fuck, but I've learned to control my anger. And cops tend not to do too well in prison anyway. You wouldn't have done well in prison. I planned on making sure of it. But see …" Josh paused, walking around Stephens who followed him as best he could with his head. "Then those fucking tapes came out. They were played in the courtroom. And I had to watch—" He stopped abruptly. "You're a sick fuck. You would've gotten everything you did to those women behind the prison walls. But not after those images. No. You can't continue to breathe the same fucking air I breathe."

"I'm a cop!" Michael Stephens shouted as if that was going to gain his freedom.

"Not anymore," I stated in a half-bored tone. "Remember? You were let go from the force while on trial."

"A fucking cop who used his badge and fellow officers to intimidate women from coming forward." Joshua's hardened face stared down at Michael Stephens as if he was dog shit on the bottom of his shoe. And he was. "Gun," Joshua ordered, holding out his hand in my direction but still staring at Stephens.

I pulled the glock nine millimeter that had been resting in my back waistband and slapped it in Josh's firm hand. He held the gun up to his face and the eeriest smile I'd ever seen extended past his lips.

"This look familiar?" he questioned, strutting in front of Michael Stephens, holding up the gun.

"Wh— Help!" Stephens yelled.

A maniacal laugh fell from Josh's mouth. "Yup, you do need help. I'm sure you'll get plenty of it in hell." And with that final statement, Josh aimed Stephens' own service weapon at him, firing one bullet to his temple, silencing Stephens forever.

3

For a long while, Josh just stood there, staring. Finally, he turned his head, peering over at me.

"Get rid of this," he stated in a businesslike tone. "Time to get your clean-up crew."

"They're already outside, just waiting on the okay to enter."

Josh nodded. "Give it. We're done with this place." And just as calmly as if he were taking a Sunday stroll, he walked right past Michael Stephens' lifeless body toward the heavy metal doors that led to the stairs, which pointed in the direction of the exit. Whistling. He was actually whistling.

I chuckled and shook my head. "Fucking Townsends."

Not many would suspect that one of the wealthiest and business savvy families in the country also held these types of deep, dark secrets. That in basements like this scattered throughout the country, Joshua Townsend not only fought in his underground fight club, but could also dole out death sentences as if he were the undertaker himself.

Of course, just like his two older brothers, Joshua had a reason. Townsends never did anything without rhyme or reason. It's what made them so good. And there was no higher reason for killing Michael Stephens than love.

CHAPTER 1

ine months earlier ...
Kayla

It's just your neighbor, I inhaled deeply, reminding myself.

"I'm coming!" I yelled from my hallway to the front door of my apartment. I rolled my eyes and sighed at the way my heart rate quickened when I first heard the knocking on my door. "It's not them," I murmured as I picked up my steps toward the front door.

I'd lived in my apartment for a few months without any problems, save for my next door neighbor knocking on my door some early mornings. I really needed to relax and get used to my new small town living.

I let out a breath when my suspicions were confirmed as I peered through the peephole and saw the profile of my next door neighbor.

I pasted on a smile and pulled the door open. "Mrs. Bevins." Despite my prior nervousness, it actually was a pleasure to see my seventy-something-year-old neighbor. When she glanced up, smiling, the edges of her eyes wrinkled, I already knew what she was going to ask.

"I hope I didn't wake you, dear."

My smile grew. "Mrs. Bevins, you know good and well what time I wake up. We've been over this."

"Oh well, I didn't want to disturb you too much. I know you've got that big important job to get to. I just had a question. My primary care physician thinks it's time to increase my insulin but I'm not sure about that. What do you think?"

I shook my head. "Hm. That's a complicated answer, Mrs. Bevins. I'd need to see your latest blood work, talk to you more about your lifestyle. But I suspect if you've been eating all of the banana loaves and muffins you're always trying to force on me, we might be able to do something about your diet before increasing your insulin."

Her cheeks grew rosy as she blushed.

"I'm Italian, you know my family likes to eat and celebrate everything with food," she giggled.

"Mhmm. I suspect your family wants you around more than they want the sweet treats. Have you been keeping up your walking regimen?"

"Sometimes."

I tilted my head and lifted my eyebrows.

"Okay, no. But who wants to walk in the rain or the snow."

"Mrs. Bevins, you've lived in Portland most of your life, as I recall. You should be used to the weather changes by now. If weather conditions are your reason for not walking, you'll never get in any exercise. What about buying a treadmill or joining a fitness class at the gym?"

She tapped her wrinkled cheek with her pointer finger, pondering. "I could do that," she replied, and nodded.

I glanced up to read the time display on my stereo system. "We can talk more about this when I get in from work this evening. Is that all right?" I asked while reaching for my light jacket from the rack next to my door.

"Oh yes, yes. Please, go on ahead. I don't want to hold you up."

I gave her a knowing look because I was certain that wasn't the last out of my neighbor. In the short period of time I'd lived in the apartment building, I'd come to recognize Mrs. Bevins as the unofficial welcoming committee. And once she'd decided she liked you, it could be a challenge getting rid of her.

Once again, I was correct in my assessment, when she held the door open, still asking questions here and there as I retrieved my briefcase and keys to head out. She accompanied me all the way to the front door of our apartment building which was two flights down from the floor we lived on, asking questions about her diabetes as well as her husband's health. While her questioning could've been perceived as annoying, I wasn't too bothered by it. Outside of work, I rarely had much contact with other people. Most of the friends I'd made in Portland were still in the city or had moved out of state. And, to be honest, I feared going back to the city much due to the events that'd transpired there, causing me to move.

Besides all of that, I honestly loved the work I did as a naturopathic doctor. I never regretted the nonconventional route I'd taken into medicine. My field was growing and more and more people were recognizing the benefits of preventive and holistic care to not just treat disease and illness, but to avoid them altogether. I'd told Mrs. Bevins my profession soon after I moved into my apartment a little over six months ago. She'd stopped by to welcome me to the building with a basket of her freshly made blueberry scones. She'd seen some of the medical books I had while unpacking and questioned me about my job. Since then, she'd been somewhat of an unofficial patient. Though I leave any prescriptions and diagnosis to her primary care physician.

I inhaled deeply once I stepped outside and I could smell the moisture in the air. The wet patches on the asphalt of the parking lot told of the rain that started and stopped in the early morning hours. Right then, the sun was shining and it had to be close to seventy degrees. It was perfect early spring weather. I thought some type of outdoor activity might be fun.

"Maybe I'll go for a bike ride," I mused while heading across the parking lot to my light grey SUV. It'd been so long since I'd spent any real time outdoors.

That thought was quickly replaced by a sense of dread when I glanced over at my car. A neatly folded piece of notepad paper was tucked under the windshield.

Maybe it's a notice from the building management, I tried to convince myself in spite of the uptick in my heartbeat.

I glanced around at the other parked cars that were in the lot and not one of them had anything tucked in their windshields. Reality was telling me what my instincts were already aware of—this wasn't a note from my apartment's management. I heard my heartbeat in my eardrums as I moved closer to the car. My grip on the canister of pepper spray attached to my keys tightened. As soon as I reached my vehicle, I angrily snatched the paper and unfolded it. I took one last look around to see if anyone was nearby before reading the note.

Primum non nocere

I felt sick to my stomach. *First, do no harm.* A saying that is memorized and quoted by doctors all over the world. A saying I once loved, now was being used as a warning.

"Bastard," I blurted out angrily. But even as my anger rose my eyes misted with fear. I blinked back the tears, refusing to let them fall. I squeezed my eyes shut as images of the last year tried to invade my sanity. I wouldn't let them.

I blinked my eyes open, hand still tight around the can of pepper spray on my keychain. No one was around but I didn't need to see anyone to know who or whom was responsible for this note. For months I'd been harassed. I'd moved three different times, eventually leaving Portland altogether, to a smaller town just outside the city, and still I wasn't safe. One night of my being irresponsible and reckless had caused all of this. It was my fault why I was suffering. I knew that. I just wanted it all to be over with, to move on with my damn life.

Was that too much to ask? Of course it was when you were dealing with an obvious sociopath.

I crumpled up the note in my hands, knowing it would be useless to take to the police. Hell, just the thought of walking into a police station made me want to upchuck that morning's breakfast. I inhaled deeply, before tossing the note into a nearby trashcan and getting in my car to head to work.

I would not let that bring me down. I had started the day in a great mood and I had intentions on keeping it that way. But even the best laid plans get sidetracked when an unhinged person has you in their sights. Halfway through the work day, I was informed by the receptionist at the front desk that I had a call. When she transferred the call, all I heard repeated over and over again were the words *primum non nocere*. I could tell the voice had been put through some sort of voice scrambler but it was him. I knew it was. Or possibly one of his fellow officers he'd recruited to aid in carrying out his dirty work.

I was unsettled for the rest of the day. He knew where I worked and where I lived. I was just starting to get comfortable in my new town and job. It'd taken me months to even feel comfortable or safe enough to decide to go out for a bike ride. I'd moved there with a broken spirit, the same way I'd moved from Williamsport to Portland. But I loved my work. Was I supposed to pick up and leave again? Where would I move to?

You could always go home.

The answer in my head came too quickly to be ignored.

Home.

I hadn't lived in Williamsport in close to seven years. I kept my visits to once a year, around the holidays to visit my parents. And even then, they were no longer than a week, and I avoided major gatherings to avoid running into anyone I knew. One person in particular. But maybe it was time to go back to the place that'd been calling me for more than a few years. My dilemma was only exacerbated when I spoke with my mother later that evening and she once again brought up the subject of my moving back home.

"Ay mija, think of all the people you could help right here in your home city. The clinic we went to that first diagnosed you is still open and in desperate need of volunteers."

My mother knew just what to say to make the biggest dent in my stubbornness. She knew all of my buttons. I supposed everyone's mother was like that. I wrestled all night with my decision, unable to

9

sleep, tossing and turning. My six month lease was up for renewal, which made this the perfect time to move if I was going to. And as much as I denied it, moving closer to my parents did fill me with joy. I'd missed them. And I'd always envisioned myself living and working in Williamsport. It was a dream for both my best friend Chelsea and I to open a joint practice one day to serve people with both conventional and alternative medicine. A dream Chelsea would never get to see.

Reaching for the top drawer of my pinewood nightstand, I pulled out the picture of Chelsea and I. This picture was from our senior prom. We were sitting, huddled together at a table, me leaning into Chelsea's bright, blonde hair as if I was about to share a secret with her. Her shining blue eyes are staring directly at the camera, so loving. Her pink lips turned up into a big smile. My mouth is covered with my hand, my red curls wild and unruly as they fall to my shoulders. My eyes are squinted, giving the camera the vixen, signature look I was once known for. That picture was the perfect embodiment of the two of us.

"I'll make this happen, Chels," I promised as I stared into the picture. I'd betrayed her once. I wouldn't do it again by failing to live out our dream. With that resolution finally made, I was able to turn over and get some sleep.

* * *

JOSHUA

"This better be a goddamned emergency." My tone was sharp as I answered my ringing phone. I hadn't even opened my eyes fully but through the cracks of my eyelids I knew it was before seven in the morning. I wasn't a morning person. Most people in my life knew it. My current project manager damn well knew it but here he was waking me up bright and early as hell.

"Mr. Townsend, there's been an incident at the Crestview property."

That made my eyes pop open fully. "Was anyone hurt?"

"Yes."

Fuck. "What happened?" I demanded at the same time I threw the blanket and sheet off of me and swung my legs over the side of the bed. I listened earnestly to my PM as I moved into the bathroom, brushing my teeth and readying myself to head out the door. I didn't like what I was hearing. And now, I had to take a two hour trip to the Crestview property Townsend Real Estate had just broken ground on two weeks prior, in order to sort this shit out.

Coffee.

I was definitely going to need a huge cup of coffee in order to deal with this. Luckily for everyone involved, I had just the stash I needed. Twenty minutes after first waking up, I entered my kitchen in a fresh suit with the jacket slung over my arm. I used my free arm to open the cabinet that held my various gourmet coffees. I honed in on my favorite flavor and quickly began brewing a pot while I thumbed through my phone for any emails or messages I'd missed during the night. Aside from the standard stuff, there was a reminder voicemail from my mother reminding me of the hospital charity event that was in two days. I grunted at the sight of that reminder. I loved my family but as of late, my mother and father had been on my case about settling down.

My two eldest brothers had married within the previous year and a half, and both of their wives were on the verge of popping out kids. You'd think that'd been good enough for my parents, right?

Wrong.

Very fucking wrong.

Whenever I was in my mother's presence she was trying to pawn off some daughter of a friend of hers for me to take out. I rolled my eyes at the thought. I'd never had trouble getting women. Not with my six-foot-one height, dark hair, green eyes, and these fucking Townsend freckles women seemed to swoon over.

Nope. Getting pussy wasn't the problem.

It was getting them to leave that was the real issue.

But I couldn't exactly explain that to my mother. And as I looked at the reminder message from my mother, my chest tightened with the memory of exactly why I'd kept my distance from anything that resembled a relationship as well as why I felt compelled to donate such as huge amount to the oncology department of the hospital.

I didn't have time to think about any of that right then. Nor did I care to make the time. Shaking off those memories, I poured my coffee into my mug, and screwed the top on. Minutes later I was out of the door of the home I'd only recently moved into, that was in fact, one of my own company's projects.

I lived only a few doors down from my two oldest brothers in Cedardwoods, right outside of the city of Williamsport. We'd all purchased homes in the same neighborhood. I may not have wanted a family of my own, but that didn't mean I didn't want to be close to my brothers and their families.

Due to growing rush hour traffic it took me the full two hours to get to Crestview. As soon as I stepped out of my car, the frowning face of my PM greeted me.

"How's Ron?" I questioned Dennis, my project manager, not bothering with greetings.

I breezed past Dennis to head toward the lot where the accident had taken place, leaving him to trail me.

"He's fine," he began explaining from behind me, walking quickly to keep up with my pace. "A bump on the head from his fall so he's taking the rest of the day off. Medics didn't think there was a concussion."

"He went to the E.R. just to make sure, right?" I leveled a look at Dennis over my shoulder.

"Yeah."

I nodded. "We'll take care of the cost. The last fucking thing I need is a lawsuit from this shit," I grumbled and glanced up toward the dug up dirt where the tractors and other equipment sat. I noticed a few of the workers mingling around the equipment. Everyone had orders from me not to touch anything until I'd arrived.

"Did you get pictures of the tractor?" I questioned Dennis, my eyes still focused on the sight before me.

"Yes, as you instructed."

I nodded and slowed my steps as we grew closer.

"Ron said he arrived e—" Dennis' words were cut off when I gave him a withering glare over my shoulder. I didn't need his commentary at the moment. I trusted my instincts more than anything. I would let them lead me to find out what the hell was going on.

I glanced around the construction site, noting there were only fifteen workers who stood around. "Where's Joseph?" I finally asked Dennis.

He squinted, looking around. "Joseph?"

"There're fifteen guys here, plus you, makes sixteen. Ron is at the hospital. Seventeen. There're eighteen guys who're supposed to be on site today. I know the names of every single one. Where's Joseph?"

Dennis blinked, stunned, and began scratching the back of his head.

I narrowed my eyes on him. This was my first time working with him as my project manager. I didn't like the unsure look he was giving me regarding the absence of one of the workers.

"That's a lot of workers. How'd you know how many—"

"Dennis, do you have children?" It was a bullshit question. I knew he had two.

He nodded.

"And you know the names of your children, right? Who they play with? You protect them by knowing who you let around your kids, right?"

"Of course."

I nodded. "As do I. Townsend Real Estate is my baby. I protect it as would any parent their child. I run background checks on every single person who works on my sites. I know every project Townsend touches, like the back of my hand. I know exactly who is supposed to be on site, when, and for how long. That said, Joseph should've been here an hour ago. Where is he?"

"He called saying his kid was sick. Had to take him to the doctor," a voice called from the group of men who were milling about.

I glanced over at the man who'd spoken. "Thanks, John." I turned back, glaring at Dennis. "And you didn't know that because …"

13

"He probably called and left a message. I haven't checked them yet seeing as how I was dealing with this issue with Ron as soon as I arrived."

I ground my teeth, rolling over Dennis' explanation in my head. I also knew Joseph had a six month old baby at home. I stored that information in the back of my mind for later. Pivoting, I turned and headed over to the tractor, observing it.

It laid on its side, obviously having tipped over. The only good news was that Ron hadn't been inside of the damn thing when it did. He'd turned the tractor on but gotten out to check on something when the it lost control, causing him to jump out of its way. He'd hit his head on the landing and the tractor came to an abrupt stop as it fell on its side.

"What're you looking for? Obviously Ron got sloppy," a voice called out. This one was different than the one that'd spoken earlier about Joseph's absence.

I looked over my shoulder before standing. I narrowed my gaze on the guy who now stared at me. He was average height, sandy blond hair, and dark eyes. *James.*

"You were here when it happened, James?"

His eyes widened slightly at the use of his name. He shook his head and shrugged. "No, but—"

"No, but …" I let that hang in the air for a moment. "So what you're saying is, you weren't here when the tractor tipped over and Ron was injured but you just *happen* to know that *obviously Ron got sloppy.* Is that what I'm hearing?" Tension filled the air around us all as I quietly stared at the worker who was also new to Townsend Construction. From what I was seeing, he wouldn't last too long with my company either.

"Ron has worked with Townsend Real Estate for the last six years. Not once, have I known him to get sloppy with a tractor. But, of course, if you know some information I don't, I'd be happy to hear it." I stopped, tilting my head to the side and raising an inquiring eyebrow.

Silence.

"Didn't think so." Turning back to the tractor, I let my eyes rove over the tractor's underbelly, ensuring that everything was as it should've been. Within a few minutes of my observations, I could tell that everything wasn't right.

"Dennis, what'd you say Ron got out of the tractor for?" I questioned without taking my eyes off the tractor.

"He said he got out to check something."

"I bet he did. Look at this." I stepped to the side and pointed at the loose screws and wiring I saw.

Dennis' face pinched.

"When was the last time all of your equipment was inspected?"

"I'm not sure," he answered hesitantly.

"Isn't that one of our *first* rules of safety? Equipment is to be checked weekly."

"Nobody does that." That same fucking voice.

I turned sharply, my eyes shooting over to James yet again. *This fucking guy.*

"Nobody?"

His lips pinched. "We check as often as possible, but—"

"Another fucking but," I griped before gritting my teeth together. I rarely lost it in front of my employees but this guy was pushing my limits. "Well, this time around it almost cost your head foreman his fucking life, James.

"Now," I turned to Dennis, "this needs to be marked. Nobody touches this tractor until I have my investigators out here to check it over. Your first order of business today will be to get a security team up here to install cameras in your trailer. I'm shutting this site down for the rest of the day. By tomorrow morning, every inch of this community needs to be visible on the security feed.

I turned about to walk away, leaving Dennis to follow me when I stopped. "James, you can come with us." I turned swiftly, walking back to the construction trailer.

I paused, letting Dennis move into the trailer and stepping in front of James just as he was about to enter.

"You can hand over your hard hat and name badge." It was difficult to keep the growl out of my voice.

James' eyes widened considerably. "Seriously?"

"I don't joke about firings."

This guy gave me a bad vibe, right off the bat. Not only had he taken our safety precautions as a joke, but he'd insulted one of my top foremen. Good workers were hard to come by in the real estate business and I wasn't about to let this guy talk shit on Ron. There was also something in his eyes I just didn't like. And I always trusted my instincts. They'd never failed me before.

"You'll be paid through the end of the week," I informed him. "But you are dismissed from Townsend Real Estate. You can give Dennis your hat and badge." I turned on my heels and walked up the three steps into the trailer, and jutted my head for Dennis to take James' belongings.

"You sure about that? He seemed like a good worker."

I glanced up from the files I was looking through to Dennis who now stood in the center of the trailer, badge and hard hat in hand.

"Then I'm sure he won't have a problem getting hired somewhere else," I grunted, looking down at the files.

"I need to review your numbers," I informed Dennis as I sat down behind his desk to pull up the information I was looking for on his screen. I scrolled through the numbers of how many lots that'd had deposits placed on them. So far, there'd been ten deposits put down on homesites, but even more stunning was the fact that four people who had put down deposits had pulled out. That was not a good sign.

"You've got bigger fucking problems than one employee being fired," I informed Dennis.

He frowned, giving me a confused look. "What?" He came to look at the computer screen.

"Four depositors have pulled out over the last month."

"But we were able to quickly replace them with new deposits."

"That's not the point. The problem is there is a reason why these people are pulling out in the first place. Did the sales agent bother to ask them why they were pulling out? I don't see it in the notes."

Dennis shrugged. "I don't work with the homeowners as far as deposits go. Just the building."

Angling my head, I stared at him for a few heartbeats. "You think that's an acceptable answer?"

"Susan is the—"

"I know Susan's role in my company. Trust me when I say I will be speaking with her." I moved from behind the desk and headed to the door. The sales office was across the parking lot in another trailer. "From now on, I want you and Susan communicating regularly about the sales count. You need to understand what's going on with this site just as much as she does."

I waited for Dennis' nod before leaving out of his trailer to go speak with Susan. I had to tear into her for not informing me of the high turnover rate that was occurring with the development. After some digging, I'd found out that three of the former depositors had heard the crime rate in the area was spiking and the school system was failing, which led them to choose another location to build. It was a total fabrication and served as more proof that someone was targeting my company.

"Susan, from here on out, I want bi-weekly sales reports and if you hear anything else about crime rates, failing schools, or any other issues, you let me know immediately."

Once she agreed, I headed back over to Dennis' trailer to speak with the security team I'd had Dennis call. I had them spend the morning going over every detail of the work site over the past twenty-four hours.

Before heading back to my main office in Williamsport, I stopped by the hospital where Ron had been taken. Turns out the knock to the head was rather minor but I still made him take the next few days off. I wasn't about to risk my foreman getting re-injured because he came back to work too soon. That was bad for business. And my gut was already telling me there was a storm that was brewing on the horizon.

What happened to Ron hadn't been an accident. The faulty wiring and loose screws at the bottom of the tractor had told me that. The number of residents who had pulled out of their deposits because of false information being spread throughout the surrounding neighborhoods was another check on my bullshit meter. Something was going down.

And whatever it was was starting to make my left hand twitch. My left hand twitched when something was wrong or I was about to beat the shit out of someone in a fight. I was definitely going to need a few rounds in the ring after everything was said and done.

CHAPTER 2

*J*oshua

"Enjoying yourself, hun?"

Despite my annoyance with the week's events at work, my lips parted on a smile upon hearing the soft tone of my mother's voice. I used my smile to disarm the thread of worry I heard in her voice also. She always carried it when we attended this particular charity event.

"Yes, Mother. How about you?" I asked, staring down into her cerulean eyes that my eldest brother, Carter, had inherited.

My mother's tanned cheeks from the three-day weekend trip to the Bahamas she and my father had just gotten back from wrinkled as she grinned at me. "As long as my boys are doing well, I'm great," she answered, turning from me to stare across the room at Carter and Aaron who were both dressed in tuxedos similar to the one I wore, with their beautiful wives at their side. I watched my mother's eyes soften as they drifted downward to peer at my sister-in-law Patience's bulging belly. She was pregnant with her and Aaron's second set of twins.

I shook my head and took another sip of my champagne. I certainly didn't envy her.

"I'm so glad they worked out their differences."

I snorted. "Worked out? More like your second oldest bullied his wife into marrying him." Love makes men do foolish things apparently.

"Don't let Patience fool you, she may've been reluctant but she wouldn't have married Aaron if she didn't love him." My mother turned back to me and for a second I felt the nerves in my stomach grow.

"Good for her," I quipped, rolling my eyes. Just after taking another sip of my champagne I caught my mother eyeing me. "Don't even start," I warned, in a softer tone than I would've used on anyone else.

My father had already started hinting about marriage, love, and importance of one's own family legacy, earlier in the evening. I was more straightforward with him. Telling him that he could forget it. I'd tried that love shit once and after having my heart ripped out of my chest, I was over it.

I let my eyes drift downward to meet my mother's when she'd gone eerily quiet for more than a few seconds.

Finally, she stated, "Tyler should be arriving soon."

"He's on his way over now. Plane landed an hour ago. He needed to get home to change," I commented, on my youngest brother's arrival, grateful for the change in topic.

My father made his way over to us, stealing my mother away so that he could introduce her to some people. I, too, made my rounds, talking with some of the fellow donors and attendees. Formal events weren't really my thing. I got my adrenaline rush from breaking ground on a property, scouting out the next Townsend Real Estate locale, and from in the ring. But I was a seasoned professional at looking the part at these types of events. With a last name like Townsend, I had no choice.

"You almost look as good in a tuxedo as I do."

"You fucking wish you looked this good in Henry Poole & Co.," I cockily replied while brushing off my shoulder before turning to Damon.

His mocha-colored cheeks wrinkled as he smiled and held up his hand. I met his right palm with my own and we pulled each other in for a half-hug greeting.

"Thought you weren't going to make it," I stated as we pulled apart.

"You know better than that. Work held me up."

"Yeah, plus you didn't want to face me after that beating you got a week ago," I jibed.

"Never that." He stood up straighter, as if I'd bruised his ego. "That young kid had no idea what was in store for him. But I did want to tell you, your right hook was looking a little lackluster the other night. Hope you're not getting soft in your old age."

My eyebrow peaked. "Ask your woman how *soft* I am."

"Fuck you," he retorted.

"No thanks, your woman's got that taken care of. And by the way, my right hook has met your jaw enough times for you to know it's not to be messed with." I narrowed a challenging look at Damon. We were friends, but fierce opponents as well.

"Those were lucky blows you got in. Don't let this tux fool you."

"Yeah? Name the time and the place."

Before Damon could respond, we were interrupted. "Well, look at these two pansies."

My eyebrows lifted as I pivoted and saw Connor O'Brien staring down at the both of us. The guy was easily six-five and stuck out like a sore thumb, dressed in the suit pants, button-up top, and a fucking leather jacket on.

"Only Connor O'Brien shows up to black tie events wearing leather," I commented.

"What's the matter O'Brien, gym not making you enough money? Can't afford formalwear?" Damon teased. "I bet Townsend here wouldn't mind spotting you the bread."

I shook my head. "This guy makes enough off of our joint ventures to have paid for this entire event by himself. He just has no sense of style."

"Screw both of you," Connor retorted.

"I'll pass."

Fighting had brought all three of us together. We each had our own reasons to fight. Mine had also led me to the very event we were in attendance at.

"Well, hello," Damon spoke.

I followed his eyes to across the room to where a group of women were eyeing the three of us. Two wore appalled expressions when they cast their gazes on Connor's choice of clothing. In true Connor O'Brien fashion, he noticed and blew the ladies a kiss before baring his teeth, causing them to quickly look away.

"Asshole." I shook my head, grinning. "If you two will excuse me, I'm going to go introduce myself," I stated, not taking my eyes off of the brunette who was ogling me.

"Yeah, as if she doesn't know who you are already."

"She obviously does."

Connor and Damon responded at the same time.

I ignored them both. I'd intentionally showed up solo to the fundraiser that night. Too many women got to thinking we were actually a *thing* once I'd brought them out to public events with me. But just because I'd shown up alone didn't mean I needed to leave that way. I placed my champagne flute in the hand of a passing waiter.

"Gentlemen." I nodded before sauntering off. I examined the woman as I grew closer. She was cute. About five-five, slim waist, her hair was neatly tucked into some type of style in the back. She was doable.

"May I?" I questioned smoothly with my hand held out. She took it, of course, lowering her lashes demurely. I led her to the center of the ballroom where a number of couples were already dancing. "Are you enjoying your evening?"

She nodded. "Yes."

"Good. A beautiful woman should always be happy," I responded, laying it on just thick enough.

She giggled. It was only slightly off-putting.

"I thought I knew all of the beautiful women attending tonight but I see your name on the list escaped me. I'll have to speak with the coordinators about that. But I won't let it stand in the way of our evening. What's your name, beautiful?"

"It's Denise," she answered airily. "Denise Waters."

"Pleasure to make your acquaintance, Denise."

She laughed as I stepped back to twirl her around.

"You're quite the dancer," she acknowledged.

"One of my many talents." I winked at her, and her cheeks turned crimson. This one was good. She could even blush on demand. I might actually be able to convince myself to get lost in her for the night.

As we continued to dance, I found out Denise was one of the oncology nurses at the hospital. All of the staff had been invited. The smiles I threw her way gave the impression I was hanging on her every word when that couldn't have been further from the truth. In my head, I was calculating the amount of time it would take me to convince Denise to leave this event early. I wouldn't take her back to my home. Nobody went there with me, but I had a condo close by that I reserved for my dates.

Just as Denise was getting to a story about a patient of hers that was helped by money donated to the facility, something at the entranceway caught my attention. A flash of red had me doing a double take. Without even realizing it, I'd completely stopped dancing.

"What the hell?" I questioned out loud, staring straight ahead at the woman in the entranceway.

"Is everything all right?"

I frowned, lowering my gaze to the woman whose name I could no longer remember. "No ... yes. Hell," I grumbled, turning back to the entranceway. A buzzing sound started in my ears as my eyes danced over every inch of her.

Kayla.

The hell is she wearing? was one of my first thoughts. She was dressed in an understated short sleeve black dress that fell a few inches below her knees and a shawl for Christ's sake. What twenty-eight-year-old woman wears a goddamn shawl? Especially, not Kayla. Her style was always much flashier than this.

I furrowed my brows as I damn near gawked, the familiar anger rising in my belly. *She left me,* I reminded myself. My legs, on their own accord, began carrying me closer as I continued to stare, observing. The auburn curls were gone. She now wore that wild mane of hers straight, pulled back in a bun at the nape of her neck. I noticed it when she turned her head to the side, seemingly looking for someone. The cinnamon tone of her skin shone brightly on her five-foot-six frame, made a couple of inches taller by the black pumps she wore. Though the dress was simple, it outlined her lithe body well.

My gaze narrowed when I saw her bite her bottom lip and use her hand to smooth back her bun as if an invisible curl had escaped. This was Kayla, I was certain of that, but something seemed off. Something about the uneasy way she slicked back her hair yet again, told me this wasn't *my* Kayla.

Where the hell had that thought come from? Since when had I thought of Kayla as mine?

I didn't have time to assess the answers to those questions since Kayla turned and looked me dead in the eye. Her eyes doubled in size, exposing every part of her chestnut irises. I could see the wheels in her head moving, contemplating her out.

Not this fucking time.

I moved to stand directly in front of her, blocking any escape she might have considered taking.

She's the puzzle piece I never knew was missing until it arrived. My brother's words from a conversation we'd had in his office months prior echoed in my head. Not until much later, would I pick apart why that particular conversation chose to replay in my mind. At that moment, I had other things to tend to because right then, Kayla's and my eyes clashed for the first time in seven years, throwing me back to the day I learned she'd up and left.

* * *

THEN …

"This is fucking ridiculous!" I spat out before angrily tossing my cell phone against the leather sofa in my living room. It'd been a month since I dropped Kayla off in front of her house and she was still refusing to take my calls. The final straw had been a recorded message alerting me that her number had been changed.

"Fuck this," I grunted, throwing a baseball cap on my head backwards, and grabbing my keys. She could tell me face-to-face to fuck off, but this silent treatment bullshit needed to end. I'd been feeling like I was losing it for weeks. This shit had to end.

I made it down the stairs from my third story condo and to my car in the garage in record time. Before I knew it, I was peeling out of the garage on my way to Kayla's. Normally, the drive took forty minutes to get to her parents' house. This time I was there in twenty-five.

I parked right out front, slamming my car door shut and charging up to the front door, banging on it.

"The hell?" I heard a male grumble from the opposite side of the door. Kay's father. A second later the door was pulled open and an angry looking Mr. Reyes stood there, staring me down with a deep wrinkle in his forehead and daggers shooting out of his chestnut eyes. Those eyes reminded me so much of Kayla's.

"Mr. Reyes, I need to speak with Kay." I tried to sound as respectful as possible but it was difficult.

He folded his arms across his burly chest. He was a few inches shorter than my six foot one height, but he was wider. As he stood there sizing me up, the hint of resentment I'd always felt come from him was no longer in hiding.

He began shaking his head. "No."

My anger flared. "Mr. Reyes, I don't know what your problem with me is and I don't care, but I need to speak with—"

"I said no!" he barked, widening his stance to prevent me from seeing inside of the house.

Our height differential made his endeavor null and void. I could easily see behind him into the house. My eyes readily searched for any signs that Kayla was inside. I'd seen her car parked in the driveway as soon as I pulled up.

"I know she's home. She won't answer my calls. Just let her know I'm here," I insisted.

"Ay, dios!" he commented in his native Spanish. "Que no entiende ese hombre!"

"I understand quite well that you're hiding Kay from me. The reason why, however, is beyond my understanding."

His eyes widened. I guessed he'd forgotten I was fluent in Spanish. His daughter had taught me. She was extremely proud of her Afro Latina roots.

He sighed, angrily. "Kay doesn't want to speak with you. Just leave my daughter alone!" He stepped back and went to shut the door in my face.

Too bad for him, the door slam was stopped by my foot in the door.

"Listen, son …" he growled.

"Where the hell is Kayla? I know she's here!" I shouted, feeling close to unhinged.

"She's not here!"

"Bullshit!" I shouted, forgetting that both of my parents had raised me to be respectful toward my elders. To hell with that, they weren't there, and I felt as if I was coming apart at the seams. I'd already lost Chelsea, I couldn't lose Kayla, too.

"Watch your mouth, son!" Mr. Reyes shouted. "This little friendship you've had with my daughter is over. Kayla's moved. She's in Portland."

I paused, the grip I'd had on the edge of the door slackened, and Mr. Reyes was able to get the door closed with me on the outside of it.

"He's lying!" I insisted to the open air. I began pounding on the door with my fist and ringing the doorbell incessantly. "Open the goddamn door!"

"Leave here now. I don't care how much money your family has, I will call the police!"

"Call 'em!" I didn't give a shit at that point. I continued to bang on the door and when that got me nowhere, I moved to pounding on the windows at the front of the house. "Kayla, come out here!" I shouted, moving toward the back of the house, to the window I knew belonged to her bedroom. She had to be in there. In the background I could hear Mr. Reyes had emerged from the house, yet again. This time he was on the phone calling the police.

Let them come, I thought. Every ounce of decorum I'd had abandoned me. I was known as the rational and even charming Townsend brother. But at that moment all I felt was anger mixed with pure pain. Those two emotions had driven me to behave like a caged animal over the last month.

"Sir. Sir, you need to come with us." I distinctly heard behind me in a firm tone. My arm was being pulled. That was when I took the first swing at whoever was grabbing at me. I needed to get to Kayla.

"We will arrest you!"

"Get the fuck off of me!" I growled, yelling and still swinging.

The vague knowledge that it was the police who were talking didn't calm me down. Next thing I remembered, I was being carted off the Reyes' property, my head being pushed into the back of a police car. I locked eyes with a furious Mateo Reyes as the squad car drove off. My gaze narrowed as I stared just as aggressively at him, my arms locked behind my back at the wrists by the metal handcuffs.

"WHAT A MESS you've gotten yourself into."

I barely acknowledged my father's words, rolling my eyes and snatching my belongings from the officer behind the desk. I squinted against the sunlight as I passed through the police station door behind my father. I wasn't in any real mess, not legally anyway. I wasn't formally arrested or charged with anything. The police captain did my family a solid by personally calling my father and having him come pick me up. The rest of my life had felt like it was going to shit, however.

"Look at me, Joshua."

Begrudgingly, I lifted my gaze to meet my father's stormy eyes. Usually, any look of disappointment I saw reflected in his gaze directed at me, would cause me to straighten up and get my shit together. But right then, I just didn't care. I could barely see straight through all of the anger I was carrying.

My father had just explained to me, before we left the police station, that Mr. Reyes hadn't lied. It was true, Kayla had moved to Portland to start medical school a month early. She left me completely and utterly alone. Fuck her.

"Son ..." my father tried to console, placing a firm arm on my shoulder.

I didn't want to hear it. I shrugged off his hand and proceeded to his awaiting, chauffeured SUV. I waved the driver off and opened the door myself, climbing in. My father rounded the vehicle and got in on the other side after a few hushed words with the driver.

He didn't say anything for a while.

I was thankful for the silence. I wasn't in the mood to hear or discuss how upset this would make my mother, or how it would be an embarrassment if this got out to the public. But, per usual, my father surprised me when he finally did speak.

"You've always been my slow to anger son."

I pivoted my head in his direction but he stared straight ahead.

"People know to stay out of Aaron's way when they see him coming. Carter doesn't wear his anger on his sleeve the way Aaron does, but his temper is quick. Ty is my unpredictable child. But you ... you've always been the steady, even-keeled one. At least," he paused, turning to face me, "that's what you wanted everyone to believe. You've got that intensity in you just like every other child of mine but you mask it with that easy-going charm. It'll serve you well as you build our real estate division." He paused, finally turning to me. "If your anger doesn't take you down first."

I remained silent, still feeling too consumed with resentment to even speak.

He nodded slightly. "Yeah, that's what I thought." He sighed.

A few minutes later we were pulling up to an unfamiliar brick building in the heart of Williamsport.

Frowning, I watched my father get out and fold his arms over his chest, waiting for me to do the same. I pushed out a breath and slid over to get out of the car on the side closest to the sidewalk.

"We'll be a little while," he spoke to the driver before looking to me. Silently communicating that I was to follow him.

I did so as he pushed past the glass doors of the building. I was surprised when instead of heading toward the elevators he moved to the stairwell. He headed downstairs instead of up.

"You've gotten in three fights over the last month," he stated, continuing down the steps.

I remained silent because the truth was I'd actually gotten into more but he'd obviously only heard of three.

"So now, we're going to put that energy to use." He stopped at a large metal door that read "Private" in black spray paint.

He knocked three times in quick succession, pausing for a heartbeat and knocked two more times. Some type of coded knock.

"Robert," a large man with sandy blond hair greeted. He wasn't friendly looking, but he obviously knew my father. What was really odd, was that he looked to be in his mid-twenties, closer to my age than my father's. Most men my age referred to my father as Mr. Townsend.

The guy let his gaze rove over me, causing me to feel defensive. I stood up to my full height, which was still a few inches shorter than this guy.

"This him?" he questioned, still staring me down.

"Don't ask dumb questions, Connor," my father retorted.

I squinted. Connor O'Brien. I recognized him. He'd been an up and comer in the boxing world.

He motioned with his head and stepped aside, allowing my father and I to enter. I was hit by the humidity in the room—not from the summer weather outside, but from the many bodies in motion around the room. Before my eyes was a large room that had been converted into a boxing gym. At the center stood a large ring where two guys were circling one another. To the far right hung a row of heavy bags, three that were in use at the moment. Behind the ring was another row of speed bags, two of which were being used. Opposite the heavy bags, to the far left, were two makeshift fighting squares where two men were locked in some sort of ground battle. An older man stood over them, yelling directions.

"A boxing gym? Fucking seriously?" I turned to my father with a scowl on my face. The hell was he doing bringing me here?

Both Connor and my father shared a look. I narrowed my eyes, not liking the feeling of being left out.

"This," my father finally began, "is your new training spot."

My head shot backwards. "Come again."

"You'll be training here."

"Training for what?" I glanced around skeptically.

"Life," my father stated.

"What?" I glared at him as if he'd lost his damned mind. Because obviously he had.

"Listen," he began, grasping me by the shoulders tightly, "you need to learn how to channel that anger and grief because it's eating you up. I know losing Chelsea has been rough. Obviously, Kayla leaving was another hard blow. This place," he nodded to the surrounding gym, "is where you will go to let all of that shit out. No more bar fights or threatening to beat up your friend's father."

I should've been ashamed for that last part. Threatening Mr. Reyes was never my intention but he'd gotten in my way.

"Aaron takes his aggression out at work, Carter has the military, Ty has football, and now you have fighting." He loosened his grip and took a step back.

Connor, who'd been watching us quietly, stepped forward. I noticed a pair of lightweight boxing gloves in his hand. "Let's see what you got," he said as if he didn't expect much from me, tossing the gloves in my face.

I caught them easily, never taking my eyes off of him. I felt my lips turn up into a snarl. I didn't like the appraising look he was giving me.

"What the fuck!" I yelled and ducked, just narrowly missing

Connor's massive fist. I barely had time to recover from the first swing, when I was ducking and swerving again, dodging the second one.

"He's quick," Connor tossed over my shoulder to my father.

"I told you."

"Ah, shit!" Connor growled when one of my fists landed in his stomach.

I felt the bruising of my knuckles against the muscles of his abdomen, but much more satisfying was the thrill of landing a solid punch. I went to swing again, but my arm was caught in a vice grip.

"Not so fast, Townsend. You've got a lot to learn before you can take on the head guy."

I turned, coming face-to-face with the older man who'd been yelling at the two grappling men at the other end of the gym. He appeared to be in his mid-fifties, but the strength in which he held my arm spoke to just how seasoned he was to be in a place like this.

"Don't touch me," I seethed through clenched teeth.

He nodded his head, and took a step back before releasing me. "Your father was right. You've got a lot to learn." He turned to my father and nodded. "We'll keep him."

"Good. I'll be back in a few hours."

I glanced at my father in confusion, but didn't say anything. I wasn't about to beg for him to stay like I was a scared little boy. Instead, I moved toward the center ring. The two men who were in there when I first entered had vacated it, leaving it empty.

"Ah, no. Not on your first day," the older man stated from behind me.

"Take him to the bag, Buddy."

"I don't take orders from you, O'Brien," he growled. "Let's go, kid. The heavy bag is your first stop."

I lifted a brow.

"You need to learn how to throw a proper punch."

"I know how to fucking punch."

"Yeah?" His eyes lowered to my hands.

"Been in plenty of fights and haven't gotten my ass kicked yet," I affirmed, cockily.

"You keep punching the way you are and you're going to have more than some bruising on those knuckles. To the bag!" he ordered.

I narrowed my gaze and took another look at him, assessing him. After a minute's hesitation, I reluctantly moved in the direction of the punching bags. I silently followed his instruction on how to land the proper punch, as to avoid the most damage to my own hands, while still causing plenty of damage to my opponent. After a few run throughs, he taped up my wrists and hands, handed me back the pair of gloves, and stood opposite me, holding the heavy bag in place to allow me to wail on it.

"That's it!" he yelled when I would hit the bag to his liking.

"Is that how the fuck I taught you?" he'd yell when I'd revert back to my old punching style.

"Now you're just getting sloppy!" he yelled when my anger rose, causing me to throw punch after punch, clumsily.

On and on it went. I punched and punched. I don't remember how long it took for the flashbacks to start coming, but they did. The flashback of the first day I met Chelsea in kindergarten. The day she introduced me to the new girl in school in sixth grade. I remembered being in awe seeing Kayla's naturally auburn hair against her cinnamon skin for the first time. The smile she gave me when we met had me tongue-tied. I swallowed and hit the bag harder as my memory took me to that horrible day in Chelsea's doctor's office when she cried in my arms upon hearing her cancer diagnosis. *A rare and aggressive form ...* The doctor's words echoed in my head and I hit the bag harder.

"That's it!" Buddy called, oblivious to the fact that I'd zoned out, at least I thought he was oblivious. "Let the anger out. Put it into the bag."

He knew what I was doing.

By the time my father arrived two hours later, my arms felt like lead and my lungs burned from all the exertion.

"See ya tomorrow, kid," Buddy called.

I nodded. "Tomorrow," I agreed in between gulps of air and sips of water. I had nowhere else to go. My career with Townsend Real Estate didn't hold the same appeal after Chelsea's death. Kayla was gone, off living her life in Portland without so much as a good-bye. The two closest people to me in the world were gone. My family was there but they didn't get it. Besides, they each had their own lives. I might as well return to that dark room where nothing mattered but fighting. *This is what I need*, I thought as I followed behind my father as we exited the gym.

* * *

JOSHUA

"Long time no see." My voice was cold as I pulled myself from those long ago memories and refocused on Kayla in the present.

"Joshua." Her voice was just above a whisper.

"Hey, Joshua."

An instant glower covered my face at the intrusion of the male voice to my right. Still, I kept my eyes trained on a squirming Kayla.

"Dr. Carlson," I stated as he appeared in my peripheral, moving next to Kayla, who'd taken a step back.

"I see you've met our new naturopathic doctor."

I cocked my head to the side. "Really?"

Kayla noticeably swallowed.

"Yes, Dr. Reyes comes highly recommended all the way from the West Coast."

My belly filled with a warm anger I fought hard to keep from showing on my face. This man knew more about Kayla than I did. That didn't sit well with me at all.

"Dr. Reyes and I are old friends," I told Dr. Carlson, briefly looking to him before putting my full attention back on Kayla, who remained uncannily silent. "Luke, how about you let a pair of old friends catch up?" I tossed him a friendly smile, while reaching for Kayla's hand. I got the sense she was just on the verge of trying to get away but I wasn't allowing that.

Out of the corner of my eye I saw Dr. Carlson narrow his gaze but eventually shrugged it off and left us. I pulled Kayla a few feet into the ballroom, still clutching her hand in mine as I turned to her.

"Cat got your tongue?"

She lowered her head before lifting it again, squaring her shoulders. "I-I'm just surprised to see you here."

"That wasn't the greeting I was expecting," I noted.

She gave a shy smile and something in my chest shifted. "Hi, Joshua," she stated in that raspy voice of hers.

One second I was staring down into those dark brown eyes that were framed by long lashes and the next she was wrapped in my arms. The anger I felt was there, but a need to know she was real and standing in front of me, became more important than my anger.

For the first few seconds she remained stiff, but eventually she melted into my hug.

CHAPTER 3

*K*ayla

Home.

My eyelids floated closed and I became wrapped up in the scent of lavender and cardamom with a hint of cedar. I inhaled deeply. This hug felt more like a homecoming than the taste of my mother's pasteles.

I'd been back in Williamsport for a little over a month. Had been staying with my parents for that same amount of time. However, I hadn't truly felt as if I was home until the exact moment Joshua Townsend wrapped his arms around me. That wasn't good news.

I don't know who broke the hug first. It probably was Joshua, if the hard glare he was giving me was any indication. How he could go from hugging to grilling me was beyond me. But that darkness that I remember seeing in his eyes as a kid was still there and right then it was focused on me.

For what felt like forever he just stared down at me; that beautiful jaw of his, which was decorated by neatly trimmed hairs, was rigid.

"Seven years you've been gone without a word and just show up to my fundraiser?" His voice was so full of accusation.

I glanced around, searching for a comeback. "I didn't know this fundraiser was hosted by Townsend—"

"Not Townsend, *me,*" he corrected. "The oncology department of Williamsport General."

A pang in my belly and my eyes briefly closed. Yes. It made sense why he'd have a fundraiser for this hospital's oncology department. We'd spent a lot of time in these halls once Chelsea got sick.

"I didn't realize—"

"You would have if you'd stuck around."

His sharp tone stung almost as much as my guilt had but I squared my shoulders and looked him directly in the eye.

"I was working on my medical career to be able to help people."

"Is that what you were doing?" he asked snidely.

"Yes."

"Looked more like you were running, from my vantage point."

I narrowed my gaze on him. "And where exactly is that vantage point? From the crack of your—"

"There you are, Joshua," a slender brunette interrupted my reply.

For a split second, Joshua looked just as annoyed as I felt at seeing the woman. But within the blink of an eye his annoyance was gone so fast that I was sure I'd imagined it.

I wish I could say the same for my own feelings. My lips pinched as I watched the woman place a perfectly manicured hand on Joshua's forearm. I took a step back when something inside of me wanted to push her away. Joshua wasn't my possession … hell, we weren't even friends anymore, obviously. That was my fault, and I knew it. I'd take responsibility for the ending of our friendship.

"Denise," Josh murmured.

She had to be his girlfriend. She looked like his type. Beautiful and demure enough to fit in with his high society crowd. I wasn't surprised to see Joshua had moved on. It had been seven years and he was a very good-looking, wealthy man in his prime. I had to refrain from observing too closely just how good looking he was in the tailored black and white tuxedo that draped over his fit and lean body. His chiseled jaw was evident even through the light coat of the beard he now wore. The contrast of the darkness of his hair and the sparkling green of his eyes was still enough to cause a weakness in my knees. And those fucking freckles. *Jesus.*

"I'll leave you two alone," I commented just loud enough to be heard before I sauntered off, grabbing a champagne flute from a passing waiter.

Unfortunately, I lasted at the charity event for another hour. My aim had been to go, make sure a few of the doctors I worked with saw me make an appearance, and get the hell out of there. Just as my luck would have it, my boss insisted I meet with a few of her patients, which turned into more questions on my field and the type of medicine I practiced. And of course, as often happened with my line of work one of the traditional doctors I was introduced to took the time to challenge my credentials. I wasn't a stranger to doctors who believed naturopathy was the way of quacks. It wasn't *real* science in their estimation. My degree was a joke. And every one of these doctors that I'd come across had a story of a patient who knew of a friend of a friend who'd listened to a naturopathic doctor and ended up dying from their very treatable form of cancer. It was bunk. I would've told him that, too, if it had been a few years prior. Instead, I just smiled and restated the rehearsed defenses of my practice before gracefully bowing out.

I managed to get away from my colleagues when I looked across the room and saw Joshua dancing with the woman from earlier. A weird sound escaped my mouth when I saw him lean down and say something meant only for her to hear. Just as he rose, he looked up and our eyes met again. My belly quivered, not for the first time at the sight of those emerald eyes, which held just a hint of danger in them. Without my permission, I was thrown back to the last day I'd seen those eyes up close.

* * *

THEN

The heaviness in my heart grew with each passing step as I hiked

37

through the wooded trail. A few feet ahead of me, Joshua kept up a steady pace, but his head was hung low. The burden of what we were doing on this trail weighed us both down. We were getting closer. The thunderous sounds of the waterfall grew louder with each step. My heart rate quickened in anticipation and the load on my chest doubled. I'd waited for years to finally see this place and the one person I wanted to see it with wouldn't be there.

That wasn't entirely true. Technically speaking, Chelsea was there.

My eyes misted as I gazed up ahead in Joshua's direction and saw the beautiful gold and ceramic urn he held carefully in his arm.

"You okay?"

I inhaled and peered up, my gaze clashing into emerald green orbs that were devoid of their usual shine.

"Yeah." I nodded, lying.

His eyes continued to rove over my face, assessing my mood.

Guilt swirled in my chest. He was hurting just as much as I was, if not more, but here he was looking out for me.

"We're almost there."

I nodded again, unable to speak when an unfamiliar warmth flooded my veins when he took my left hand in his. I sucked in air and let him lead me the remaining distance to the waterfall. He was right. In less than five minutes of us walking hand in hand, I glanced up and my breathing hitched. There stood a twenty-foot waterfall, spilling into crystal clear water. I could actually count the smooth, earth-colored stones that sat at the bottom of the lake, undisturbed by the rushing water above. My eyes danced around the forest surrounding us. The greenery was still dripping with water from the thunderstorm that'd passed earlier that day. Inhaling my lungs filled with the scent of the moss and trees mixed with the dampness in the air.

"She said this place was majestic." A lump formed in my throat when I felt Joshua's hand tighten around mine. I was about to pull my hand from his, but when I looked over my shoulder to see his profile, I thought better of it.

In spite of the sadness written all over his handsome face, he chuckled. "Leave it to Chels to use words like *majestic*."

"Yeah," I laughed, too. "She was such a geek … and a romantic." I'd meant it to be funny but my voice broke on the last word and a sob escaped my lips, the tears now coming. I can't recall how or when but I found myself bracketed in strong, muscular arms. His hold was tight, almost too tight, but for some reason, not tight enough. I gulped in air, trying to force myself to stop crying. That time my nostrils filled with the odor of lavender, cardamom, and cedar. His signature scent.

I could stay here forever.

Thankfully, that thought alone shook some good sense into me and I pulled back, albeit reluctantly.

"I'm sorry. This is hard for you, too. You shouldn't have to comfort me." I wiped away the tears that'd fallen but they kept coming.

"Don't be sorry," he affirmed, cupping my chin and raising my gaze to meet his.

I swallowed the lump in my throat, as I peered up into his eyes, that held a darkness I always found intriguing. I stepped back and looked around.

"I hate that she's not here." Sighing, I ran a hand through my unruly mane of curls. "She talked about this place so much when you two first found it. She promised to bring me as soon as my doctors gave the approval after my transplant." But then she got sick. I unconsciously ran my hand over my abdomen, feeling the two-year-old scar that ran down the entire length of my stomach. I hated that my illness had stolen so many moments of my life.

"Don't do that," his deep voice urged, thick with sadness.

I looked up. "Do what?"

"Blaming yourself for time lost. Chels would be pissed if she were here."

I blew out a frustrated breath. "I know. I just … wish it could've been different. She loved being outdoors but she spent so much time inside with me when I was sick or in the hospital."

"And you returned the favor."

I gave him a weak smile but didn't say anything. I wouldn't suck him into my regret. Instead, I watched as he carefully shifted the urn from his left to his right arm, and began rooting around in the pocket of his shorts. I wrinkled my brows when he pulled something out, but then I gasped when I realized what it was. In between his thumb and pointer finger he held a stunning diamond ring, that to my untrained eye looked to be at least two carats. The band was surrounded by smaller diamonds.

"I bought it the day before she was diagnosed." His voice was as heavy as the grief I felt. I reached out, grasping his hand for comfort the same way he'd done to mine earlier. "I was going to wait until after graduation …" He paused, angling his head, looking at the ring as if it held the answers to some mystery.

"But then she got sick," he continued. "I put off asking, wanting the timing to be right."

The timing was never right. Months before we were scheduled to graduate, Chelsea—Joshua's girlfriend and my best friend—was diagnosed with an aggressive form of ovarian cancer. She spent most of her senior year at Williamsport U in and out of the hospital undergoing extreme chemo and radiation treatments.

The worst part was, no one saw it coming. I was the sick one. She and Joshua were always the ones comforting me in hospitals.

The three of us had been close since middle school, all of us having attended Excelor Academy where my mother was a teacher. I remember being nervous the first day, wondering if I'd fit in with the rich kids that went to the school. Though we were firmly middle class, my parents could've never afforded to send me to Excelor if my mother hadn't taught there.

On my first day at Excelor a bright-eyed, blonde-haired girl named Chelsea Armstrong introduced herself, welcoming me to the class. We became thick as thieves almost over night. I met Joshua that same day when our teacher assigned the three of us to a group assignment. I couldn't stop myself from staring at him. Though his smile was easy and disarming there was something about his eyes that easily pulled me in. The way even some of the upperclassmen moved out of his way while walking down the hallways, not because of his last name, but because of the assuredness with which he moved through life, was intriguing. I'd never met a twelve-year-old boy with such confidence.

That same tween boy, grew up to be an incredible man. I wasn't the only one who'd noticed either. During our junior year, Chels revealed to me that she'd grown a crush on our long-time friend.

I'm going to tell him, she'd said that night in our dorm room.

I swallowed down the "No" that wanted to escape and plastered the most sincere smile on my face I could manage and told her, "*Go for it, you only live once.*"

And she did.

The two became a couple soon after, Joshua deciding to let go of his philandering ways to commit to Chelsea.

They were the perfect couple. Both from well-to-do families. Each of them were probably what the other's parents had in mind for them when they grew up and married. I couldn't stand in the way of that. So, I encouraged their relationship.

"No use for this now." His voice pulled me back from my ruminations. Joshua took one last look at the ring before standing and flinging it in the water.

I was shocked but didn't say anything. Just silently watched him as he sauntered back to the boulder, sitting next to me. My heartache grew and my gut twisted with guilt, and just the tiniest bit of jealousy.

I inhaled and pushed my petty emotions down. Leaning over, I rested my head on his shoulder. "This place looks just the way she drew it." I sighed. "Remember when she decorated my hospital room with all of her pictures of this place?" For the first time in weeks, there was a lightness in my voice at the sharing of the memory of my best friend.

"She spent hours drawing this place to decorate your room," Josh continued.

We reminisced over the next hour of memories of Chelsea. Josh even teased me about getting her into trouble when I convinced her to sneak me in my favorite fudge brownies during one of my hospital stays.

"Your nurse flipped her shit." He laughed, causing me to as well.

"I know, but I wanted one sooo bad and Chels could never say no to me." I giggled. That's how it was with us. I may've been the sick one, at first, but I was the mischief maker while Chels was the quiet yet loyal one. Josh was the charmer of the group. "But you stepped in and easily disarmed Nurse Ratchet's temper."

His laughter bubbled up from his chest and my heart squeezed. I lowered my head, feeling ashamed for some reason.

After a lull in our conversation, Josh retrieved the urn that he'd lowered to the ground, onto his lap. The heavy mood as to why we were there in the first place returned. This is where Chelsea insisted we leave her ashes.

"I want to be outside, not left on a shelf or a mantel. I want to be a part of nature's regrowth."

She'd said those words just days before she died, making Joshua and I promise to carry out her wishes. I'd promised but had my doubts as to whether I could honestly ask Mr. and Mrs. Armstrong for their daughter's remains. She was the light of their lives. But, once Joshua Townsend made a promise to do something, he carried it out, full steam ahead. Even if it broke his own heart to do so. And from the tremor I heard in his breathing, I just knew it was tearing him apart.

I silently watched as he pulled the lid off of the urn.

"We'll do this together," he stated, glancing down at me.

I nodded, obediently.

We stood and walked closer to the waterfall, where the water was a little more rough. We paused at the same time, a feeling overtaking us that this was the right spot. I felt the spray of water hitting my face and bare arms.

"Ready?" he asked.

I shook my head. "No … but it isn't up to me." I reached out to cup the urn, and Josh maneuvered his strong hands over mine.

"Rest in peace, Chels."

"Rest in health, Chels."

We stated at the same time as we set her free. A second later, my knees went weak as I heard the thud of the now empty urn falling right by my feet before I was again embraced in capable arms. We held onto each other as we cried. I'd never cried so much, not even when I believed my own death was inevitable. The tears felt like they would never end.

* * *

"Thanks for driving," I stated, foolishly. I turned my head to stare out the passenger side window of Josh's car. I squeezed my fingers when I felt his intertwine with mine for the umpteenth time that day.

"Like I would've trusted you to drive."

My lips twitched. He was right. I was a terrible driver. I attributed it to my late start behind the wheel. I'd only had my license for a year.

"Jerk," I retorted at the same time as we pulled up in front of my parents' home.

Josh snorted. He turned off the car and pressed his head against the leather headrest, closing his eyes and pushing out a breath.

"This shit hurts," Josh grunted, shaking his head.

I lowered my head. The tension and bereavement in his voice nearly shattered me. But I knew what he meant. Life without Chelsea Armstrong just didn't make sense. We'd graduated from college a month prior and had our whole lives ahead of us.

"We were supposed to go to med school together," I added. I looked up when his hand tightened around mine. My throat squeezed at seeing his eyes boring into mine.

"You'll make it." His voice was so low, but steady and reassuring.

"But not with her. We had so many plans together. Graduate college, med school, travel ..." I trailed off.

"All of which, you'll still get to do."

I shook my head. "I'm thinking of postponing med school," I nearly whispered.

Josh sat up fully, his head moving closer to mine. "What?"

His voice was so hard I flinched a little.

"I-I just don't think I'm ready. Chels was the smart one—"

"You graduated with a four point oh, top of your class. What are you talking about?" His voice was unyielding.

43

I ran my free hand through my hair, feeling anxious. I knew I wasn't making any sense. Being physicians had been both my and Chelsea's dream.

"I'm not saying forever, just a year ... or two."

"Or *two*? Chels would kill you. Hell, *I'd* kill you. You were born to help people, Kay."

My lashes lowered at my nickname on his lips. The fluttering in my belly started and suddenly it seemed as if someone had sucked out all of the air in the BMW.

"Don't quit on this."

I pinched my lips. "What about you? You were supposed to start at Townsend Real Estate last week and you weren't there," I charged, needing to turn the attention off of me.

His lips tightened. "That's different."

"How so?"

"It just is."

I gave a mocking laugh. "Real estate is your passion. You were drawing up luxury home plans at fourteen. Practically had your own office in Townsend at sixteen. But now you're blowing off work and telling me it's different than delaying med school for a while," I accused.

"It just is!" he yelled before clamping his mouth shut. His jaw ticked as he stared out the windshield.

Thick silence filled the car. I stared at his profile and my belly fluttered. Instinctively, I reached up and ran my hand along his jaw, then cupped the back of his head.

He lowered his forehead to mine, closing his eyes. He was silently apologizing for yelling. He could save it. I didn't need it. We both were dealing with a broken heart. Mine was broken for two reasons but he didn't need to know that.

"We'll figure it out." Sighing, I opened my eyes, which had drifted closed. I realized our lips were mere millimeters apart. I looked up to see Joshua's eyes were still closed. I berated myself even before I made a move.

This was wrong.

These feelings.

But common sense, loyalty to my dead best friend, and just plain ol' decency be damned. Half a second later, I found myself moving in just a hair closer, connecting our lips. *Oh my!* They were soft, so soft and comforting. A feeling I'd never felt before shot up from my midsection and I pressed my lips into his even more. It had to have been my imagination when his mouth fell open and my tongue met his. That was the moment that sobered me up.

"Oh God!" I squealed, pulling back and covering my mouth with my hands. *What the hell was I thinking?*

Josh stared at me, mouth agape, confusion rolling around in those emeralds.

"Shit!" I cursed. "Josh, I-I'm so sorry," I repeated over and over in between sobs and tears. I hurriedly reached for the door handle to free myself from the car. Even once I got the door open, the fresh air hitting my body didn't provide any comfort. I needed to get in the house, behind closed doors.

"I'm so sorry, Josh!" I stated again before slamming his car door and rushing off to the single story, ranch-style home my parents had built right on the outskirts of the city of Williamsport.

I didn't look back as I removed the keys from the small backpack I'd brought with me. I fumbled and dropped the keys. Quickly yanking them from the ground, I inserted the key into the front door at the same time I heard Joshua's car pull off. My heart sank deeper and I felt lower than dirt.

"What did I do?" I wailed in my hands, covering my face as I pressed my back against the door.

"Mija?"

My mother's consoling voice only made me slide to the floor. But she was there, wrapping her arms around me. I leaned into her and didn't even try to stop the tears.

"I know, mija. I know," she consoled. "You loved her very much." My mother referred to Chelsea. She knew I'd gone with Josh to release her ashes. I didn't answer her, only cried harder against her chest. I couldn't find the words to tell her my tears weren't only for my late best friend but because I'd betrayed her in death by falling in love with her boyfriend.

* * *

Kayla

I groaned inwardly, at the memories of the past. I'd hated myself for so long for what'd happened between Josh and I in that car. I'd betrayed two friendships that day. And as I stared across the ballroom, eyes locked with Josh's, I realized how different they were. Harder. Less disarming than the twenty-one year old I'd left in that car.

Questions swirled in my head on what'd changed that, but I clamped my jaw shut. Instead, I decided it was time for me to go.

Thankfully, I'd driven myself to the event. As soon as I made it to the valet booth, I handed them my ticket and impatiently waited for the valet to pull up with my car. The sooner I was away from that place the better.

I sighed in relief when my car pulled up. After tossing the valet a tip, I hopped in my SUV and quickly pulled off. If I'd had my own place I would've gone home to soak in a warm bubble bath.

"I really need my own place," I mumbled to myself as I drove.

CHAPTER 4

Joshua

She'd run off again.

I watched as she lowered her eyes and turned, making a beeline for the door. My instinct was to ditch Denise and stop Kayla from walking out of that damn door. But fuck that. I didn't chase women. Not even ones I'd had a ten year friendship with.

"Anytime I have the look in my eye that you've got, there are only three options: fight, fuck, or build. Which is it for you?" Damon's deep voice sounded from behind me.

My eyes narrowed. "Someone did tell me I needed to work on my right hook," I commented, staring straight ahead at the entrance as if it would make Kayla reappear.

"Fighting it is," Damon retorted. "I've been in the ring with light-weights for weeks anyway."

I grunted in response, feeling the blood rush through my veins at just the mere thought of releasing this pent-up tension through fighting.

"I'll see you in an hour."

* * *

I PANTED HEAVILY, sweat pouring into my eyes, stinging them. My vision was blurred but I didn't need to see clearly to know my way around a ring. Damon and I circled one another. He had a cut just above his right eye. I was sure blood was pouring into his eye, but he was just intent as I was.

"How's my right hook feel now?" I taunted, baring my teeth.

"'Bout as good as my left uppercut," he tossed back.

Just the mention of his uppercut caused my right ribs to ache. But the pain only made me grin, similar to the way Damon was grinning back at me. In the ring we didn't feel any pain, just the thrill of the fight and the need to take the other guy down. I'd long since moved on from the dank gym my father first brought me to seven years earlier. We were now in what would be considered a world class gymnasium on the outskirts of Williamsport. Connor technically owned the building, but I was the backer, as I was with a number of these underground fighting rings around the country. The network was extensive and extremely secretive.

Yeah, just like the movie, the first rule of our fight club was you didn't fucking talk about fight club.

"You two pussies going to keep talking or fight?" Connor yelled from the side of the ring.

"Suck my cock!" I growled.

"He's got a point. I have a date later on," Damon said just before lunging at me. He attempted to use one of his infamous takedowns and he nearly succeeded in getting me down, but as usual, I was too quick for him. Just as he was about to swipe my right leg from under me, I did a spin move and ended up getting behind him. I went to put him in a chokehold but he elbowed me in the same spot in my ribs where his uppercut had caught me.

"Shit!" I grunted, falling to my left knee. I quickly rebounded and sent one of my own uppercuts to his jaw. He pivoted his head at the last second, causing me to just clip him. I'd made contact but it wasn't enough to do any real damage. Not to Damon, at least. A lesser fighter would've felt it.

We kept at it for another three rounds before Connor finally made us call it. Damon and I always ended our fights like this. In a damned tie. I fucking loathed ties.

"I'm gonna beat the shit out of you one day," I warned as we touched gloves.

"Not before I whoop your ass," he returned.

"Ah, both of you are full of it!" Connor grunted as he removed our gloves. "My grandmother could whoop both of your asses. With her eyes closed."

"Oh yeah? Why don't you invite her over to my place." Damon winked.

I chuckled while Connor threw him a middle finger.

I stretched out my fingers from the gloves and ducked under the ropes of the ring to climb down. "Who's next?" I shouted to the ten or so guys who were present and watching the fight between Damon and I. An array of hands went up.

"You and you." I nodded at two separate guys who looked to be about the same height and build. I watched as the two men sized each other up, carefully searching for each other's weaknesses as they moved to the ring.

A smile tugged at my lips.

I, too, loved the sizing up of an opponent before we stepped into the ring. Most times I'd already won the fight in my head long before first contact was ever made. Fighting was definitely just as mental as it was physical. Most sports were.

"This should be a good one. Doc's been out of the ring for weeks due to his injury. He's itching to pop someone."

I turned my gaze over my right shoulder to peer at Damon who was now standing next to me, but staring ahead at the ring, as he sipped from a bottle of water. I nodded.

"I don't think the poor guy knows what he's getting into," I retorted.

Damon chuckled. "At least he's a real doctor. After Jacob kicks Daniel's ass, he can stitch him up before he sends the new guy home."

I nodded in agreement, carefully watching as both men entered the ring. Daniel was new to our group. Damon and I both took a few steps back, joining the handful of other guys who began intently watching the start of the next fight.

Fighters.

That's who we all became once we got down there. In these rooms, we weren't our professions. I wasn't Joshua Townsend, born into a multi-billion dollar empire with a silver spoon in my mouth. Damon wasn't the former drug dealer turned real estate mogul. And the guy currently beating the hell out of one of the newer members of our group wasn't an up-and-coming plastic surgeon. We were all warriors. Catering to our base instincts. Working to get out the stress and pressure of the day, week, year, whatever. It was either fight, or we'd explode on someone out there and sometimes that wasn't an option.

I watched as Jacob—the doctor in the ring—circled his opponent, taking him down with a surprise leg sweep. It was a beautiful move, that landed the doc on top of his much slower opponent.

"Hey, you need to ask Jacob to teach you to do a leg sweep like that. Yours was sloppy as shit." Damon laughed.

"Fuck off," I grunted.

I continued observing the fight, but to my dismay, my thoughts began drifting. The initial adrenaline rush of the fight had begun to taper off and long ago memories of my former best friend started to resurface. I'd worked hard to forget about Kayla for years now. She'd left me during the saddest time in my life. So why the hell was her being back an issue for me now? Why had I already decided to have my family's security team get me the contact information on where she was now living and working?

"Hey, I'm out," Damon stated, interrupting my thoughts. He tapped me on the arm and held out his hand.

I slapped my hand in his and we briefly pulled on another as our usual custom when departing. My gaze flickered between Damon's retreating back and the fight still happening in the ring, but my mind was still caught up on Kayla Reyes. Something was off about her. I'd noticed it from the first moment I laid eyes on her.

Seven years of separation and my own best efforts hadn't

completely submerged any and all memory of her. What I'd saw earlier that night wasn't the same Kayla I knew growing up. My mind shifted to the way she'd worn her hair at the fundraiser.

If they don't like my big hair, they can kiss my ass.

Those had been her exact words one time after an argument she'd gotten in with her mother about straightening her hair. I never understood what the big deal was, but I agreed that her hair looked best loose and curly. At the fundraiser she'd had it straight and pulled back in a bun. Not only that, but her demeanor was ... off. As if she'd been unsure of herself. Something didn't feel right. The one moment it felt like the old Kay was back had been when she was about to hand me my ass for calling her out. But instead, she'd clammed up when Denise interrupted us.

My growing need to find out what had brought such a change about was winning out over the voice in my head that tried to convince me to stay away. In the end, I already knew I wasn't about to keep my distance. She'd walked back into *my* city. Even against my own better judgment, I'd go to the ends of the Earth to pursue what it is I wanted.

Hell, I figured I owed it to Chelsea to at least ensure that the woman who'd been her best friend was okay. After that, I could walk away without another thought. Just as Kayla had done.

CHAPTER 5

*K*ayla
This cannot be happening! I threw up my free hand, pacing the carpeted floor of my office, while holding my cell phone to my ear with my other hand.

"Isn't there *something* you could do?" I implored through the phone to Darla, my real estate agent.

"Not if you don't want to live in a place where the building could collapse on you at any moment."

I rolled my eyes, lifting my head to the ceiling and pushing out a hard breath. I resisted the urge to tell my agent she was being just a *little* dramatic. Yeah sure, an appraiser had come in to do an appraisal which resulted in Darla making this phone call. But really, what were the chances of the building actually falling?

"Do you really want to risk it?"

My realtor's dry voice made me realize I'd stated that question out loud. I pushed out another breath of air.

"I need to get out of my parents' house," I mumbled, causing Darla to laugh.

"Listen, Kayla, I know this is a bummer, but I'd rather you have a safe place to live that you had to wait just a little longer to find, than to sell you a place that was unsafe."

"I know. I know," I mumbled some more, sounding like a child. "And I appreciate your help."

"I've got to go, but I am emailing over a list of places I think might be a good fit for you. We'll review them the next time we talk and then start visiting within the next week, okay?"

"Yeah, all right." I sounded defeated to my own ears. I had loved the spacious two-bedroom condo that I'd put an offer in on the week before. Everything was looking on the up and up, until a second appraiser came in and questioned the building's structural integrity. Whatever the hell that meant. A new contractor had been brought in and found the same issue, essentially condemning the building, leaving me with no place to live. Well, that wasn't entirely true. I was still living with my parents, who'd made it abundantly clear I could stay as long as I'd liked. I knew they enjoyed having me around full-time again, but after seven years of living on my own, I'd gotten used to my freedom. And, although my parents weren't nearly as bad at smothering me as they were when I was a child, I still got knocks on my door at six a.m. from my mother or father asking if I'd taken my medicine yet that morning.

They meant well, I knew they did, but I needed more breathing room. I tutted and tossed my phone on my desk, barely looking over my shoulder when a strange feeling crept up my spine.

"Trouble finding a place to live?"

"Holy shit!" I jumped, startled at the sound of his deep voice. That feeling in my spine intensified and burst in my belly before I even turned around. When I did, I had to stop myself from swallowing my own tongue. *Breathe, Kayla,* I reminded myself when I started to feel as if I were suffocating. Oh, but why did my next inhale fill my nose with his scent? He smelled the same as he did the other night. And he was still standing at the door, halfway across the room. Not standing really. More like leaning against the doorjamb, his feet crossed at the ankles, looking devilishly delicious in a silver suit that perfectly contoured his muscular frame.

His eyes scanned me from head to toe, the smirk on his face telling of his obvious enjoyment in the fact that he'd startled me.

"You scared the hell out of me."

His eyes narrowed and my toes curled in the black pumps I wore. Was he reading me?

"The Kayla I remember wasn't so jumpy." He lifted an eyebrow, standing up completely.

"A lot has changed."

"What was that?" He moved farther into my office, looking around.

"Nothing. What are you doing here?"

"Oh no, I don't need a seat. I'll stand, sure," he commented snidely, eyeing the chair across from the desk I stood behind.

I blinked and chided myself. Exhaling, I lowered my shoulders slightly. "Sorry, I didn't mean to be rude. I just got some not so great news from my realtor."

"So I heard."

"How long were you standing there?"

"Not long. That building was shit anyway. I could've saved you the cost of getting it appraised. That is, if you'd come to me from the beginning," he responded, before moving in front of the chair, unbuttoning his suit jacket, and taking a seat, then folding one leg over the other. He looked so comfortable that for a moment I'd forgotten this was my office and not his.

He'd been listening long enough to have heard which building I was to have bought into.

"I have a very capable realtor."

"Who didn't know that building was a piece of junk to begin with."

My top lip curled. "Not everyone's a real estate mogul."

He shrugged. "Too bad for them."

Silence drifted between us for a half a minute.

"What was wrong with the building?" Josh finally asked.

I let out the breath I'd been holding and unfolded my arms from my chest, slowly sinking into my leather chair. "Something about the structure of the building. I don't know. You'd probably understand it more than I would."

He made a snorting noise and shook his head. "I knew the contractors who'd constructed the building were garbage. The owners are cheap and use subpar contractors."

I nodded. "Yeah, well, I've withdrawn my offer and my realtor's sending me a list of more places."

He regarded me for a long while. "Where're you staying now?"

"Casa de Reyes," I sing-songed.

"Home sweet home," he commented.

"It ain't Townsend Manor, but it's—"

"Nothing's Townsend Manor."

I nodded

"I could make some calls on your behalf?"

I sat up, eyebrows raised. "You'd do that?"

For a heartbeat, I watched as Joshua's eyes darkened, before returning to their normal emerald color. But the way his eyes narrowed I felt my question angered him. Why that was, I wasn't sure.

He shook his head. "Yeah, Kay, I would."

Why did his answer feel like a slap across the face?

I shook my head. "That won't be necessary. So, uh, what are you doing here? Did you have an appointment with one of the other physicians?" Certainly, he wasn't there to see me. I was very aware of every patient or potential patient I had on my schedule that day.

"I had some business in the area." He let his eyes linger on my face for a half a second before standing and moving around my desk.

My breath caught in my throat when I thought he was moving closer to me. Instead, however, he went to the back wall, staring up at the degrees I'd hung there. My hand flew to my abdomen when I watched his full bottom lip curl upwards.

"Be it known to all that, Kayla Reyes, N.D., has hereby fulfilled all of the qualifications ..." he read my degree out loud, pride mixed with a tight rigidity in his voice, while I kept my gaze locked on him. When he finished reading, he turned his head slightly, staring down at me;

his eyes held a coldness that almost made me shiver. "Congratulations, Kayla. Sorry I missed your graduation."

I lowered my gaze and swallowed the lump that had formed in my throat. I also swallowed the words that were fighting to come out. The ones that would tell him that he was one of the first people I wanted to call the day I graduated with my degree.

Slowly, I moved my gaze from him to my degree on the wall. I stood. "Josh, I—"

"I've got a place where you can stay," he interrupted.

"I— What?" I turned to him, confused.

"You need a place to stay. You said living with your parents is growing uncomfortable, right?"

I hesitated. Had I said that? Yes, on the phone with Darla.

"Yes, but I couldn't stay at one of your houses. I can't afford the luxury homes you build. And besides—"

"It's not one of my developments."

I frowned. "An apartment you're renting?" I questioned, cautiously. Joshua loathed apartments as real estate properties.

He frowned. "I haven't changed that much in the last seven years."

"Okay," I breathed out. "So, what place are you talking about?"

"My house."

My eyes must've expanded to two times their size. "Your house? As in, where you live?"

He tilted his head to the side, which caused me to recognize how silly I sounded.

"Yes."

I began shaking me head. "I couldn't put you out like that."

"I wouldn't invite you to stay if it was putting me out. I have six bedrooms, only one of which I use. Five and a half bathrooms, again, only one in which I use regularly. I travel often for work, so you might make better use of the place than I would." He pulled a card from his pocket, flipped it over, and snatched a pen from my holder on the desk, scribbling something on the card.

"Here." He thrust the card in my hand and tapped it with the end of the pen. "Head over after you get off tonight and I'll show you around and give you the access code to the house and the gate."

"The gate?" I questioned, dumbly.

"Yeah, I live in the gated community in Cedarwoods. I'll show you once you get there tonight. Just text me when you're on your way."

I frowned, furrowing my brows and looking for some way to tell him I would not be staying at his place. "I … uh, are you certain your girlfriend will be okay with this?"

He stilled, eyeing me carefully. "Girlfriend?"

"The woman from the other night. Danielle, or Diane, something."

His gaze soon filled with recognition and a smile formed on his lips that had my heart sinking. "Oh, Denise."

"Yeah, Denise," I mumbled. In reality, I'd remembered her name. I was just being childish.

"I'm sure she'll be fine with it. I'll see you later. Don't forget to text me."

I went to tell him I didn't have his cell number, but his head gestured to the card in my hand. Looking down, I saw that he'd written it in beneath his address. I went to make one final attempt to refuse his offer but the words fizzled on my lips when I looked into his eyes at the hard glare he was giving me.

Daring me to refuse.

My mouth opened but no words came out. Strangely, that seemed to satisfy him, and the glare turned to satisfaction. He nodded and turned for the door, giving me one last glance over his shoulder before exiting.

I fell back into my chair, wondering why he'd seemed to suck all of the air out of the room when he left. And more so, why I hadn't flat out turned down his offer. Maybe I really was just sick of living with my parents. It'd only been about six weeks but I was so ready to move out. I loved being this close to my parents again, but my own space was needed. I could stay with Josh for a week or two until I found my own place. If worse came to worst, I could rent a place for a while until I was ready to buy.

* * *

JOSHUA

I pushed through the double doors that led to my brother's outer office and was greeted by his grinning head assistant.

"Mark."

"Mr. Townsend." He nodded in greeting from behind his desk.

"Cut that out. Mr. Townsend's your boss and my father." We'd been over this many times prior.

Mark shook his head. "I'll refer to you as Joshua under one condition."

I peered down at him through a narrowed gaze. His brown eyes sparkled in mischief and I just knew I wasn't going to like what was coming from his mouth next.

"No," I shook my head and said before he could get the next words out.

"Come on," he urged, bending and turning his head to peer down the hall. My guess was to make sure Aaron wasn't coming around the corner.

"Mark, no. You said the last time was enough."

"I know. I lied."

Even I had to chuckle but I quickly straightened up and shook my head.

"What's the big deal? You know I can handle my own."

Sighing, I ran my hand through my hair. "You handling your own isn't my concern. You know your brother would do his best to kick my ass if he found out I was letting you fight." I wasn't afraid of Connor's wrath. I more so despised the feeling of sneaking behind his back.

"What Connor doesn't know won't kill him … or me." He grinned.

"You both are fucking pains in my ass," I said low through clenched teeth.

He wriggled his eyebrows. "You don't even mean that."

"Younger brothers are the biggest pains in the ass."

"Aren't you a younger brother?" he retorted.

"That's exactly how I know. But I've got nothing on Ty," I stated, referring to my youngest brother.

"Look, I'm itching to get in another fight. It's been almost two months since my last one."

I sighed. I heard the yearning and desperation in his voice. I should've told him no, flat out, but I sensed he needed this just as bad as the rest of us who fought. Hell, I'm sure he had some type of pent-up animosity working with my brother all week.

"You'll fight under one condition."

He frowned. "What's that?"

"You tell Connor about your fighting. I'm not doing this sneaking around bullshit. I've got more important shit to worry about."

Mark looked as if he was about to refuse but thought better of it when he looked at me again. His shoulders sank. "Fine, but after my next fight."

"He'll be out of town for a while, anyway. Next Friday, ten p.m. down at the lounge. Don't be fucking late," I stated sternly, pointing a finger at him.

His face morphed from an almost pleading desperation to utter elation in the span of two seconds.

"I'm always on time." He grinned. "Now, let's get you into your meeting with the big guy."

I watched as he rolled his chair out from behind his desk and turned to head down the hall toward Aaron's office. I silently followed behind Mark's wheelchair, pausing for him to knock on Aaron's door.

"Mrs. Townsend is in with him, but he wanted me to let him know as soon as you arrived."

I nodded, and then looked up from Mark to Aaron who'd opened the door.

"Thanks, Mark." I moved into my brother's office, a smile touching my lips when I saw my sister-in-law. She was sitting at the conference table at the far side of the room, her feet propped up in a second chair. Her right hand, lovingly caressed her swollen belly.

"Patience," I greeted. "No, don't get up," I insisted, but she waved me off.

"No, I need to stand anyway to stretch out my back and legs. How're you, Josh?" she asked as I bent down, giving a kiss to her cheek.

I grinned and gave her a wink when I heard Aaron grunt his disapproval behind me. Patience smirked as well, peering over my shoulder at her husband.

"Calm down. He's not the brother you need to worry about anyway."

"I'll kick Ty's ass if he touches you again."

She giggled. "He just does it to get a rise out of you."

"True. Ty likes pressing all of our buttons," I added.

"He's a jackass," Aaron retorted. Despite his harsh words, the softening of Aaron's face revealed the affection he held for our kid brother.

"I know you two have a meeting. I was supposed to head out fifteen minutes ago," Patience commented, eyeing Aaron. "*Somebody* wouldn't let me leave."

"Heading out?" I questioned.

"Lunch with Michelle. She's going a little stir crazy waiting on the baby to arrive, so we're going to eat to get her out of the house while Carter's on shift."

I nodded. Both of my sisters-in-law were pregnant. Michelle, Carter's wife, was two days past her due date while Patience was about four and a half months along with her second set of twins.

"I should go—"

"No," Patience stated sternly, cutting Aaron off. "You are *not* coming with us. This is a girl's lunch. You obviously have business to tend to with Joshua. I will be *fine*," she emphasized. "Besides, I still think you intimidate the hell out of Michelle."

I snorted at that. Aaron intimidated the hell out of a lot of people.

I glanced at Aaron and saw his eyes lower to her belly and then back up to her face. He was blatantly warring with the idea of Patience venturing out without him by her side. He'd been like that for the last few months ever since she was attacked. She still hadn't returned to her job as a librarian, instead spending many days at

Townsend Industries. I would say that Aaron was overreacting, but hell, I'd be just as protective if it were my wife that had been kidnapped and almost taken away from me by a deranged madman. I couldn't blame my brother.

"Fine, but—"

"I am going with my *two* security guards. One of which will remain in the car and the other will be discreetly located in the restaurant while we eat. After finishing I will be driven by my security slash driver to Excelor to pick up the children, and we will stop by Townsend to pick you up on our way home."

Aaron's chest deflated as he pushed out a breath. He stared for a while longer, eventually nodding.

"How's she doing?" I asked once Patience left.

He gazed at the door longingly. "Better than me some days," he admitted.

"Love," I grunted out, shaking my head. It made even the strongest men I knew weak. Both of my older brothers and father were the most capable men in the world, to me, and even they could be brought to their knees faced with the idea of losing the women they loved.

Been there, done that. No thanks, I thought as I patted Aaron on the back before moving to take a seat at the conference table.

A flashback of the night just about six months prior came back to mind. He and I were in this very office. It was dark and Aaron had been drinking, which he rarely does. As soon as I saw the bottle of aged scotch and the look in his eyes, I knew it had to do with his wife. That was the type of behavior love could drive someone as strong as Aaron to. I didn't need it.

"Something on your mind?"

I wrinkled my brows and glanced up to see Aaron glaring at me.

"A man can't have his own private thoughts?"

He squinted. "He sure can. In his own damn office. Off company time," he deadpanned.

I rolled my eyes and stood. "Jackass."

Aaron grunted. "I've been called much worse."

I shook my head. "Yeah, I know. I've called you much worse. Anyway, let's discuss what I came here to talk about."

Aaron hesitated for another minute but eventually got down to business. "What's going on with your properties?"

I began to run down all of the issues that'd been coming up in the last three months at my developments around the area. I included the incident in which one of my workers had been injured the previous week, as well as the deposit cancellations. I told Aaron about my suspicion that the tractor had been tampered with but I couldn't be sure until a full investigation was done. Those weren't the only incidents that made me feel as if something bigger was going on.

The previous month, at a different division, we'd had trouble getting the zoning paperwork to go through. I'd been in the business since I was a teen, I knew the necessary zoning regulations within each district I built in, but for some reason, it'd taken twice as long to get approval. Things were starting to feel like these seemingly separate incidents weren't coincidences.

"Keep an eye on it. Now what's going on with Detroit?" Aaron questioned, switching topics.

When I'm in a business meeting or discussing real estate matters, rarely am I easily distracted. In fact, it *never* happens. I'm typically laser focused on the tasks at hand, and always thinking of the next project. It's what has kept me a step ahead of my competition. So when I found my eyes wandering off, checking the clock on the wall for the time, I became agitated at myself. Not because I wasn't focused on work but because I knew my underlying anticipation was of seeing Kayla that night. Not just seeing her, but having her stay with me.

* * *

MY HOME IS MY SANCTUARY. It's my respite from the world. My place of refuge from working and fighting, when I need a rest. I don't invite people in that I don't know or like. Hell, aside from my immediate family, the *only* people who've been invited in were Damon and Connor on the rare occasion. So why I chose to invite Kayla, not only over to my place, but to actually *live* with me was beyond my comprehension.

She must've felt the same apprehension I felt because as soon as I opened my front door she asked, "Are you sure this is a good idea?"

My eyes traveled to her plump bottom lip as she bit down on it, and an urge to pull that lip into my mouth almost overtook all of my good sense. I must've needed to get laid. It had been about two months.

"Probably not," I answered her question while simultaneously reaching for the strap of the duffle bag she had slung over her shoulder. I eyed her up and down in the dark grey button-up shirt she wore paired with the black slacks.

"I can go back to my parents'."

"You're here now." I stepped to the side to allow her entrance into the foyer of my home. I kept my eyes trained on her profile as she stepped inside and her head tilted upwards as she looked around. Not for the first, or the second time, I noted how the red undertones of her skin made it appear as if she was wearing makeup when I could tell she wasn't. Again, her natural auburn curls had been suppressed by a flatiron and pushed back into a bun at the back of her head. My fingers twitched as if they had a life of their own.

"This is just what I imagined your place would look like."

I quirked an eyebrow and continued to stare. "How so?"

When she turned toward me, something in my chest tightened as I realized the mischief that had always hung out in her eyes was gone—now replaced with a reserved look.

"When we were kids. It was no secret you loved luxury homes. I pictured the brick siding because it gave the home a traditional look and the inside would be lined with marble floors." She made a show of staring down at the white and grey coloring of my marble floors. She was also correct about the brick siding.

Unlike my brothers, I'd chosen brick as my siding because I did appreciate the traditional look it gave.

I made a tilting motion with my head, silently stating that she'd discerned correctly.

"Is that all you brought?" I questioned, referring to the duffle bag I held.

She shook her head. "I've got more in the trunk but I wanted to wait until we talked. I mean, until I asked again if this was really okay. Don't feel obligated to let me stay here just because you offered earlier or because we were friends once. If you've changed your mind since then, I'd understand. In fact—"

"Feel obligated?" I chuckled. "I don't do anything out of obligation. The only thing I'm loyal to is my family and Townsend Real Estate. I do what I have to to ensure the success of both. Outside of that, anything I choose to do is because I *want* to. Just so we're clear," I affirmed.

Kay looked stunned but she quickly recovered. "We're clear."

"And we'll get to your *used to be friends* comment a little later. For now, let me show you around."

"You still like to be in charge."

"Only because very few people are more capable." I tossed her a cocky wink. "Your room is up the stairs, second door on the right. Give me your keys. I'll bring in the rest of your stuff and then show you around."

Taking the keys from her, I watched as she ascended the stairs and turned down the hall in the direction I told her. My gaze lingered for a half a second longer and then I pressed the key in my hand to open her trunk. I went and retrieved the few suitcases she had in the trunk before sealing it shut. After dropping all but two of her bags at the entranceway, I carried a suitcase and the duffle bag up the stairs.

"I can help with that," she started as I entered the room.

"I'll handle it," I insisted. "I'll get the rest later. Let me give you the tour and tell you the codes so you can come and go as you please."

"Yes, let's do that," she agreed, pushing out a heavy breath.

"This is the biggest guest room, and you have your bathroom," I pointed out, moving to open the door to her bathroom in the guest room. "Anything in there is yours to use." I walked out, and gestured for her to follow. "This floor has the master bedroom, another guest room, and a lounge area," I pointed out as we passed them heading down the stairs. "You obviously know where the entrance is, but follow along back here and we come to the solarium."

"I bet you love this room in the spring," Kay admired, looking out at the tree that stood in the front yard, which could easily be seen from the solarium.

I nodded in agreement. "Farther down the hall, is the kitchen which extends into the dining area. There's a smaller dining space on the opposite side of the fireplace."

"I love that it's separated," she noted. Why her love of my place mattered to me I have no idea, but for some reason her approval sat well with me. Too well.

"I'm pleased with the way it came out."

"You should be."

I continued the tour, showing her the rest of the house's main floor and the back patio which was accessible from the sliding glass doors of the kitchen. I gave her the access codes for the house's alarm system, as well as the number for the private security company that patrolled the community. I ignored the voice in my head that asked why I was allowing someone who'd been out of my life for the past seven years such access to my home. I reasoned that I'd already had my security do a background check on her, getting all previous addresses, criminal history, and education records over the past seven years. She wasn't a threat to me in any way. And she was right in one regard. We *had* been friends once upon a time.

I shut my overthinking off as we made our way to the garage area. "There are four garages to the house, only three of which are occupied, so you have space to park your car."

"Still love driving yourself, huh?"

"You remembered," I answered. I hated being driven by anyone else. I derived peace from being the one in control, behind the wheel.

"How could I forget? You never let Chelsea or I drive anywhere."

"Cause you suck as a driver. Hope your skills have improved," I retorted. And they had. Her driving record hadn't indicated any car accidents over the past seven years, but I kept that information to myself.

"I'm a great driver." She rolled her eyes and stepped past me as I flicked on the light in the garage.

I peered over at Kayla when I heard a low whistling sound.

"Lotus Evora four hundred. Is this a 2017?"

Making a disgusted sound with my mouth, I gave Kayla a sideways glance as I moved closer to my beauty. "She's a 2019."

"Of course. Because Mr. Joshua Townsend just *has* to be a year ahead of the rest of us."

The hairs on my arms stood on end when she broke off into a giggle. I felt a little lighter in that moment.

Once she sobered, she looked around, stating, "This must be your work car." She was looking toward my dark grey series 3 BMW. "And the Lexus is for ..." She broke off, looking back to me for an answer.

I glanced over at the cream luxury SUV. "For the family."

Kayla frowned, giving me a perplexed look.

"The family's growing, so I wanted something that could carry them when we have events."

My chest tightened a little when Kayla's face softened and those full lips stretched into a smile that I'd missed over the last seven years. I held back, refraining from moving closer to her to take her hand in mine, although my instincts dared me to. More often than not, I trusted my instincts, but this time I just knew they were guiding me down a dangerous path. One that could lead to more than just rekindling an old friendship. I didn't need that shit in my life.

"Let me show you the rest of the house." My voice sounded strained.

I shut the light out and left Kay to follow me as I moved back inside of the house. I showed her the rest of the bathrooms and lounge area on the first floor, as well as informing her of the code to get in and out of the house. There was no key; instead, my security system had the backing of the team that patrolled the neighborhood, which was also backed by Townsend's privately hired security company.

"What? No basement?" Kayla folded her arms across her breasts.

The button down blouse she wore separated just slightly, exposing more of her smooth skin. My mouth watered.

"You want to see my basement?" Again my tone had taken on a mood of its own.

Kayla bit her bottom lip and I forced myself to look away. Yeah, I definitely needed to get laid.

"Come on," I insisted, turning toward the back staircase that led to my basement. Part of my downstairs housed my home office where I worked on days I didn't feel like or have time to go into Townsend Industry offices. However, the main part of the basement remained unfinished. And was furnished with a punching bag, speed bag, weights, treadmill, a mat, and other equipment. Just the way I liked it.

I heard Kayla gasp behind me. I turned and from her profile, as she glanced around, I could see her forehead contort into a wrinkle of confusion.

"It's not finished? Did you move in early?" she questioned.

"No."

"So you wanted it like this? With concrete walls and floors. You could've had a state of the art gym down here. Instead …"

"It's got everything I need."

She looked to me, tilting her head and stared for a moment before saying, "Yeah … it suits you."

I lifted an eyebrow meant to encourage her to continue.

"It's a little jarring at first. From the outside and first two floors of the house, everything is immaculate. Beautiful marble floors, granite countertops, guest rooms that rival many hotel rooms in luxury. But then you come down here and it's unfinished, or not unfinished, but *raw.*"

"Raw." I ran the word over in my mind, glancing around at my basement gym.

"Yeah, untamed. Kind of looks incomplete but it is completed. Finished just to your liking. It's kind of like … you."

"Explain," I encouraged.

Her shoulders raised on a shrug. "It reminded me of my first impression of you, in sixth grade. You remember?"

In spite of myself a smile touched my lips at the memory. "How could I forget?"

She dipped her head and flattened her bun with her hand.

Again, my fingers twitched to run them through her hair and mess up the perfectly tamed hairstyle.

"I remember thinking, of course *this* kid is a Townsend. He looks the part. Tall, even for sixth grade, perfectly cropped hair, and cute. I just knew you were going to be a douche."

I snorted.

"Anyway," she paused, glancing around for a moment before moving closer to the punching bag that hung from the ceiling, "do you box?"

"A little."

She glanced back around the room. "My guess is more than just a little."

I remained silent, folding my arms across my chest.

"Are you any good?"

"Why, you think you can take me?" I teased.

Something flashed in her eyes just before she turned her head from me. I wondered what the hell that look was about but chose not to question it.

"Could you teach me?" Her voice was light, deceptively so. As if she wanted to make it seem like the question was no big deal, but there was something in her eyes …

"Teach you to box?"

"Yes. Fight. Self-defense."

I stared, blinking, angling my head. The questions began flooding my mind. Kayla had been one of the most self-assured girls in our class. She always had a confidence about her. So, her standing there asking me to teach her self-defense rattled something in me. My gut was telling me there was something more to this than meets the eye.

Moving closer to her, I let the silence encompass us both. I stared down on her, still not responding.

"Forget it, I just—"

I caught her by the arm as she tried to walk away. "I'll teach you."

Three little words. But there was a promise in them. And once it was made, Kay's eyes sparkled for just a moment, and I'll be damned if a warmth I'd only experienced once spread throughout my chest.

"Damn, I've missed you, Kay." A truth that fell from my lips before I could tell my mouth to shut the hell up.

"I've missed you, too."

Her words were sincere, honest, which prompted me to ask, "Then why the hell did you leave in the first place?" The accusation was written all over the question.

Her shoulders sank and she pushed out a breath. "I had to, Josh."

"Why? Say the words," I insisted. I already knew where this was going but I needed to hear the words out loud.

"The kiss."

"In my car."

She nodded and averted her gaze, turning her head.

"That's the only reason?"

She turned back to me, eyes wide. "That wasn't enough?" She paused, taking a step back, and this time I let her create space between us. "I should apologize. I'm sorry for doing that, especially after where we had just been. I don't know what I was thinking."

"You were upset."

"So were you, but …" She looked up at me. "No hard feelings? For the kiss, I mean. It won't happen again. I'm sure your girlfriend wouldn't like that."

I grinned inwardly. She still thought Denise was my girlfriend. "I don't have a girlfriend."

"Really? I thought Denise—"

"Is a woman I met the night of the fundraiser." *Why the hell am I explaining myself?* Not my typical M.O.

"Oh, well that's good, I guess. So, no hard feelings?"

I ran my tongue across my bottom lip, pondering before I shook my head. "No hard feelings."

"Great, when do we sta—" She was cut off by a phone alarm.

"What's that?"

"Time to take my pills. You have a bottle of water?" she questioned while pulling her phone from her pant's pocket to turn off the alarm.

"Flat or sparkling?"

"Flat."

I turned and headed up the stairs, listening as Kay's footsteps followed me.

"Good, you didn't take up the bag with my medicines yet." She headed for one of the suitcases remaining in the foyer.

I pulled out two bottles of water from the fridge, placing them on the granite top of my kitchen's center island. Kay returned with a large case in her hand, placing it on the island. A sour feeling rose in my stomach as I watched her open the various lids of the case that held a different type of medication. I counted, there had to be at least five types of drugs, but some dosages had more than one pill for them. Kayla carefully counted out each pill and proceeded to open her bottle of water. I remained silent, watching as she swallowed the pills with her water.

"You still have to take those every day?" I asked her but was staring at the labels for each of the pills. She'd typed up the different pill names and placed them on the sections of the pill box.

"Yup. Some I take twice a day, others only once," she stated casually, closing the pill box.

"You don't get tired of taking them?"

She looked at me carefully. "Not really. This might seem like a pain in the ass, but remember, I was the girl who was sticking myself with needles by the time I was ten. Sometimes, up to ten times a day when my blood sugar wouldn't stabilize. I woke up in pools of blood more times than I care to remember from pulling my insulin monitor out in my sleep. Nearly passing out or fearing going to sleep because I might not wake up …" She broke off, shaking her head, obviously remembering the horrors of a childhood with Type 1 diabetes. "Now all I have to do is take some pills a few times a day combined with a healthy lifestyle. I'll take that any day of the week."

I swallowed the lump in my throat. "I remember."

"Shit, I'm sorry, Josh."

I peeled my attention away from the now closed pill box to a guilty looking Kayla.

"I didn't mean to remind you of …" She didn't finish her statement, too busy scooping the pill box off the counter, into her arms as if she was hiding it from me.

"Chelsea?" I shook my head. "You didn't. I'm heading out for a few hours. I'll be in late but the alarm has already been set and security is just one button press away."

"Oh, okay."

"You finish unpacking," I instructed as I stood from the stool and moved to pass Kayla. My eyes found the box of medicine and my chest squeezed, something ugly blanketing me. I gave Kayla one last nod and headed for the garage.

I hopped in my Lotus and backed out of my garage. Whenever this darkness overcame me, I headed to the one place I could let all that shit out.

CHAPTER 6

*J*oshua

"What the fuck was up with you tonight?"

I turned my attention from the unfurling of the wrapping on my right hand to peer up at Connor standing over me, arms folded. There was an impressed look on his face.

I turned my back to him. "Liked what you saw?"

He whistled low. "I can't remember the last time I saw you do three takedowns back-to-back."

"Two years ago, the night after I lost the biggest deal of my career. *Thought* I lost, anyway," I answered. A deal to purchase a huge piece of land to convert into a luxury community had gone south and it seemed like my main competitor was going to swoop in and get it. Fortunately, things turned around in the end.

"Yeah, whatever. You looked like you might have a shot at taking me on someday." Connor's gruff chuckle echoed off the tiled walls of the bathroom.

"You won't fight me because you don't want the guys to see you get your ass kicked."

Connor gave a disbelieving snort. "You wish. I know fighting and I know that most men who come through our doors fight like you fought tonight when something heavy is weighing on them."

Tilting my head to the side, I stared up at Connor. "Don't get fucking mushy, O'Brien," I grunted.

"Fuck you." Connor waved me off. "I've got enough of my own shit to deal with. Kid brother of mine keeps asking me to let him fight."

"Is that right?" I packed my wraps in my bag. Obviously, Mark hadn't told his brother the whole truth.

"Yeah, so I get it. Listen, my flight leaves tomorrow morning. Do me a favor and keep an eye on Mark while I'm gone, will ya?"

"You know Mark's a grown man. He's pretty good at taking care of himself."

Connor became silent behind me.

I peered at him over my shoulder. "But, as always, I'll keep an eye on him for you."

"That's all I ask. See ya in a week and a half."

I nodded and watched as Connor exited the bathroom. I glanced around the specialty bathroom that only a handful of patrons were allowed to use in this gym. Connor was the name and the face of the gyms we owned together, and the underground fighting rings we ran, but this, much like my home, had my signature all over it. From the outside, the gym was the classic boxing gym. No frills, punching bags, speed bags, a ring, and equipment, but the spacious bathroom in which I sat belied it all. It was luxury and the only ones granted access were the owners and those who fought with us after hours.

It was like Kayla stated earlier.

The raw mixed with luxury.

The charm and the dark side.

It was me.

Finally deciding to head home, I packed up my belongings. It was well after midnight. I'd had three separate fights that night, and like Connor said, I'd had takedowns in all three, back-to-back. My energy was running on all cylinders that night due to the extra charge I got from having Kayla in my space. Her presence alone had awakened something in me that I'd thought had become a casualty of my growing up.

As I entered my home, I carefully placed my duffle bag on the floor next to the door. I was preparing to carry the rest of Kayla's suitcases up the stairs when I looked down and saw they weren't there. I forced out a gush of air, pissed when I realized she had taken it upon herself to carry the rest of her bags up the stairs after I'd explicitly told her not to.

"Stubborn woman," I groaned as I charged up the stairs. I had every intention on heading to my bedroom, and just ream Kayla out in the morning for not listening, but my legs had different intentions. They ended up carrying me to the doorway of the guest room in which Kayla was staying in. I placed my hand on the doorknob and realized that the door was slightly opened. I pushed the door open slowly. As soon as it was fully opened, I made out her light snores coming from the bed.

That warmth I'd felt earlier started up again. Kay laid across the bed, sleeping peacefully. Her hair had been removed from the bun and though it still remained straight, loose strands spread across the pillow.

My grip on the doorknob tightened and I forced myself not to go in any farther. My eyes roamed over her body as if my very hands were caressing her. Most of her body was covered by the light blanket she slept under, but the outline of her frame was apparent. The dip in the blanket from the curve of her hip had my groin tightening. When my eyes reached her lower half, I could see that her bare leg stuck out from the blanket. It was the same cinnamon color as the rest of her skin and looked smooth to the touch. Her toes appeared uncolored but the shine on them revealed they were painted in a clear polish. Just as my mouth began watering, a small moan escaped her lips when she turned onto her back, exposing even more of her body, as she pushed the blanket from her. The rise in the button-up pajama top she wore revealed a small part of her lower abdomen.

Get your shit together, I admonished myself, pushing a hand through my hair. I stepped back from the doorway, pulling the door shut behind me.

This was Kayla.

I'd spent the last seven years somewhere between being pissed as shit at her and trying to forget her altogether. Now she was in my damn home, at my insistence.

I traveled farther down the hall to my own bedroom. Removing my clothes, I made my way into the shower and my hand immediately went to my already stiff cock. When my hard-on had even occurred was a mystery to me.

I really need to get laid, I thought not for probably the hundredth time that night. As my come spilled from me in the shower that night, I made a mental note to make a date with one of the women in my phone. I obviously had some sexual tension I needed to work out. Maybe once I'd gotten that out of the way, these feelings I was starting to feel for Kay would return to normal.

* * *

"WHAT THE FUCK?" I grumbled, rubbing my eyes as I blinked them open. Stretching out my arm, I rooted around for my phone on the nightstand next to my bed. "The hell?" It was barely six o'clock in the morning, yet I was hearing sounds coming from my living room. I stumbled out of bed, forgetting that I was only dressed in a pair of boxer briefs. I stormed through my bedroom door, still rubbing my eyes as I made my way down the stairs and to the living area.

The only time a woman should be waking me up this damn early is if my cock is in her mouth, I thought as I squinted my eyes to see an image of some woman dressed in spandex leading a group of women in some cardio move. A hand flying through the air, off screen, caught my eye and I refocused. My mouth watered at the sight in front of me. Dressed in a pair of runner's shorts and a sleeveless tank top was Kayla, sweating and breathing heavily as she easily kept up with the women on the screen. My eyes had a mind of their own when they dropped low, planting my gaze on Kayla's rounded bottom. *When the hell did Kay get an ass like that?* I watched as it jiggled beautifully as she began doing jumping jacks, following along. Her toned legs spoke to the effort she put in to keep herself in shape. It reminded me of what she'd said the night before when I asked her about taking the medication. Apparently, she was serious about maintaining a healthy lifestyle. And it was paying off in more ways than one.

My eyes narrowed on her slim waistline that expanded into the curve of her hips. I noted that this was the first time I was really seeing the outline of Kay's body since she'd been back. The night of the charity event, the dress she'd worn had been slightly form fitting but she'd paired a shawl with it. A flashback of Kay dressed in short shorts and tank tops, even after having major surgery, popped into memory. Kay had never been shy about what she wore. From her hair to her clothing. Something had changed.

"Oh shit!"

Her curse snapped my attention back to the present. My eyes found hers wide, the remnants of fear beginning to recede to the background as she took me in. What had been fear just a second ago, swiftly turned to something else, as those brown eyes darkened. I watched as her eyes lowered from my face to my chest, stopping at the boxer briefs I wore. She ran her tongue along her bottom lip and my chest tightened. That's when I remembered I was damn near nude. But I wasn't about to cover up. Something was starting to burn between Kayla and I, and I was quickly losing track of the reasons I needed to do my best to ignore it.

"I didn't know you were there."

"So I see." I sauntered over to the remote that was on the glass coffee table, which Kayla had pushed to the side of the room.

"Sorry about that. I just needed space to workout."

I clicked the remote, turning the television off. "Not a problem. It's time for your first lesson anyway."

"Lesson?"

I tilted my head. "You wanted to learn to fight, right?"

She nodded. "Yes."

"Since you woke me up, it's the least we can do at this ungodly hour," I grunted but turned back when I heard a laugh fall from Kay's lips.

"I forgot how much you hate mornings."

"Yeah? Well, you're about to hate mornings as much as I do in about five minutes. Meet me downstairs." I turned and headed up the stairs to change into a pair of shorts and T-shirt.

* * *

Kay

"Ouch! Goddammit!" I yelled as my back slammed against the mat for probably the fiftieth time that morning. "I thought you were supposed to be teaching me self-defense!" I growled, standing up. I chose to brush off and fix my clothing rather than stare at Josh. A very thin sheen of sweat had formed over his pecs and abs, visible only because he'd chosen to remove the T-shirt he'd first come down the stairs wearing.

"I am teaching you. Man up!" he taunted, doing that damn boxer shuffle thing he first taught me as part of this lesson. The move was supposed to keep a person light on their feet to easily move out of the way or dodge a punch.

Harder to hit a moving target, he'd said.

"I'm not a man," I countered, rolling my eyes. "And I'm hungry," I practically whined. The truth was I was hating how helpless all of this was making me feel. Josh was extremely strong and fast as hell. Though I felt safe with him, it just reminded me of how helpless I was against a real opponent, or in my past.

"Come back to me."

I blinked. "Wh-what was that?" I looked at Josh's emeralds staring intently at me.

"You zoned out." He paused, continuing to watch me.

I shook my head. "Yeah, just thinking about the million and one things I need to take care of at work today. New patients, updating records, etc. I'm sure you understand how busy work can get." I ran a hand through my hair, hating the feel of my roots frizzing up. Even with the sweat-wicking headband I'd donned, it was still a task to keep my hair straight while working out.

"Indeed, I do," Josh responded to my work comment. "Let's go over one basic defense move before we close this out. Come here." He didn't wait for me to move, instead pulling me closer to him by the waist.

My legs went willingly.

"The elbow," he stated, slapping his right hand against his left elbow, "is one of the strongest and quickest defense moves. And you don't have to aim it at someone's head to make is effective. Most guys try to make the biggest impact by landing a punch to the face. It's the knockout move most widely shown in movies and shit. But it's bullshit. A well executed elbow to the ribs can turn an entire fight around, if not end it altogether."

I listened intently and followed along when he demonstrated how to complete an elbow strike. We practiced over and over, Josh reminding me constantly not to use my forearm but my elbow. After I don't know how many rounds on the punching bag, striking elbow after elbow, he held up hand pads. I then practiced uppercut elbows with him for a while.

By the time we were done, I'd worked up a good sweat but I didn't feel as defeated as I had in the beginning. Something began to shift inside of me.

"We'll always end on a high note."

His voice felt like it surrounded me on all sides. But instead of feeling trapped it warmed me from the inside out. Making me feel ... safe. I hadn't felt safe in a long time.

"I appreciate this," I finally got out, turning to stare at him. I stumbled a little when I caught his dark eyes already on me. But strong arms came out, holding me upright. "Thanks." I sounded breathless. "So," I began, squirming out of his arms, "when did you learn to fight like this?"

He handed me a bottle of water that he'd brought down earlier. "Here and there," he stated casually. "Still hungry?"

"Starving. I'll cook," I offered. "I had a few groceries delivered last night after you went out. Scrambled tofu okay?" I questioned, tossed over my shoulder as we ascended the stairs.

"You trying to fucking kill me?" he practically snarled.

A giggle fell from my lips. "You'll like it. Trust me," I encouraged.

He narrowed his eyes on me once we reached the kitchen.

"Trust isn't something I dole out easily."

Why did that feel like a warning?

"Nor should you," I countered. "But since I'm already living in your house ..."

He nodded. "Touche. I'm going to go shower."

"Breakfast will be ready by the time you're done."

I watched his backside as he strode off in the direction of the stairs. My eyes were glued to him. I quickly had to remind myself of the promise I'd made to him the night before. I wasn't about to ruin our rekindled friendship by letting some minor attraction get in the way. I was no longer a twenty-one-year-old kid. We were adults now. We were friends, or at least becoming friends again. I wouldn't mess that up.

* * *

"Hi," a cheery, young voice sounded behind me.

I pivoted from the entrance of the conference room to the corner to see the young girl I'd only met through a photograph smiling up at me. Her big, brown eyes were bright and filled with innocence.

"Hi," I greeted, smiling. "You must be Monique." She, as well as her mother, were new patients of the office. The three of us, as well as another doctor in the office, were scheduled to meet for a patient review.

Her smile doubled at hearing her name. "Yes. Are you my doctor?"

"I'm one of them. Where's your mom?" I glanced around the empty conference room.

"She had to pee."

"It's *restroom*, Monique."

I turned to see a woman who was an older version of Monique

entering the room. This was obviously Monique's mother. Her picture hadn't been in her patient file.

"Ms. Robinson?"

"Yes, but please, Sandra is fine. Dr. Carlson said we could wait in here while he gathered some of our intake forms. I needed to run to the restroom."

I nodded. "That's fine. Dr. Carlson and I met earlier about your case and we began discussing a treatment plan that we think might work well for you and Monique. Why don't we sit as we wait for Dr. Carlson."

Sandra nodded and moved farther into the room while I shut the door.

"This office is beautiful," Sandra began. "Even the lobby is so soothing and comfortable with the waterfall and soft music," she gushed.

"I agree. It's one of the things that drew me to this office when I first interviewed for the position here. We take overall wellness serious here. I was so glad to find an office in which the holistic approach to patient health was taken seriously. And as long as the methods of treatment I suggest are research and evidence-based, my colleagues have been in total support."

"That's good to know," Sandra added.

I went on to tell Sandra about my position as the office's only naturopathic doctor and how my focus was less about simply prescribing medications, and more about overall lifestyle changes and habits that she could incorporate to ensure her and her daughter's health. Once Dr. Carlson joined us, we began discussing specifics of Monique's condition. While both were our clients, Sandra was most concerned about the well-being of her daughter. Her love for Monique was evident.

"And is there a Mr. Robinson in the picture?" Dr. Carlson asked as we reviewed the forms.

"No, I don't have a daddy," Monique spoke up, answering for her mother.

I watched as Sandra began fidgeting with the straps of her purse.

"N-no, I'm not married, Dr. Carlson." Sandra's gaze shifted from Dr. Carlson to myself and then to Monique, a look of dread filling them.

"Hey, Monique, what's your favorite subject in school?" I asked to change topics.

Monique quickly answered and we began talking about the latest picture she made in art class. Sandra appeared to calm down throughout the rest of the intake interview and treatment plan discussion but I could still sense her unease.

"Can I speak with you a moment?" she questioned low enough for me to hear as she was exiting the conference room.

"Sure. My office is right down the hall." I got the sense she didn't want Dr. Carlson to be a part of this conversation.

"Monique, sit right out here while I speak with Dr. Reyes, okay?"

Monique nodded, her eyes lighting up at the tablet that Sandra handed her.

"I know it's not great to let her play on that thing but sometimes it comes in handy," Sandra stated, chuckling uncomfortably.

I laughed lightly. "As long as she's not spending all day every day on it, I don't see a problem. Balance is key."

Sandra nodded.

"Please sit. What did you want to discuss?"

I opted for us to sit on the leather loveseat that was on the far right side of my office, as opposed to sitting at my desk. I felt Sandra needed a less formal setting for what she needed to say.

"Um ..." She blew out a breath, her eyes shifting around the room.

"Sandra, whatever you need to tell me, you can say it. I'm not here to judge you, only to help you and your daughter."

Her brown eyes were filled with trepidation. "I, uh, I just wanted to ..." She paused, sighing, fighting to find the right words. "It's just, when I was asked about a Mr. Robinson? Monique is right, she doesn't h-have a father, not in the traditional way."

I nodded but remained silent.

Sandra looked toward the door. "Monique is a result of a rape. I-I was raped by my ex-boyfriend and two of his friends. I don't know which one is actually her b-bio—" Sandra couldn't finish the rest of her sentence but she didn't need to. She was sniffling as she quickly grabbed the tissues I offered her, dabbing at her eyes.

My grip tightened around the pen I'd been holding, almost to the point I feared breaking it in half. All of the air had been stolen from my lungs as a mixture of emotion filled me. As much as I wanted to go into that dark hole of emotion, I had to remind myself that this conversation was about my patient.

Not about me.

I pushed back in my seat and cleared my throat.

"No one knows. Not even my family."

"I see." I reached out to pat her hand, comfortingly.

"That's why I can't answer questions about her hereditary history."

"I understand, Sandra. You don't have to explain any further if you don't want to."

She nodded. "I just wanted to tell you why. I'm not some irresponsible mother who'd have a baby with a guy I didn't know. Not on purpose."

"I would've never thought that of you. It's evident how much Monique means to you. You're an excellent mother. And I want to thank you for being comfortable enough to share this with me. The circumstances of Monique's conception will never hinder the type of service I give to her or you, okay?"

Sandra nodded, relieved. She stood, as did I.

"Sandra, I understand your hesitation in talking about this." I paused, inhaling deeply. "Trust me, I really do. I know all too well—" I stopped just before the truth tumbled out of my mouth. "What I mean is, I imagine it's not easy experiencing what you've been through and raising a daughter with an illness as serious as Type I diabetes all alone. We at the office are here to help, but you might also want to seek out some form of counseling. We work with some great ..." My voice trailed when I caught the alarmed look in Sandra's eyes.

She shook her head vigorously. "No, I'm fine. I just wanted to tell you so you knew. That's it. What happened was a long time ago. Almost ten years."

"Okay, okay," I soothed, deciding to back off. I understood the reluctance. In fact, part of me felt like a hypocrite even making the suggestion. "I won't bring it up again."

"Thank you." She nodded and moved to the door.

When it opened, Monique peered up from her tablet, giving her mom a smile. I watched as Sandra took her daughter by the hand and led her out of the office. I both admired Sandra for her strength and hated that she had to be that strong.

Shutting my office door, I leaned my forehead against it and closed my eyes. Strength. That was what I'd lacked for so long. I couldn't remember the last time I felt strong. No. That was a lie. Just that morning, practicing with Joshua. I'd began to feel just the tiniest bit of control over my own life that'd been stripped away over the previous two years.

CHAPTER 7

*J*oshua

She's different. That was the conclusion I'd come to after staring out of my nineteenth floor office window for that past ten minutes. Every moment I'd spent with Kay in the past week ran through my mind. From the moment I'd first spotted her at the fundraiser to that very morning, practicing with her in my basement. She was different.

Of course, we all change over the course of seven years, but this wasn't a good change. She was less vibrant somehow. More closed off. The Kay I'd grown up with was always willing to be the life of the party. Her personality was a big as her hair. The very same hair she'd now kept straightened and tucked away in a neat bun.

It wasn't her.

Kay had always loved her big, red, bouncy curls loose. Hell, I'd kicked a kid's ass in the seventh grade for thinking he could make fun of Kayla's hair. I'd always been protective of her and Chels that way. After that, no one dared to make fun of Kay for her hair or for her sickness, which had caused her to miss many days of school. Anyone who dared would have to deal with me. Most people didn't want that. They still didn't.

So as I sat in my office pondering the ways in which Kayla had noticeably changed in the past seven years, I also was reminded of how timid she'd been during our training that morning. She was hesitant with her punches, unsure of herself, which easily led me to taking her down. Again. That wasn't the Kayla I'd grown up with.

My musings on the woman now living in my home were interrupted when a knock on my door sounded.

"Come in."

A second later my door opened to reveal my assistant. "You didn't cancel the permits in Washington, did you?" Katrina questioned, looking at me through confused eyes.

"Of course not," I answered. "I'm heading out there in two days. Why would I do that?" We were breaking ground on a project in Washington state and I was scheduled to head out for a few days to oversee a couple of things.

"I didn't think so," she sighed. "We may have a problem."

I narrowed my eyes on my highly competent assistant. She didn't get rattled easily and she'd been with me for nearing on a half a decade. She'd seen a few problems throughout her time with me, so if she said we might have a problem, I knew some bullshit must've been brewing.

I sat up in my chair, now turning my full attention on Katrina. "Get Aaron's office on the line and let him know I won't be able to attend this afternoon's meeting. Then make arrangements for the plane to be gassed up and ready to head to Washington tonight," I ordered before directing my attention to my desktop to begin sending out emails, alerting my staff in Washington of my early arrival. "When you're done with that, gather everything we have on this deal because we're going to go through it with a fine tooth comb before I get on that plane tonight."

"Sure thing." Katrina nodded.

My hands paused over the keyboard. "Katrina."

"Yes?"

I hesitated, looking to my assistant before shaking my head. "Never mind." I went back to typing, dismissing her. Once the door was closed and the emails sent, I pulled out my cell phone from my desk drawer.

"Hey."

Her voice was breathless but I ignored the chill that ran down my spine.

"Are you busy?"

"No, I'm on my lunch break and decided to pick up a few things for dinner. Since you hated the scrambled tofu, I'd thought I'd make a proper carnivore meal for you tonight. Grilled steaks, roasted potatoes, and grilled veggies."

I inhaled at the thought of the sound of the meal. And for the first time in … forever, I regretted my damn job. That was not a good sign.

"Sounds delicious but I'll have to give you a raincheck. Duty calls. I need to head out of town a few days early for work." Again, I ignored the voice in the back of my head that reminded me that I *never* took the time to explain to a woman my comings and goings. I just consoled myself with the knowledge that this particular woman was living in my home, and that we weren't anything more than friends … old friends.

"Liar."

I sat up. "What?"

The sound of Kay's giggles pushed through the speaker of my phone and my grip tightened around it.

"You're just leaving so you don't have to put up with the early morning workouts, huh? Liar."

I pushed out the breath I'd been holding, chuckling. "Keep laughing, I'll have you flat on your back in no time, again."

A sharp inhale on the other end of the phone silenced the laughter. Tense silence filled the space where her giggles had once been. I probably should've regretted my words; I realized they could've been interpreted a number of different ways. And the quiet coming from Kay's end told of just how she was interpreting them, but instead of backing off, something deep inside of me urged me on. So I pushed some more.

"Cat got your tongue?"

"N-not even close. Someone once told me I've got a pretty killer elbow strike. A takedown won't be so easy," she retorted saucily.

We were no longer talking about self-defense. Or were we?

"I'm betting I could handle it."

"You're a betting man these days?"

"My whole life, sweetheart."

Shit! I silently cursed when my assistant knocked on my office door. For a few short moments, I'd forgotten I was at work. Something that'd never happened to me before.

"I've gotta go. I'll call you when I'm in Washington."

I disconnected the phone before Kay could even respond.

* * *

Kayla

It wasn't the same there without him. That became apparent as soon as I'd stepped over the threshold into Joshua's home. The house was immaculate, beautiful, and with every luxury I could possibly want. Josh had more than made it clear to me that anything inside of his home was at my disposal should I need it, but still. It didn't have the same appeal without his energy present.

I thought about going down to the basement to work some more on my punches and boxing, but in all honesty, it felt a little creepy down there, especially without Joshua. I remembered what he'd said about Aaron and Carter living nearby. He'd pointed out both of their homes when we'd done a tour of the neighborhood. Though I knew both men, I didn't feel comfortable going to either one of their homes, despite my not wanting to be alone. Aaron had always intimidated the hell out of me, and Carter, though more relaxed than Aaron, still seemed more serious than I'd like. The fact that both men now had wives and children almost pushed me out of the door. Maybe I could befriend either Michelle or Patience. I would love having more friends in Williamsport. I'd given up all of my friends once I moved away because the two that mattered most—Chelsea and Joshua—were either dead or pissed at me.

"No." I shook my head and pushed the door that I had just opened in my contemplation shut. I'd have to meet Michelle and Patience another time. The truth was, I wasn't in any mood to socialize, though I wanted company. I just wanted to be in the presence of someone who I didn't need to introduce myself to. As I started up the stairs toward the guest room, my phone buzzed in my pocket. I pulled it out and I felt like my silent prayer had been answered.

"Hey," I answered, casually for the second time that day.

"Hey, Kay."

My grip on my phone tightened and I reached out with my free hand to hold onto the shiny wooden bannister of the stairwell as my legs sank to the plush carpeting of the stairs. I plopped down on my butt. *Joshua.*

"How's it going there?"

"Well, the party doesn't start until ten, but the keg and beer pong table are just arriving now," I joked.

"Beer pong? A little immature for your age range don't you think?"

"Are you calling me old?"

"I might be."

"That's rude as hell."

A deep chuckle had me dipping my head. "I've said plenty worse. Trust me."

"I bet you have," I mumbled.

"What're you doing tonight?" he asked smoothly.

Starting to feel comfortable, I leaned back against the stairs. "I was going to introduce myself to either Patience or Michelle but then thought better of it. It might be too late. So, I'll just crack open a bottle of wine and eat a grilled steak and veggies."

"Sounds fucking delicious." The deep moan in his voice mysteriously caused my nipples to stiffen.

"I-I'm sure the luxury hotel you're staying at has steak," I stated.

"But it won't be prepared by *you.*"

I swallowed the saliva that'd pooled in my mouth.

"So you're not a vegan then?"

I perked up, thrown off by the question. "A vegan … oh, because of the tofu."

"Yeah, that." His voice hardened but I smirked.

"It was good though."

"I had to choke it down."

"Liar!" I charged for the second time that day. "You ate it and you liked it."

"There are much more interesting things I'd love to eat."

The air caught in my lungs as my mouth dropped open. It was almost as if I forgot how to breathe. Thank God for automatic body responses because due to no mental effort on my part, my lungs began to work again.

"Wh-what's happening here?" I nearly got out on a whisper.

"I'm pretty sure it's obvious," his blunt reply came.

I cleared my throat because I had no words to say in response.

"I'll see you when I get back. Don't hesitate to reach out to Carter or Aaron if you need anything. *Anything* at all, all right, Kay? My brothers can be assholes but they'll be there if you need them."

Why did his words feel like a punch to the gut?

"Why're you extending yourself so much for me?" The question slipped out before I could stop it.

"I asked myself the same thing."

I should've been caught off-guard by his honesty, but I wasn't. Joshua was nothing if forthright and honest.

"You left town without so much as a fuck off—"

"I told you why—"

"Yes, you explained. And I get it. I don't like it but I get it. It's over and done with. You're back in town and needed something I could help with."

"Two things," I retorted quickly. Too quickly.

"Two?"

"The self-defense teaching."

"You *needed* to learn self-defense." It was a statement but I heard the pensive way it came out. He was considering my words carefully.

"Why hadn't you taken classes before? Most major cities have self-defense classes."

Yeah, and just about everyone is taught by police officers. Thankfully, I caught myself before that admission could spill from my lips.

"I, uh, just never felt comfortable until now." A partial truth that was met by total silence on the other end. Not silence in the way when the person on the other end has checked out. No, silence that meant the wheels were turning in Joshua's mind. I could just imagine his green eyes, narrowing on me, deciphering every word I'd just said.

"I'll be back in a few days. We'll continue our lessons then. In the meantime, reach out to Carter or Aaron if you need to."

I nodded even though he couldn't see me.

"I'll give you a call tomorrow night."

And just like that, the opposite end of the phone went dead. I was already looking forward to the next evening. That was when I realized, that hearing Joshua's voice was the safest I'd felt all day.

"Tomorrow," I repeated out loud to the empty house. I glanced around, standing to go prepare the very meal I'd told him I was having for dinner. It felt easier moving through his home after that conversation. Out of nowhere, I found myself smiling at the idea of hearing him again the next night. It occurred to me just how much I'd missed Joshua over the years.

And then it hit me like a ton of bricks.

Guilt is heavy like that. I wondered if the stories my mother told me about loved ones who've passed on, watching us from heaven, were true. Because it was starting to feel like I could sense my best friend's eyes on me at that very moment.

* * *

Joshua

"What actual the fuck?" I growled staring at my phone when I saw Aaron's name pop up onto my screen. I knew this wasn't a social call. It'd been five days since I left on my business trip to Washington state, and even though as head of Townsend Industries he was privy to all of the updates I gave, my brother wanted to discuss the issues I ran into face-to-face. Normally, I wouldn't have a problem with that, but it was just after six p.m. on a Friday and I would've much rather been stepping into my own home to see Kay's face.

I'd never been this damned anxious to get home from a business trip. Yeah, the comforts of my own bed were appealing. But what I really wanted to see was *her*.

We'd talked every night I'd been gone. Every evening after business meeting after another bullshit business meeting, handling problem after problem, I'd gone to my hotel, completely depleted. Telling myself all I needed was a shower and a warm bed, but somehow I found myself dialing Kay's cell, feeling reenergized whenever I heard her breathless "hey" as she answered.

Something in me just wanted to make sure she was still there. Still around. That she hadn't run yet. I'd never taken Kay for the skittish type, but I'd obviously been off on that assessment. Now that she was back, something was driving me to see to it that she stayed close.

Shaking off those thoughts, I pressed the answer button on my phone.

"Yeah, Aaron. I'm on my way." I didn't even give him time to ask.

"I'm at the office."

"See you in ten. I'll make it short and sweet." I damn sure wasn't going to keep it short on his behalf. I had shit of my own I needed to sort out. I hung up and directed the driver to take me to Townsend Industries. Aaron wasn't going to like what I had to tell him but I wasn't about to sugarcoat anything.

"What the hell is this?"

I peered across the table, staring my brother directly in the eye. Aaron and I weren't biological brothers, but out of the four of us, he and I looked the most alike. Aaron was actually my cousin but had been adopted by my parents after his died in a car accident. He and I both had dark hair and the signature Townsend freckles, but he had about an inch on my six foot one frame, and whereas his eyes were hazel, mine were green. And at that moment, his hazel irises were burning a death glare into mine. I felt his same anger at the file I'd just pushed across the table for him to look at.

"Exactly what it says. It's the security report from the incident a few weeks back."

"And you're saying your early departure to Washington was the result of even more sabotage?"

I nodded, blowing out a breath. Sitting back in the leather chair at the wooden conference table, I folded one leg over the other, masking my growing agitation at the situation. "Appears so. Initially, I believed the sellers were backing out because the deal wasn't to their liking."

"But?"

"But, it became clear in talking to them they'd gotten some false information."

"What type of information?"

"The kind that made them believe Townsend Real Estate uses subpar equipment and materials to construct our homes."

Aaron's frown deepened as he sat forward. I could see the next question forming already so I decided to answer before it was even asked.

"And why would they even care about something like that?" I asked for him. "Because, they were also given the impression that having been the company that sold us the land, if any injuries were to occur, they could also be held liable."

"That's bullshit."

"Not really." I shook my head. "There's a precedence for this type of thing. A case in which a former landowner was also held responsible for injuries sustained after they sold a property. I don't know all of the details but it showed that they could've been held responsible."

"How the fuck is that even legally acceptable?"

I shrugged. "Lawyers."

"You should've went to law school to understand all of this shit."

"No thanks. I was too busy learning the ins and outs of real estate. Ty, he's the one you need to blame for not going into law."

Aaron grunted.

"Anyway, the real problem is someone is going around spreading the bullshit about Townsend using subpar materials for our constructions. That's the shit that if it gets out to the public could be a disaster."

"It's not true, right?"

I angled my head, glaring at my brother. Now, he was just pissing me off. "Who the fuck do you think I am?"

"Just wanted to see your reaction."

I narrowed my gaze.

"I know you wouldn't jeopardize the Townsend name like that."

"You better know it. Anyway, I was able to straighten the confusion out and prove to Jensen Industries that all of our shit was on the up and up. They finally signed the papers. The property is ours. And the permits are back in the application stage. It'll take longer than we'd hoped but we'll get them."

"When do you break ground?"

"Two to three weeks tops."

Aaron nodded. "And what are we doing to prevent this from happening again?"

"I've already got Brutus all over it. I've got a gut feeling this is connected to the incident a few weeks ago at my other site."

"Where your employee was injured?"

I nodded.

"Shit, Josh," he growled. "This is a growing problem. I don't like problems."

"Fuck. You think I do? I'm handling it. Townsend Real Estate will not be brought down by anyone or anything. You worry about running the rest of the company."

We both stood, peering across the table at one another. Aaron sized me up. I knew he was wondering if I really had things under control. In spite of the confident, self-assured look I was giving him, there were a million scenarios running through my mind as to who was behind this sabotage. And while I was plenty efficient at running Townsend Real Estate, and knew I could go up against any competitor or would-be enemy, I still had a need for my older brother to trust in my abilities. Aaron may appear cold and callous to most—that was how he liked it—but he was family, and loyal beyond words. Letting him or any other member of my family down just wasn't an option.

"You can handle it," he finally stated.

"Don't ever doubt it." I gestured toward the door. "It's close to seven. I'm surprised you're letting Patience and the kids be home without you this late."

Aaron raised his brow, giving me an *are you out of your mind* expression. "They're over Carter and Michelle's."

"Ah." I nodded. Aaron trusted Carter with his family when he was out late. "Michelle still ready to pop?" I questioned as he grabbed his briefcase and shut off the lights in the office.

We strolled to the elevator.

"Apparently."

Michelle was more than a week past her due date. I would've headed over to Carter's with Aaron to see everyone since getting back, but a drive unlike any I'd felt pushed me to get back to my own home.

"Somewhere you need to be?" Aaron glanced over at me as I looked down at my watch.

"As a matter of a fact there is." No use lying but I wouldn't give him all of the details.

"Fighting tonight?"

I shook my head. "Not tonight. Since when did you become Miss Chatty Cathy?"

He glared at me. "Fuck you, Josh."

I grinned. "There's the asshole I know and love." I chuckled. "Give Patience and the kids a kiss for me."

"I'm not giving my wife shit from you. She gets plenty from me."

I shook my head. "Whatever, asshole. I'll see you on Monday." I climbed into the back of the town car I'd taken from the private airport. The closer I got to home the more anxious I began feeling. I hated that fucking feeling. To ease my own nerves I pulled out my cell phone to call Kay but received no answer. I chose not to leave a message, figuring I'd see her soon enough. That wasn't to be.

CHAPTER 8

*J*oshua

"Kay! You here?" I called out as soon as I entered my front door. I'd already gotten the impression that she wasn't home when I saw all the lights in the house had been turned off from the driveway. Since Kay usually parked in the garage, I couldn't see if her car was there or not.

"Kay!" I made one last attempt as I turned on lights and moved farther into the house, toward the kitchen. My stomach began growling, reminding me of my hunger. When I entered the kitchen and turned on the light a piece of paper on the island caught my attention. I picked it up immediately recognizing Kay's handwriting.

Having dinner at my parents'. They wouldn't take no for an answer. See ya later!

I crumpled the paper up and tossed it into the garbage, pissed. It was ridiculous. She was a grown woman, able to come and go as she pleased. I shouldn't expect her to be waiting on me. So why the hell did it piss me off that she wasn't?

I tapped my fingers on the granite of the kitchen's island, that energy of frustration beginning to pulse through my veins. There was only one thing that helped this feeling when I couldn't take on the *real* issue. And at that moment, I couldn't drag Kayla back from her parents' house so that we could sort out what was going on between the two of us. That left me with one choice.

I thought about making a sandwich before heading out but was too keyed up for food. Within fifteen minutes I'd changed and was out, speeding down the highway in my Lotus, my duffle bag full of my fighting gear accompanying me in the passenger seat. It wasn't too late and I figured I could get in a fight or two before I called it quits and carried my ass back home.

"Came to see me fight?"

I blinked, shocked to see an excited Mark grinning up at me. I'd forgotten that night was the night I told him to come down to the gym to get in a round. Good thing Connor was still out of town.

"Wanted to see if you'd lost your edge or not."

"I've always got my edge. Maybe once I'm done with this guy, I can give you a run for your money."

Grinning, I peeked over at the ring in the center of the dark room. A guy was already in the ring, dancing around, shadowboxing.

"He looks tough." I lowered my gaze to Mark.

He turned his head, looking over his shoulder. "Think so?" He didn't sound worried.

"Aaron will try to kick my ass if his head assistant has to take time off to recover from a fight."

Mark gave me a cocky smirk, reminding me of his brother. "Afraid of your big brother?"

I snorted. "I said he'd *try* to kick my ass. Not succeed."

"I don't know, that brother of yours seems to have some tension he could let out down here," Mark suggested.

I looked Mark dead in his eyes. "Aaron's been in much darker rooms than this. He has a better outlet for his tension now."

"Which is?"

Love.

The word came instantly to mind. Despite appearances, Aaron now had a calmness about him that he hadn't had before marrying.

"Patience," Mark answered his own question.

I gave a one shoulder shrug. "Anyway, let's see what you've got."

I held out my fist, to which Mark fist bumped it. I watched as he turned himself around in his chair and rolled toward the ring. I followed behind, nodding at the ten or so guys I knew. Reaching the front of the audience, I stood with my arms folded, ready to watch Mark do his thing. I saw the expression of surprise on the other guy's face when he realized Mark was going to be his opponent.

"You're shitting me, right?" the guy asked, holding up his hands, looking around until his eyes landed on me.

"What's the problem?" I lifted a brow.

"The fuck is this?"

"The fuck does it look like?" I snapped back, not liking his tone.

"Don't worry. I'll take it easy on you," Mark replied, intervening. "Let's go. I don't have all damn night."

I chuckled under my breath. This guy had no idea what he was in for.

"Whatever." He shrugged. "It's your funeral."

"I'm not even going to remove my T-shirt for this one," Mark snarked.

"Less talking and more fighting, ladies!" I called out, ready to get this show on the road. As much as I wanted to see Mark kick this guy's ass, I was more ready to get in the ring myself. I hadn't come down to the gym to watch fights. I came to get into one. The stress of the work trip I'd just returned from along with going home to an empty house had filled my veins with stress that was best let out by wailing on someone or something.

"You heard the man, boys! Let's go!" Buddy called out from the side of the ring. He was still very much a trainer in the gym, but he loved the underground fights just as much as Connor and I.

The bell sounded and I could feel the collective breath holding that surrounded me. I didn't feel nervous at all as I watched Mark move swiftly, using his hands to move the wheels of his chair, while he pivoted and ducked his upper body to dodge his opponent's punches.

"Come on. Hit me!" Mark taunted the guy.

"Just like his fucking brother," I chuckled under my breath. I could easily see where he'd gotten his fighting style from. I perked up when the guy went in for a right hook to Mark's face but was caught by surprise when Mark quickly used the guy's leverage against him, flipping him over his chair. The guy landed on his back, stunned. Mark wasn't, however, and he promptly sent a blow to the guy's chest and face. Mark backed himself up so he was able to pull the guy's arm behind his back, tugging at it painfully. At first, his opponent refused to give in, but eventually it was either tap out or have his damn shoulder ripped out of its socket. His reasoning prevailed and he used his free arm to tap out. The bell sounded and Mark released the guy to lay in a lump on the floor.

"Told you I'd go easy on you," Mark taunted.

Before the laughter spilled from my lips I heard …

"What the fuck is going on in here?"

"Shit!" I cursed at the sound of Connor's irate voice. The shit was about to hit the fan. I glanced up and over behind the ring to see Connor's eyes bulging, breathing heavy and face red as hell.

"Mark, what the hell are you doing in that damn ring?" Connor demanded as he stomped toward the ring. "Buddy, fucking seriously? You let him do this?"

"Connor, calm down," Mark implored.

"Fuck no! Buddy, what the hell is this? You let my kid brother in this fucking ring—"

"It wasn't Buddy," I interjected, moving closer.

Connor turned stormy hazel eyes on me but I didn't flinch. He could come at me if he wanted.

"Mark was itching to get into the ring. I told him the time and place."

Connor moved toward me but Mark got in between us.

"It's not anyone's fault but mine. I hadn't been in a fight in a few months, and I was—"

"A few months?" Connor yelled, running a hand through his hair. "You!" He pointed angrily at me. "You knew about this?"

I nodded. "Not only did I know about it but I condoned it." I folded my arms over my chest. I'd known Connor's reaction to finding out about Mark fighting wouldn't be too kind. I was ready for whatever the backlash would be.

"Connor, don't blame Joshua. In fact, don't blame anybody. You kn—"

"I asked you to look out for my brother," Connor seethed as he cut Mark off. "One favor. One fucking favor was all I asked. Get him the job at Townsend and now ..."

I stood up straighter, knowing Connor had just crossed a line.

"What did you just say?" Mark's voice was low, now filled with his own barely controlled anger.

Connor's head dropped to stare at Mark, a stunned look on his face. He'd just realized he'd revealed our secret in front of the one person he didn't want knowing.

"*You* got me the job at Townsend?" Mark's head spun between myself and Connor.

"Mark, listen—"

"Fuck that!" Mark spat back. He didn't bother to look at either one of us as he wheeled himself over toward the short ramp that was attached to the ring, to let himself out and down.

Connor gave me one last hard glare before he went after his brother who headed inside the door that led to the locker room at the back entranceway of the building.

"No," Buddy stated, holding me back with his arm. "You've got brothers yourself. You know this is something they need to work out on their own."

I sighed, knowing he was right. Whenever there was an issue between my brothers and I, my parents let us work it out ourselves, unless they absolutely had to intervene. I needed to let Mark and Connor figure their shit out. As for me, getting Mark the job at Townsend, if he asked about it, I'd tell him the truth.

"You're right." I nodded at Buddy. "Anyway, I need a fucking fight."

Buddy grinned up at me. "Will do." He wriggled his eyebrows and moved to the center of the ring, calling out for a show of hands of who wanted to take me on.

I didn't bother turning back to see who he selected. No matter who it was, I knew they were in for a beating. I removed the T-shirt I'd put on and started doing some shadow boxing and jumping up and down to get my body revved up.

"I'll take him."

I grinned, turning to see Jacob emerge from the crowd. "Doc, long time no see. I'd hate to mess up those hands of yours. I know they're pretty important in your career field."

"I'll take my chances," Jacob Reynolds retorted as he jumped up and proceeded to enter the ring.

"It's your call," I chided back.

Jacob's nickname around the underground fighting scene was Doc because that was his profession. But he wasn't just any doctor, he was one of the top up and coming plastic surgeons in the state. No one understood why he'd put such a lucrative career in jeopardy by climbing into the ring but everyone had their demons.

"Hope you warned all of your patients they'll need a new doctor soon."

"You fucking wish," Jacob snarked back.

"All right, you two know the rules. And fuck making it clean. Make it as dirty as possible," Buddy cheered, causing the others standing around, watching, to cheer as well.

The bell sounded and all of the bullshit with Connor and Mark, and Townsend Industries fell away. None of that mattered. Almost everything fell by the wayside as Jacob and I locked arms, dueling for supremacy over one another. But Kayla. She was still a lingering thought in the back of my mind. So much so, that when an image of Kayla laughing came to mind, I lost concentration just long enough for Jacob to sweep my right leg out from underneath me.

"Fuck!" I grunted, pissed at myself for being so damn careless. Nothing distracted me while I was fighting, absolutely nothing. Except one woman, apparently.

"Nice fight."

"Fuck off," I grumbled at Jacob while returning his fist pound. He'd won that bout and I needed to give respect where it was due. But I wasn't done. I was still filled with tension thinking about Kayla, and even more so as a result of losing the first fight of the night. I took on another fight and won that one. I thought to take on a third fight but something in me was pulling me back home. I was calling it quits for the night.

* * *

"You're home," Kay greeted with a smile as soon as I stepped into the kitchen.

I was starving by the time I'd arrived home from fighting, but as soon as my eyes honed in on Kay in a pair of skin hugging black spandex leggings and a white T-shirt that stopped right at her waist, my mouth watered for different reasons.

"Hungry?"

My gaze lifted to meet Kay's and a hunger I hadn't felt in a long time overtook me. And it most definitely wasn't for food. At least, that's what my mind was thinking. However, my body had other plans because a loud stomach growl answered Kay for me.

"You didn't eat the dinner I left?"

I gave her a quizzical look. "I didn't see anything." I stared around the spotless kitchen.

"I left a grilled steak, vegetables, and roasted potatoes. Don't worry, they're not the same potatoes from five days ago. I bought more to make since you said you weren't eating steak or potatoes until I made them for you."

I had said that. In our second phone conversation while I was away. And I'd meant it. I'd avoided steak and potatoes because Kay promised to make them for me once I arrived back home.

"Where?" I questioned, pointedly looking around but seeing nothing.

"I left the plate in the oven for you. I wrote it on the back of the note."

I frowned, trying to recall what note she was talking about. "Oh, the one about eating at your parents' house." The same one I'd crumpled up and threw out due to my not liking having my plans for the evening changed.

"Sit. I'll heat it up."

My feet moved toward one of the kitchen stools and I sat at the center island, watching Kay in those damn leggings as she brought the plate out from the oven.

My mouth watered at the sight of the plate of food and the smell of rosemary from the potatoes hit my nostrils causing them to flare. I was hungrier than I'd imagined.

"This thing was tricky the first time I used it. I thought it was the oven." Kay's words pulled me from my own ruminations.

"They do look alike," I responded. My microwave sat directly atop the stainless steel oven. Both of which were built into the wall.

"Were you out for a late night workout or something?" Kay questioned as she placed the plate of food in front of me.

I glanced down at myself, noting the workout tee and shorts I'd worn to fight in that night. "Something like that," I responded. My stomach growled again as the steam from the food hit me. "This smells delicious," I told Kay, reaching for the fork and knife she handed me.

I immediately tore into steak, cutting it and grinning when I saw that beautiful pink middle.

"Medium rare. I remembered." She grinned and my eyes fell to her plump lips.

I ran my tongue along my own bottom lip, but it wasn't because of the steak, although it was quite delicious.

"Can't see how you eat it so rare."

"I'm a fucking carnivore. No more tofu!" I warned, pointing my fork at her.

She giggled and sighed. "It wasn't *that* bad. You liked it. Come on, admit it," she taunted as she bent over the kitchen island.

My eyes dropped to the considerable amount of cleavage that position afforded me to see. "You're about to get your ass in trouble," I growled.

I plucked another piece of steak in my mouth, followed by a

perfectly roasted potato, as I continued to stare. Kay's eyes were wide, cautious. I decided to give her an out.

"How was dinner at your parents'?"

"Great. Mama made carne asada arroz con gandules y lechón. Muy rico!" she commented.

"I bet."

"I brought some home for you. I know you enjoy my mama's cooking as much as I do."

I smiled around the bite of food in my mouth. I had enjoyed a number of the traditional Puerto Rican or Dominican meals Kay's mother made us when we'd spend time at her house as kids.

"Do your parents know you're staying with me?"

"Yup. Mama is okay with is. Papi is … papi." She shrugged.

"I bet," I mumbled.

"Huh?" she asked, moving closer.

"Nothing. These potatoes are excellent, Kay." She'd obviously inherited her mother's ability in the kitchen.

"They're better fresh out of the oven, but …" She trailed off.

"They're great now. Taste." I pulled her by the arm to me and stood over her, holding a potato wedge on the end of my fork to her lips.

She was caught off guard, but after only a moment of hesitation she opened her mouth, allowing me to easily slip the tongs of my fork between her lips. Not for the first time, I imagined slipping something else between those succulent lips.

She closed her lips around the fork, and slowly I pulled the it free, watching her chew. A small sigh escaped her mouth and my groin tightened uncontrollably.

"It's not ba—"

Her response was cut off by my mouth on hers. Another sigh escaped her mouth but for different reasons. She opened up enough to grant my tongue entrance. I tasted the remnants of my meal on her mouth but there was a sweetness that was all her. I pushed the kiss deeper, harder, when I reached around and cupped the back of her head, pulling her to me. I pushed her back the few inches to the island, bracketing my free arm around her waist.

But I wasn't alone in this.

Kay gave just as much as I did to the kiss, pulling me by the arms to her, leaning her head back, granting me better access to her mouth. A shared surge of energy wrapped itself around us, cloaking us from head to toe. The only thing that mattered right then was this kiss. Her lips glued to mine, the tiny moans that escaped her mouth begging for more. The feel of her hardened nipples beneath the thin T-shirt she wore. I broke free from her lips and blazed a path down her chin to her long neck, licking, sucking, and biting. All of the stress and tension I'd felt waiting to get back home over the past five days was coming to a head.

Literally.

My cock was growing hard enough to drill through concrete. Kay's soft hand found its way to my hair, pulling my in.

"J-Josh," she moaned. "J-Josh, wait ... Josh you're ringing," she pulled back to tell me.

At first I only heard a ringing sound and thought it was coming from my own ears, until I blinked. It was as if I was coming to, out of a trance. I realized my phone was actually ringing in the pocket of my shorts.

Biting back a curse, I pulled out my phone. If someone was calling this late it must be important.

It was.

"Michelle's in labor. The baby's finally coming and he seems to be in a rush," my father said as soon as I pressed the phone to my ear.

"General?"

"Yes. If you leave now you might be able to make it before the baby arrives."

"On my way. We gotta go," I told Kay as I hung up the phone.

"Wh-what? Go? Where?" She looked as confused as I'd been a few seconds prior.

"Michelle, Carter's wife, is having the baby. They're at General." I didn't wait for her to reply. I grabbed her by the hand, looking down to make sure she had shoes on before grabbing my own keys and heading for the door. "We're going to meet my new nephew."

CHAPTER 9

*J*oshua

Unfortunately, we were too late. After my having to overcome Kay's protest of the reasons why she shouldn't be going to the hospital with me, she'd made us stop at a twenty-four hour convenience store. We picked up some flowers and balloons as a gift.

"I'll have to get more tomorrow but this will have to do in the meantime," she stated, frowning, obviously disappointed.

"More? What more could you have to get?"

She gave me a sideways glance just as we entered the hospital's parking garage. It was well past official visiting hours, but when you're staying in the luxury wing of the hospital the rules didn't always apply. Especially not with the last name Townsend.

"Baby clothes, gifts. Oh, I know!" she stated, snapping her fingers. "I'll make them some meals for a week or two."

"Michelle does the cooking."

Another side eye from Kay. "She just had a baby. Do you know how rough life is with a newborn?"

I shrugged.

"Such a guy. Sleepless nights, waking nearly every hour, especially if she has to breastfeed, and let's not even discuss whether or not the baby is a cluster feeder. She'll be too exhausted to cook, so it's customary to bring over meals for a family with a new baby. Do you think she likes casseroles? Or maybe some pasteles," she mused as I held the door open for her.

"I'm sure whatever you make, they'll appreciate. Come on." I took her by the hand—not knowing when it'd become customary for me to hold doors open for her or hold her hand, but it felt as natural as breathing. After passing through security, we made our way up to the floor where Michelle and Carter's room was located.

I rapped on the closed door we had been directed to a few times before hearing Carter's deep voice ordering us to, "Come in."

I pushed the door open. "Congratulations," I greeted, smiling at my oldest brother.

A smile a mile wide spread over his face. I couldn't recall ever seeing him so happy.

"Thanks, man," he answered, hugging me.

I returned the hug before pulling back and bringing Kay to stand next to me.

"This is—"

"Kayla," Carter greeted. "We've met, though it's been a while. Thanks for coming."

"Congratulations!" Kay added. "We brought some gifts for you." She held out the flowers, card, and balloon.

"Thank you," Carter added, pulling Kay in for a hug.

A charge of jealousy moved through me at the sight of another man's hands on her. I fought hard to tamp it down. This was Carter. Moreover, we were there to celebrate his wife giving birth. He wasn't flirting in the least.

In fact, as soon as he released Kay from the hug, he looked anxious to get back to his wife and newborn son.

"This way," he began, ushering us through the entrance portion of the room to another door where I could make out laughter and talking on the other side.

Just before Carter opened the door, he turned to me and said,

"Don't scare my son with your ugly mug."

I snorted. "Please, the only saving grace that baby has for looking halfway decent is that his mother is beautiful," I retorted.

"Don't look at my wife," Carter growled with the same jealousy I'd just experienced moments before.

"You two," Kay laughed, shaking her head.

I tightened my fingers around hers, bringing her hand to my lips just before turning and seeing the rest of my family, save for Tyler, who was out of town for work, and the children who'd been left in the care of a nanny while they slept. I quickly made introductions—or reintroductions—of Kayla to my family who was present.

"You weren't fighting, were you?" my mother whispered loud enough only for me to hear.

I pressed a kiss to her cheek. "Hello Mother."

She frowned, her blue eyes narrowing at me. My mother hated the fact that I fought. From what I heard, she practically kicked my father out of their bedroom when she first learned he was the one who'd gotten me into it. After close to seven years she reluctantly accepted it. But as she scanned my face and body looking for bruises or injury, the frown on her face revealed how much she still hated the idea of me fighting. It was the same, worried look she often gave Tyler after a game or a big tackle.

"You'll meet a woman someday who'll make you forget all about fighting." Her eyes immediately shifted to my right and a sparkle entered them at the sight of Kayla.

I sighed, refusing to inform my mother that this son of hers didn't plan on settling down. Ever. But even as I thought those words, my head shifted and I stared at Kayla who was smiling at the bundle of joy in Michelle's arms, the words seemed to lack the same passion they'd always had in the past. Almost as if I were starting to doubt my own conviction.

Instead, I gave my mother one last look and moved toward the bed where Michelle sat up, smiling just as big as Carter who now stood at her side. Aaron and Patience were at the foot of the bed.

"Hey, sis," I greeted a tired but beaming Michelle.

"Josh, hey." She smiled and turned to Kayla.

"This is Kayla."

"Nice to meet you," Kay began. "I'm sorry, if you wanted just family here I can leave."

Kay's words pissed me off but before I could say anything, Michelle spoke up.

"If Josh brought you, then you're family," she stated easily.

Kay's mouth clamped shut as she turned her head to me.

"She's right," was all I said.

I turned back to the bed. My eyes dropped to the bundle in her arms. I watched on as Carter bent over to retrieve the sleeping baby from his wife. He brought the baby over to me.

"Everyone else has already had their turn."

I stood up a little straighter, feeling pride my brother entrusted me to hold his most precious gift.

I held out my arms.

"Don't drop my son," Carter warned.

"I'll protect him with my life," I promised fiercely, meaning every word. As soon as Samuel was in my arms, his tiny lips opened and he let out a huge yawn. "You're exhausted. It's been a big day for you, little guy," I crooned.

I held and rocked him a while longer, only to look up and see four pairs of eyes staring at me.

"What?" I asked, glancing around.

"You're a natural," Patience answered.

"Whatever." I lowered my gaze back to Samuel. I could make out his features enough to know he was going to look exactly like his father. I lifted my head and stared directly at Kay. Her eyes were glued to little Samuel. I turned and looked to Carter, wordlessly questioning if it was okay to let her hold the baby.

He nodded and I shifted to pass Samuel to Kay.

"Oh no, I couldn't," she began, shaking her head.

"It's okay," Michelle urged, silencing Kay's protest.

She bit her bottom lip just before holding out her arms and easily taking the baby from me. She stared around the room wide-eyed for a moment, still unsure. But when her gaze landed on Sam her eyes lit up in a way I hadn't remembered seeing in a long time.

"Hey, little guy. You're beautiful," she cooed, rocking him gently.

I couldn't take my eyes off the sight before me. Never had I thought about having kids until that moment. Not even when I had thought I was with the woman I'd be with for a lifetime. Not until right then did I picture a future with children of my own.

I turned my head away.

A few minutes later Kay returned Samuel to the loving arms of his mother. We remained at the hospital for a while longer. But it was obvious Michelle was getting tired. We decided to head out. Everyone congratulated Michelle again before leaving them to get some rest. Carter decided to walk everyone to the elevator.

I walked out with Aaron, my father, and Carter, while Patience, my mother, and Kay stayed another minute with Michelle.

"You need to get Michelle one hell of a push present for putting up with your lame ass long enough to produce another heir to the Townsend throne."

Carter grunted. "Get out of here with that bullshit. And Sam's not sitting on the Townsend throne. He's going to be a firefighter like his father."

I shook my head. "You've already got your successor in the department covered with Diego, Townsend Industries needs at least one of your offspring. We all can see Kyle's going to be another little tyrant like his father."

Aaron grunted, scowling in my direction.

"Probably not *as* bad as you," I added just to dig at my brother a little.

Carter shook his head. "No can do. All of my boys are going to be like their father."

"That's what I thought, too."

We all turned to my father. His brown eyes shone with delight. He glanced over at Carter with proud eyes. "I had plans for my boys also but they all have a mind of their own." He looked between the three of us.

Carter grinned. He, of all people, should know what my father was referring to. Being the oldest out of the four of us, everyone expected him to take over the mantel at Townsend Industries once my father stepped down. But Carter made his own way, going into the army for six years and then into the Williamsport Fire Department. He was one of the top firefighters in the department from my estimation.

"We'll see what your sons turn out to be." My father tapped Carter on his shoulder.

"Making plans for my grandchildren already?" my mother interrupted us, turning an accusing eye on my father.

I smirked. If there was one person on this planet who could keep my father in check it was my mother.

"Just a few," my father answered, wrapping an arm around her waist and pressing a kiss to her forehead.

I watched as Aaron unabashedly did the same with his wife. As soon as I felt her at my side, my arm was extending, pulling Kay into me. A warmth settled over me when her body melted into mine as if that's right where it'd wanted to be all along.

"Townsend men tend to fall fast."

I glanced up, looking at Carter's whose eyes were pinned on me.

"What was that?"

"Nothing. I'm going back to my wife and kid. Don't call us, we'll call you," he stated before sauntering off down the hall.

By the time we made it back home that night, Kay and I both were exhausted. I barely had the energy to walk up the stairs. But when Kay went to head to the guest room, on instinct, my arm reached out, stopping her. I pulled her to my room instead.

"What're you doing?"

"I don't like sleeping alone."

She lifted a brow. "Since when?"

"Since now," I answered, kicking the door closed, slamming it.

Kay must've been too tired to ask anymore questions because when I pressed a quick kiss to her lips and walked her to the bed, she climbed in, allowing me to climb in right behind, spooning her. We fell asleep in less than five minutes, in each other's warmth.

CHAPTER 10

*K*ayla
A heavy weight over my legs prevented me from moving out of the warm, soft comfort of the huge bed. The bed was unusually inviting that particular morning. *Just a few more minutes,* I thought behind my closed eyelids. I could sleep just a little while longer. Snuggling my head deeper into the plush pillows, I wiggled my hips to get closer to the warmth that was behind me.

"You keep moving like that and your chances of leaving this bed anytime soon are slim to none."

My eyes popped open at the deep rumble of his sleepy, morning voice. My heart began racing. I wasn't in bed alone. The last time that'd happened …

I waited for the panic to set in but it never came. The same feeling of being wrapped up in safety that I'd felt with my eyes closed persisted.

Joshua.

I was in bed with Joshua.

I sat up. Panic may not have set in, but the guilt was starting to creep up in its place.

"We slept together," I stated, looking down on him, but I had to turn away. His eyes were half mast, dark hair resting over his forehead, and those damn freckles looked good enough to lick.

"Unfortunately, that's all we did," he grumbled, turning over to glance at the clock. "Seven fucking o'clock. You ready for your lesson?" He turned over, staring up at me.

I blinked, trying to remember what lesson. "Oh, self-defense. We can skip it—"

"Absolutely not. I'm up now."

"But you just got in yesterday and had a late night." My hand reached out and I ran my fingers through his dark mane. Smooth and silky.

"And don't think that means I'm taking it easy on your ass either." He sat up, giving me a pointed look before winking and exiting the bed. "Meet me downstairs in five minutes," he stated, entering the bathroom.

Since his tone had brokered no argument, I hopped out of the bed and started for the doorway to go to the guest room to change. Suddenly his bathroom door popped open.

"And make sure you brush your teeth. You're cute as shit in the mornings but not the morning breath."

I gasped and quickly grabbed a pillow from the seat of the armchair in the corner of the room and tossed it at the bathroom door, aiming for his head. He was lightning quick, slamming the door before the pillow could make its way to its intended spot.

"Goddammit!" I yelled thirty minutes later as I found myself pinned down on my back, yet again, Joshua's big body covering mine. "You're cheating!"

He chuckled and I thanked God for the sports bra I was wearing that concealed my hardened nipples.

"You weren't watching that time," he answered, standing and reaching a hand down to help me up.

I inhaled sharply when his extended hand pulled me in flush against his body. For a long while he stared down into my eyes, searching for something. When his head started to lower, I saw my chance.

I abruptly did a spin move he'd taught me, putting my back to his front. With his arm that was holding me, still tucked into my arm, I crouched low, causing him to bend low with me. I moved my left foot around his, tripping him and causing him to topple over onto his back. I thought I'd won that round but quick as usual, Joshua recovered, and somehow I was again pinned on my back, Joshua on top of me.

"I see I've gotta keep on my toes with you."

I smiled. "Rule number one, never let your guard down," I mimicked the words he'd said when we first began these lessons.

He nodded. "I like a quick study." He reached down and licked the side of my neck until he reached my earlobe, sucking it into his mouth.

A moan escaped my lips, uncontrollably. My eyes closed as my head fell to the mat and his lips found mine. This kiss was even better than the previous night. I reached up, entangling my fingers into Joshua's hair, as he fully moved over top of me, pressing his weight into my body. I took it all.

When his hand lowered to the waistband of the runner's shorts I was wearing, I instantly raised my hips. He tugged at the band, making room for his hand to find the inside of my panties. My eyes rolled to the back of my head when his long finger trailed along the outline of my pussy lips. It'd been so long since I trusted any man long enough to touch me so intimately.

Just when I felt myself getting lost in Joshua's arms, a flashback of one horrible night two years earlier appeared, stealing my very breath.

"Stop!" I shrilled.

Another flashback of my giggling uncontrollably as I was being dragged out of a night club on the arm of a guy I barely new, came to mind.

"Josh, stop," I implored in between pants.

"Wh-what's the matter?" he questioned, pulling back, alarm filling his voice.

I sat up when he moved from over top of me. I couldn't look him in his eye, instead choosing to fumble with my clothing, pulling my shirt down and shorts up.

"Kay—"

"We can't do this." I shook my head and started to stand but was stopped by a heavy hand around my arm.

"Look at me." His voice was so stern I didn't dare not follow.

His eyes narrowed when I finally met his. He angled his head the way he usually does when assessing someone or something. "What is it?"

I swallowed and looked everywhere besides in his eyes. "It's … it's Chelsea," I lied, using my dead best friend as a cover. While I did have guilt over what was happening between Josh and I, due to my loyalty to Chels, it was more so the shameful secret I'd carried with me from Portland.

"We can't betray her like this," I insisted, pulling my arm free and rising to stand. "I have to get ready for work." I quickly scurried out of the basement and up the stairs … feeling Joshua's eyes burning a hole in my back as I went.

* * *

"Come on, Darla, you've got to have something for me," I begged my realtor through the phone later that day. I was on my lunch break at work and she was the first person I'd called after my hectic morning. I needed her to help me find a new place and fast. What'd happened between Joshua and I that morning could not happen again. I closed my eyes and pinched the bridge of my nose, doing my best to stave off the memory of that kiss and the ease I'd felt sleeping in his bed the night before.

"I'm sorry, Kayla. The place I thought would be perfect for you just accepted an offer this morning. The other place is farther from your job than you want to be, and the third place you said was way out of your budget. The other three listings I sent you said you didn't like."

I groaned, hating that she was right. Biting on the top of the pen I held in my hand, I contemplated my options. I couldn't overspend just to get out of Joshua's house any quicker, and I definitely couldn't move back in with my parents.

"How about I drop by your office this afternoon with some new listings that just came up? I know you only wanted to look at condos, but there are some nice town homes I think you'd be interested in. We'll take a look, and if you're up to it, we can stop by a couple today."

I was desperate. "Okay sure. Come by around four. I have my last patient appointment at three-thirty." Darla and I said our good-byes, and I turned to hang up my phone. "Goddammit!" I startled, seeing Joshua perched at my doorway yet again. "Are you making a habit of scaring the hell out of me?"

He stared, jaw rigid, unanswering as if he hadn't heard my question. He moved into my office, striding confidently, glancing around the office, measuring every inch as if he hadn't already been there.

"You weren't always so jumpy."

I folded my arms over my chest, feeling exposed. "Things change. People change." I shrugged.

"Some not for the better." He perched himself on the edge of my desk as if sitting on his throne.

"What's that supposed to mean?"

"You're looking for condos."

"So? My move to your place was only temporary."

He eyed me, nodding.

"You're different. Now," he stated, changing the subject.

I furrowed my brows. "We're all different. Seven years is a long time," I defended.

"For some. Why do you wear your hair straight?"

My hand instantly shot up to my hair which was neatly tucked in a bun. My usual these days.

"I like it like this."

"Liar," he accused.

"I do," I insisted. "It's easier to manage. Can't have my hair in the way while trying to treat patients."

"You used to call your hair your crown. Even your mother couldn't touch it once you turned fourteen. You hated wearing pants.

Said you'd wear dresses or skirts to work everyday if you could." He made a show of eyeing the black slacks I worn with a white button up top.

I should've known Joshua would recall all of that.

"Maybe those were just the words of a young girl who didn't know anything." The world had changed me.

"Or maybe that girl encountered something or someone that made her scared. Scared to the point that she asks an old friend for self-defense lessons and runs out when things get too close."

"I don't know what you're talking about," I countered, my eyes dropping to the folders on my desk. "I told you what that was about this morning."

"And as much as I know you loved Chelsea, I don't believe you."

"I'm telling the truth! We—"

"When are you going to stop running, Kay?"

My mouth fell open but no words came.

"It's what you do. You ran seven years ago when things got too tough. You ran the night of the charity event. And I just walked in here to hear you talking with your realtor. I figured you were braver but maybe I was wrong." He stood.

This time my eyes narrowed.

"Maybe you were wrong," I stated to his back, which was now to me as he made his way to the door.

He paused for a moment before turning to me.

"Or maybe I'm just fucking tired of people thinking they can dictate my life."

"Who's trying to dictate your life, Kay?"

"You. My parents. The po—" I stopped before the words could come out.

Joshua waited for me to respond but I didn't say anything further.

"Fine." He nodded. "When you figure out who you're pissed at, come find me." And with that, he stormed out, slamming my door behind him.

I was still seething. Not with Joshua. He'd only spoken the truth. I was pissed at myself for feeling so weak. There were so many reasons as to why he and I didn't make sense. The flashbacks I'd experienced that morning, Chelsea, my lack of confidence.

I felt lost. Unable to remember who and what I truly wanted.

That feeling stayed with me the remainder of the day. After work, instead of going straight home, I aimed my car in the direction of the place that reminded me of the girl I used to be. Maybe I could find and recapture her somehow.

* * *

JOSHUA

"Dammit, Kay. Where the hell are you?" Yeah, sure, I'd put the ball in her court, but I didn't like it there. That wasn't how I worked. And now, it pissed me off as I paced between my foyer and living room, looking out the window of my house for her car to pull up. My cell phone was tightly clutched in my right hand.

Something had been off about her since she'd come back. I felt it, and what had transpired between us that morning had confirmed it. Now it was getting dark, raining heavily and a thunderstorm was on the horizon and she wasn't home.

"Fuck this." *Since she wouldn't come to me, I would go to her.* Just this once.

I hopped in my BMW and backed out of the garage and was on the road within five minutes, rain be damned. I decided to first drive past her office to see if she was still there. I already knew the answer but it was confirmed once I saw the empty parking lot. She wasn't at work. I even considered stopping at her parents but thought better of it. Besides, although I had apologized a few years later to Mr. Reyes, I still got the impression he was no fan of mine.

The more I drove, the angrier I grew. Kayla was doing it again. Running. And avoiding me. I pounded on the steering wheel with my fist. I wondered if I'd come on too strongly, but I'd exercised incredible restraint, in spite of my base self wanting to take what felt like belonged to me. Kayla's hesitance forced me to go slower than I wanted to, but I did it. But that would only last for so long. I had enough adrenaline running through my veins that night, that I knew once I found Kayla, I wouldn't be able to keep my hands off of her.

I understood her reluctance where Chelsea was concerned. The same pangs of guilt had plagued me too when I first recognized what was happening between us. But the pull between Kay and I was too strong to ignore. I learned to make peace with this budding ... whatever it was that was happening here.

Instead of heading over to her parents, on a whim I found myself pointing my car in the opposite direction. Driving to a place I hadn't been to in years. It was the last place I wanted to go but deep down I knew I'd find her there.

Sure enough, as I pulled my BMW up next to Kayla's parked car, I sighed, when I saw her empty vehicle. A need to see her drove me to push the driver's side door open and climb out against the pelting rain and the backdrop of loud, clapping thunder. As soon as I shut my car door the night sky was illuminated by a flash of lightning, only to go dark again a few seconds later. I growled angrily as I began walking down the hiking trail that would lead to the waterfall where we'd released Chelsea's ashes.

My heart grew heavier and heavier with each step I took. I didn't know if it was because of thoughts of Chelsea, or if it was because I could feel Kayla's agony, or it might've been a mixture of both. But as I cleared the pathway and the rushing sounds of the waterfall came in clearer, my eyes darted around the dimly lit space until they finally landed on her soaked body.

My Adam's apple bobbed up and down in my throat as I swallowed. It was dark but I could make out how the button-up top she wore clung to her body, drenched by the rain. Her head was down as she stared at the water below, but it popped up when a branch snapped underneath the weight of my foot. My pace increased, propelling me closer to the large rock she sat on. She simply stared at me when I reached her, glaring down on her.

"It's time to stop running." The anger was thick in my voice. I wanted to throttle her and pull her to me at the same time.

Her lips parted. "There're things you don't know about me."

"Is that supposed to be a deterrent? Scare me?"

She turned her head to look away from me.

Nope. Not this time. I moved closer, turning her by the chin to face me again. "There's nothing you could tell me that would stop what's about to happen. You might as well give up fighting it."

"Josh, we shoul—" One last weak protest that I didn't bother heeding.

I crushed our mouths together, breaking off any further protests, and dipped my tongue inside to receive the sweetness of her taste. I pulled Kayla to stand by her arms, closing out any distance between our bodies. I felt her hesitation initially, but even she couldn't deny the inevitable. Her body acquiesced and lips surrendered to mine. When she moaned into my mouth, I needed more. I reached down and cupped the ass that I'd watch jiggle as she worked out each morning, despite my hatred of early mornings. Squeezing it, I pressed her hips against my burgeoning hard-on. Kayla gasped, breaking off our kiss. I dipped my head to lower to her neck, itching to get my first taste of the soft skin that rested there. Kayla shivered in my arms when my teeth slightly clenched at the skin just below her earlobe.

"You've been avoiding the inevitable for too long," I growled in her ear. I took a step, and then another, pressing our bodies back up to the nearest tree. The rain and passing thunderstorm be damned.

"Josh," Kayla panted, breathlessly. "I-if we do this …"

"There is no *if*, Kayla. We're doing this." I crushed her lips with mine. My hands frantically began unbuttoning her shirt, peeling it away from her body, exposing cinnamon flesh my mouth watered to taste.

Kayla's hands weren't idol either. She rubbed her hands along my chest, finding the buttons to my own shirt, undoing them. Her hands on my chest had me growling with need.

"I should wait until I get you into my bed to take you but I can't."

"I don't want to wait." Kayla stared at me, biting her bottom lip, awaiting my reaction to her words.

The only reaction I had was to rejoin our lips and pull and tug at her clothing. I undid the button of her pants, pulling them down, exposing her lower half. My hands went to the globes of her ass, squeezing and kneading them. I used one hand to undo the button of the jeans I wore. I was so hard it was almost painful to pull myself free.

"Give me your hand," I ordered.

Kayla didn't hesitate placing her hand in mine. I guided her hand to my stiff member, wrapping it around me. "You're going to put me inside of you for the first time." I leaned in, licking her plump bottom lip and wrapping her left leg around my waist.

"Shit!" I grunted when Kayla's hand squeezed around my cock. "Do it, Kayla. Now!" I urged, licking her earlobe just before suckling it. My eyes squeezed shut when I felt her maneuver my cock to her wet entrance. I groaned in her ear as she began sliding me inside of her. She was so fucking tight I felt like my eyes were going to pop out of my damn skull. And I wouldn't mind one damn bit.

I brushed her hand aside and slid all of the way in until I couldn't go any deeper. I pressed my body against hers and leaned in. "You know why I had you put me inside of you?"

She shook her head, eyelids drooping as she looked at me.

"So you know we're in this together. You and me. You're just as much in this as I am, Kay." With that declaration, I took both of her wrists in my one hand, raising them above her head and covering her lips with mine. With my free hand, I gripped her waist and began pumping my hips into her.

"Josh!" Kayla screamed, throwing her head back against the tree.

"Yeah, baby. Say my name just like that." That shit turned me on like nothing else. Hearing my name fall from Kayla's breathless lips was my undoing. I reached up with the hand that had been on her waist and I tugged at the band at the back of her hair that was holding it in place. A few seconds later, long, curly strands fell around her shoulders. I lowered my face to the crook of her neck, inhaling her scent.

"Josh, you feel so good. Harder, please!" Kayla screamed.

I released her wrists and placed both of my hands at her hip, holding her body in a way that gave me enough leverage to drill into her the way I really wanted to and the way she obviously needed me to.

"Shiiiit!" she panted as I swiveled my hips and pumped harder.

I almost lost my footing when I felt the muscles of her pussy tighten around my cock. "Fuck, Kayla! If I'd know your pussy was this good there's no way I would've let you run from me as long as I did." The truth fell from my mouth, spurred by the euphoria that was engulfing my body.

"We're in this, Kay. You and me!" I declared, pumping so hard I felt her body bouncing off of mine. "Come for me, baby." I reached down to rub her clit with my thumb.

Kayla let out a moan that rivaled the thunder from earlier.

I felt her tighten around me and her walls began convulsing as she orgasmed. Her speech was incoherent but I didn't need coherent words to know that she was coming.

I continued to glide in and out of her as she came. My grip tightened around her ass when my own orgasm took hold of me.

"Fuck!" I lifted my head and shouted as a full body orgasm overtook me. I felt my come release inside of her. Even before the last vestiges of my orgasm disappeared, I knew I'd never felt more whole in my life. I dropped my head to Kayla's shoulder. We stood like that for a while—her rubbing her hand up and down my back, while I caught my breath.

Finally, I lifted my head and stared at her. "You're coming home with me."

She blinked away the sex-induced fog that had settled over her eyes. "B-but my car—"

"Will be fine until we pick it up tomorrow."

I didn't wait for her response. I pulled myself free, both of us moaning as I deserted her still gripping pussy. After I stuffed myself back into my jeans, I helped Kayla get redressed. With no words, I took her hand in mine and led us both toward the trail until we reached the parking area. I held the door open for Kayla who paused before reluctantly getting into the passenger seat of my car.

We drove mostly in silence back to my house. Out of the corner of my eye, I caught Kayla fidgeting with her hands in her lap. She was having second and third thoughts.

I pulled up and directly into the garage door, not for the first time thankful for the garage door opener I kept in my car. I turned off the car and immediately turned to Kayla, placing my hand on her headrest and my other arm on the steering wheel.

"I need you in my bed tonight."

She began shaking her head. "Maybe that's not a—"

"That wasn't a request," I implored. I gave her one last glare before getting out of the car and moving around to the passenger side, helping her out.

"I've already explained, Kay. We're in this together."

CHAPTER 11

*K*ayla

Five days. That's how long it'd been since I had taken up residence in Joshua's bed each night. I kept waiting for more flashbacks to happen but they never came. The guilt, on the other hand, was a different story.

"Quit it."

My body instantly heated at the sound of his voice behind me. I rolled my head over to look at him. The rest of my body was constricted, partially trapped under his long, thick leg and arm.

"Your eyes aren't even open."

He grunted. "Don't need to see you to know you're awake and thinking … loudly."

"How can I think loudly? That doesn't make sense."

His eyes popped open and I swore then I'd never get tired of the sight of his eyes, especially when they held the intensity they were holding right then.

"You don't feel weird about all of this?" I questioned, sitting up and pressing my back against the wooden headboard, my left hand pulling the sheet up to cover my naked body. I watched as Joshua's eyes dropped from my face to the tops of my shoulders then lower. His lips turned into a frown at the sight of my covered breasts. My nipples hardened the moment those green eyes, darkened with lust, moved back up to mine.

"Should I?" His voice was deeper than usual.

"Yes," I answered. "*We* should. Chelsea is—"

"Dead."

I gasped.

"For seven years now, Kay. Chelsea's been gone. We aren't betraying her."

"Joshua—" I began, but was cut off by his kiss. His lips on mine had my eyes closing as a wave of pleasure moved through my entire body. My pussy clenched, desire to be filled overwhelming me.

Joshua pulled back just as I was getting revved up. He put his forehead to mine.

"Now, does that feel like something that's wrong or shameful?"

I pushed out the air from my lungs, shaking my head. I knew what the wrong touch felt like. For a touch to be filled with disgust. I loathed that I knew that but I did. Joshua's touch was nowhere near that at all.

"I—" I broke off, shaking my head because words became impossible to speak when Joshua's big hand moved to cover my now aching sex.

"I can understand your guilt but Chels wouldn't want us to refrain from living our lives."

I sighed, knowing deep down he was right. Chelsea had the biggest heart of anyone I knew. I don't know how she'd feel if she were alive and this was happening between Josh and I, but in her absence, I think she'd want us to be happy.

"Now that that's out of the way," Josh's deep voice continued. "I want you to come with me to visit one of my properties today."

I blinked, turning my head to stare at him, wondering what the hell he was even talking about. He'd just wrapped me up in a sex-induced haze, and now he was talking about property visits.

"One of my divisions. I need to visit and it's going to take up a large part of my day. Come with me." His lips were a half an inch from mine.

"Is that a question or a command?" I grinned, staring him in his sparkling eyes.

"You'll figure that out, once we're done with practice."

"Wh-whoa!" I yelped when, with lightning speed, he leapt from the bed and picked me up over his shoulder. "What the hell are you doing?" I screeched.

"Just cause you woke up in my bed doesn't mean I'm going to take it easy on you in the gym. Let's go. We've got a busy day," he growled, slapping my ass as he carried me into the guest room to change. "And don't even think of trying to straighten your hair!" he insisted as he finally lowered me to the floor.

* * *

Two hours later, I found myself entering one of Townsend Real Estate's unfinished luxury homes.

"You said this place used to be a golf course?" I questioned, looking around.

"Yes. The manmade lake was the biggest appeal for this particular piece of land. I had the architects divvy up the lots and the roads in a way that half of the homes in this section would face the lake while the other half had their backyards open out to the lake. This is one of the homes that faces the lake."

We were standing in what would become the living room of the house, and I could see out of the huge center window. The lake was the main view and it was stunning. Whoever would become the owner of this home, would undoubtedly love it. My breathing hitched when Joshua took my hand in his. I was becoming more and more familiar with his touch, and with each instant, I grew more comfortable. Not for the first time a shockwave ran through me at feel of his skin against mine.

"Let me show you the upstairs. The view is even better up there," he announced with radiant eyes. His excitement was palpable; his love for real estate evident. I swallowed and averted my eyes, realizing that I yearned to have him gaze at me with that type of admiration and radiance.

"This is gorgeous. How many square feet is this house?" I asked to take my mind off my own personal yearnings.

"Just over forty-two hundred. It's one of the smaller models." He released my hand and moved closer to the wall, stooping low. "The hell?"

I glanced down, worried. I couldn't see anything that was the matter. But Joshua looked up and down the wall, sizing it up.

"Fuck," he grunted.

"What's the matter?"

"The spacing is off. I'm going to have to talk to my foreman." He pulled out his phone and went about typing something in it. His fingers began flying over the keypad.

"Looks fine to me," I mumbled because it really did.

Joshua grunted as he continued typing. "They also put a vent right in front of the door, where you enter the house. Assholes," he cursed, shaking his head.

I didn't envy whoever was on the other end of that text.

I moved around the lounge room that was on the second floor.

"To the untrained eye it looks okay," he started explaining once he put his phone back in his back pocket. His voice taking on an ominous tone. "But it only takes a minor problem to throw everything out of whack. Thankfully, I notice everything."

I turned to face him. His gaze was intent on me and it was then I realized we had somehow moved on from talking about real estate.

"What's that supposed to mean?" I asked carefully, feeling like I needed to guard myself for some reason.

"It means ..." he began, moving closer, crowding my space.

I wanted to step back and pull him closer at the same time.

"Exactly what I said. There isn't much I miss when it comes to property or the people I care about." He took another step closer and it was then that I felt my back pressed up against a wall. I hadn't even realized I was moving backwards until I no longer could. "I'm the most observant out of my four brothers. It's been useful when it comes to business. I can tell when a structure's off by even an inch. It's how I've made Townsend Real Estate the best in the industry and it's how I know something' off with you."

"What do you mean *something's off?*" I shifted my gaze to stare off into the distance over his shoulder.

"The bullshit reason you gave the other week for why acting on the attraction between you and I was a bad idea. The way you wore your hair when you first came back, as if trying to tone it down, to become more obscure. The dowdy clothes you try to hide behind."

I resisted the urge to reach up and feel my curls, just to point out that I hadn't worn my hair straight since that night we'd first made love in the rain.

"Dowdy?" My voice was incredulous.

"I said what I said. You used to love vibrant colors and dresses to show off your legs. Now ..." He trailed off, pointedly staring at my somewhat loose fitting jeans and sleeveless T-shirt. It was a decent outfit but far from what I used to wear.

"If you don't like my clothes—"

"This has fuck all to do about not liking your personal style and you know it." His voice was calm but underlined by a hardness that caused me to flinch and turn away.

I clenched my jaw, hating feeling this vulnerable.

"Look at me."

I inhaled, swelling my chest and blowing out the air that'd filled my lungs before pivoting my gaze to his.

"What happened, Kay? What brought you back to Williamsport?"

I did my best to act casually. "Nothing. I just missed home. That's all."

"You're still lying. And running."

I couldn't tell you what stung more. The truth of his words or the disappointment I heard in his voice.

"It's not as easy for me as it is for you."

"What's not easy?"

"Sharing my secrets. Especially when they're my own fault."

His head shot back and his expression became perplexed. He wanted to know more. Was about to demand more, but a loud banging downstairs caught us both by surprise. Josh growled low in his throat when he realized someone was knocking on the door.

"Fucking coming!" he shouted, agitated.

I chose to follow him down the stairs, thankful for the interruption. That is, until he opened the door. I stopped short, stumbling backwards. My breathing became shallow at the sight of our new visitor.

"Mr. Townsend," the officer at the door greeted.

"Officer Alonzo, how's it going?"

I took another step back until I bumped up against the bottom step.

"Originally, I stopped by to check-in on the area, and the guys at the office said you were here checking out one of the properties. I need to speak with you."

"Sure. Officer Alonzo, this is Kayla." Joshua turned, holding out his arm to introduce me.

I tried to steady my breathing, but my heart rate remained erratic. Somehow, however, I managed to move closer to the two men, though everything in my body wanted to run in the opposite direction.

"Kayla." The officer nodded.

Bile rose in my throat.

"P-pleasure."

He held out his hand but I couldn't force myself to meet it for a handshake. The very thought had me wanting to throw up.

"I think I left something upstairs," I explained before turning and heading in the opposite direction of the two men. Only once I got back up to the second floor and entered the room Joshua and I had been in before did I release the breath I'd been holding. Closing my eyes, I counted backwards in my head down from one hundred, steadying my breathing. It took me until I reached the mid-forties to feel calm enough to open my eyes. Right then, I heard the door close and Josh called my name as he moved up the stairs.

Wiping my forehead and straightening myself out, I emerged from the room with a shaky smile on my face.

My smile immediately dropped when I saw the expression on Joshua's face. "What's wrong?"

Joshua's jaw worked and his eyes squinted as if he was contemplating on what to share.

"Someone's fucking with Townsend Real Estate." His voice was dark.

"What does that mean?"

"I just received a crime report that says crime has increased twofold in this neighborhood over the last six months. It's bullshit."

I inhaled, checking over Josh's shoulder to make sure the officer had left. "And where there's crime, people don't want to move."

"Not the type of people who are willing to drop high six to seven figures on a house," he responded.

"I need to contact Brutus." He pulled out his phone. "I'll be a minute," he told me.

"Take your time." I waved him off, feeling relieved that both Officer Alonzo had gone and Josh had other things on his mind rather than the conversation he'd started before the knock on the door.

Bad news for him had sort of become my saving grace at that moment. I wasn't ready to spill the details of what had me running back to Williamsport with my tail between my legs.

* * *

JOSHUA

This shit was coming to a head. I could feel it. More and more problems had been occurring with Townsend Real Estate. The unexpected visit from Officer Alonzo at one of my divisions was just further proof that something was up. That's why, hours later, after dropping Kay off at my place, I was down at Townsend Industries' offices, in the ground offices where our head of security's offices were.

"And you're saying this is legit?" I questioned Brutus as we stood around his office desk, police records, that were likely obtained illegally, on his desk. I didn't give a shit about the legalities of the situation. I knew Brutus and his company sometimes needed to step over the boundaries of the law in order to protect Townsend's interests.

Brutus, who towered me by about five inches, shook his dark head. "The records look legit enough to someone who doesn't know any better. A prospective client decides to do a little background research on the neighborhood and surrounding community and it seems as if the crime rate has gone up."

"And our clients are the type to do that exact research." People looking to buy a home from Townsend Real Estate were usually at the top of their field. Earning high six figures to a couple million per year, easily. They were thorough, diligent, and knew what they wanted. Something like crime rates would be one of the first things they looked at when researching a home purchase. And I was sure whoever was behind all of this knew that.

"But these numbers are inflated," Brutus continued. "Look here. Compare numbers over the last five years, the rates being reported this year nearly doubled. But economic growth as well as income averages have increased as well. These two things rarely happen concurrently."

"Tell me something I don't know, Brutus," I stated impatiently.

"If we can get in touch with my guy down at department headquarters he may be able to tell me what's going on."

"*If?*" I lifted my head and questioned him sternly.

"When."

"Make it sooner rather than later. This shit is getting worse. I can feel it. I don't like where this is going." Instincts. My instincts were telling me this was a set-up. I wasn't about to sit around and wait for the other shoe to drop.

CHAPTER 12

Kayla

"He's so beautiful," I cooed at the baby in my arms before lifting my gaze, looking toward a beaming Michelle. After Joshua dropped me off at the house, I got restless and decided to finally make the arroz con gandules and baked chicken I had decided to take over to Michelle and Carter's. To my surprise, when I arrived, Patience, Aaron's wife, was also at their place, with her two kids.

Michelle's oldest son, Diego, played with the twins in an upstairs playroom, while the three of us oohed and ahhed over the baby.

"Thank you," Michelle stated. "And this is delicious. Either that, or I'm just starving. I feel like I haven't eaten since this morning."

"That can't be good," I mused.

She waved me off. "I did have a lunch, but I think I was just running around while I ate it so I forgot. They tell you to sleep while the baby sleeps but I forgot what it's like to have a newborn. That's impossible."

"I wouldn't have minded watching Sam for you while you rested, Michelle. Besides, I thought Carter had taken off a couple weeks to be here with you and the kids," Patience added.

"You have your own little hurricanes to deal with, plus two more buns in that oven." Michelle pointed at Patience's swollen abdomen. "Carter is off but they were short down at the station today and there was a big apartment fire." Michelle's light brown eyes filled with worry as she bit her bottom lip.

"I'm sure he's okay," Patience added, sensing Michelle's concern as I had.

Michelle sighed. "He is. He just called a little while ago. He's back at the station for a debriefing. He'll be leaving soon. I just worry. Ever since Corey got injured ..."

"Corey?" I questioned, looking between the two.

"A colleague of Carter's. He was hurt in an apartment fire. Carter had to help pull him out, but ..." she hesitated, "Corey's leg had to be amputated."

"Oh my goodness," I breathed out.

"Tell me about it."

I shook my head.

"Anyway, I'm surprised your husband let you out for the day," Michelle quipped looking toward Patience.

Her brown eyes narrowed on Michelle as she pushed her long sisterlocks over her shoulder. "Aaron had a business meeting."

Michelle grunted. "Hence the two huge security guards standing in my door, watching everything like hawks."

I had noticed one huge guy dressed in black standing out front of Michelle's home when I got there. She had already been standing at the door when I arrived since I'd called ahead. The guy didn't say anything to me, just stared ahead.

"That's your security?"

Patience nodded.

"I only saw one—"

"The other one's at the back door," both women said at the same time.

I frowned, wondering why the heck so much security was needed in a neighborhood like this.

"Aaron, uh, takes my and the children's security seriously."

I didn't miss the tense look that passed between Michelle and Patience.

"So, you knew Josh in high school?" Michelle asked, rising from her chair to take the baby.

I handed her a sleeping Samuel before answering. "Yeah, we kind of grew up together. I started at Excelor Academy in sixth grade. That's how we met."

"That's nice," Michelle stated as she began rocking the baby. "What brought you back to Williamsport?"

"Um," I hedged.

"Townsend men have that appeal," Patience chimed in and laughed. She peered at me and winked.

"You would know. It's not like you had a choice in returning from Oakland." Michelle chuckled as she sat back in her chair.

"You lived in Oakland?" I questioned Patience who was giving Michelle the stink eye.

"I did. For a few years."

"Yup, and after Aaron found out about the twins, her ass wasn't going back. Sorry, baby," Michelle cooed to the baby for cursing while laughing.

I lifted an eyebrow. "Wait, so …" My gaze bounced between the two women. "Aaron didn't know about the twins?"

"Nope," Michelle answered.

"There'd been a slight miscommunication," Patience spoke up, clearing her throat.

"And you've met Aaron Townsend. I'm sure you've figured out by now, he didn't take that *miscommunication* lightly."

No, I didn't think he would.

"Yeah, well my husband didn't show up in the middle of the night in my bedroom like some damn stalker."

I gasped and look to Michelle who'd stopped smiling and trained a sharp gaze on Patience.

"Both of your husbands seem a little extreme," I spoke up, causing both women to point their attention on me. "No offense." I held up my hands in mock surrender.

After a few seconds of silence the pair began giggling.

"You've got one now, too. You'll find out how extreme these damn men can be."

I angled my gaze at Patience, scrunching my eyebrows, wondering what she was talking about. Joshua could be intense, sure, but he wasn't *that* intense. At least, not about me ... right?

I continued talking and laughing with Patience and Michelle for another hour, fixing us all a cup of hot tea. I stayed until Carter arrived home. His crystal blue eyes came alive when they landed on his wife and son. Needless to say, that was both my and Patience's cues to leave.

"Hey, you should come over some time. I'd love the company since I'm not working much these days," she offered. I knew Patience had worked as a librarian but for some reason, she'd stopped.

"I'd like that. I need to get out and explore the community a little bit." For the life of me, I couldn't figure out why, however. My stay with Joshua was only short-term and once I'd found my own place, I'd be moving out. Plus, I was sure I wouldn't be moving in anywhere nearby since the homes were well out of my price range.

"It's a great place to live."

"I can see that. Josh was telling me about the different model types of the homes. He said Tyler's place is on the next block over. Didn't want to be too close to his brothers." I laughed.

"Yeah, but he didn't want to be too far either. He's still building though, taking his time" Patience laughed along as we walked down Michelle and Carter's driveway, accompanied by her twins and the two security guards.

"Guess he's not ready to settle down," I added, speaking of the youngest Townsend brother.

"Hmm. I think we'll all be surprised by Ty."

I lifted an eyebrow, questioningly, but Patience just smiled. "You always travel with an entourage?" I questioned, looking at the burly men in front of us.

Patience glanced ahead at the security guards. "Aaron's particular about our protection." Her eyes filled with an emotion I was all too familiar with. Fear. I'd seen it in my own mirror. But a second later, she blinked and it was gone.

"With good reason, I'm sure."

She nodded and gave me a half smile. "They're good like that. Protective over what's theirs. Sometimes it can be strangling but they do mean well."

My mouth dropped open. "What's theirs?" I shook my head. "I'm not … I'm not, Joshua's. We're friends."

Patience paused on the sidewalk, giving me a curious look. "The words might not have been spoken just yet but it's there," she added cryptically. "Come on, you two, let's get inside. Daddy'll be home soon," she said to her twins who cheered at hearing about the impending arrival of their father. "Don't forget to stop by soon. You have my number," Patience said, extending her arms for a hug.

"It's a date," I agreed, returning the hug. I watched as all of them turned up toward the driveway of their home. Patience had Kennedy by the left hand while Kyle skipped ahead, declaring as the man while their father wasn't around he had to watch out for his mom and sister.

I turned my head, laughing at how serious he seemed to take his duties. A few feet from Joshua's front door, I pulled out my cell phone to see if I'd had any missed calls from him. I didn't.

The driveway and front porch lit up as soon as I stepped onto the property. I appreciated that safety aspect of his home so much. As I entered the house, I thought about fixing something for dinner but wasn't particularly hungry. That's when I decided to head downstairs to work on the punching bag for a while. The basement had become decidedly less creepy to me after weeks of practicing down there with Joshua.

About fifteen minutes later I was down in the basement, playing some hip hop music on my phone to help energize me through the workout. I'd wrapped my hands exactly the way Joshua showed me but decided against using the gloves on the bag. I figured since in the real world, chances were I wouldn't be wearing gloves if I ever needed to defend myself, better to practice for a more realistic scenario. I'd just keep my punches light enough on the bag to avoid injury.

What I hadn't counted on, was about twenty minutes into my workout, I'd look up in the mirror to find an angry looking Joshua staring at me in the mirror.

"I taught you to always use gloves on the bag." His words were deep and imploring.

* * *

JOSHUA

"You could've injured yourself," I stated slowly as I stalked toward her. My body was filled with urgency to touch her, feel her. I'd already been pissed off since having to bring her home to deal with work bullshit. But then arriving home and seeing her going to work on my punching bag, turned my agitation to a deep need that I was ready to fulfill.

"I'm wearing wraps." She held up her hands as if to show me. She was in the perfect position.

I moved quickly, reaching out and taking both of her wrists into my one hand, pulling them over her head and backing her body up against the mirror.

"Wraps aren't the same as gloves, sweetheart," I said, my lips grazing hers. If she went to protest anymore, it got lost in the searing kiss I planted on her. A low moan escaped her mouth. I sucked her bottom lip into my mouth, biting down on it with my teeth before releasing it and making a trail of kisses down her neck and back up to her ear. "Do you know how fucking hot it makes me watching you punch the shit out of this bag?"

"N-no, but you can show me," she moaned, her body coming alive under my touch. She struggled to break her hands free from my hold. "Josh, I want to touch you," she begged.

I shook my head. "No. Tonight you're on the receiving end of everything I have to give."

I pulled back and quickly spun her around, ignoring the tiny gasp of shock. I ran my hands down the side of her body, reaching to lift the workout shirt she wore before moving on to lower the running shorts, tugging them down. I growled in the back of my throat upon feeling the soft flesh of her thighs and backside.

I moved my hand around to her front at the same time I leaned in and nipped at the skin of her neck with my teeth. A sharp intake of breath was my undoing. My cock grew rigid in my pants. Kayla's hand reached back, searching for the zipper of my pants, but I swatted her hand away.

"Do it again and I will have to tie you up," I growled in her ear, nipping at her earlobe. I ran my fingers through her hair, yanking her head back.

"J-Josh," she groaned in a way that sent chills through my body.

"I need to see you when I enter you."

I moved us away from the mirror, bringing both of our bodies to the mat we usually used for her practices. That night the mat was getting a different type of workout in. It took only a few minutes to completely strip Kayla of her clothes, and another minute to do the same for myself.

"All fours," I ordered.

"What's the magic word?" Kay taunted, giving me a saucy grin.

"Now."

She began shaking her head and moved like she was about to rise. *I don't think so.* I caught her by the waist, pulling her body into position on all fours so she faced the mirror.

"Watch us in the mirror as I make you mine tonight." I had one hand entangled in her hair and the other at her waist while I positioned myself at her entrance. I moved my hand from her waist to her opening, feeling the moistness that would coat my cock as I plundered her.

"Seems like you're ready for me."

"Always," she purred.

My hand tightened in her hair and around her waist, my cock surging into her. We both stiffened at my entrance; a feeling of a thousand electric volts couldn't have been more powerful than this coupling. A mewling sound broke free from Kayla's lips and all I knew was that I needed to hear more of that. Knowing that I was the one doing it to her.

I rotated my hips, searching to hit every angle of her pussy, making her completely mine. I had no idea when this possessive streak around Kay had occurred but it was there, making me want to possess her in ways I'd never wanted to with a woman.

"Oh my Godddd!" she moaned, her eyelids falling heavy.

"Open your eyes!" I ordered. "Watch me make you mine." I caught her eyes in the mirror and refused to let them go as I worked her pussy like it was my own personal playground. Because it was. I rocked in and out of her, eliciting mewls and moans set to the rhythm I'd created. Kay arched her back and began moving to our own private dance, while keeping her eyes on us in the mirror.

Her auburn curls were sweaty, some plastered to her forehead, her mouth hung ajar on a silent scream, eyes squinting but opened. The expression of awe and pleasure written all over her face was almost my undoing.

She was beautiful.

The bullshit with work fell away as my only thoughts became about pleasing her. When her pussy walls started trembling around my cock, that was my hint that I'd lived up to my expectations.

I reached around with both hands, feeling for Kay's breasts, squeezing her hardened nipples while pulling her flush against my chest.

Within seconds, Kay's moans grew loudly and her walls were clamping ferociously around my dick as she came.

I buried my head into the crook of her neck, licking and sucking at her skin, salty from her sweat. "If I'd known it'd be the good between us, I wouldn't have let you stay away for the last seven years."

"You said that before," she panted.

"Because I mean it."

CHAPTER 13

*K*ayla

"Can you open your mouth up wide for me?" I asked little Monique as she sat on the exam table. When she did, I took a look into her mouth with my light, using my tongue depressor to clearly see down her throat. "Yeah, she is a little red down there," I stated, turning to Sandra and shutting off the light I held in my hand.

"She was coughing all night. I let her sleep with me so I could keep an eye on her insulin levels."

I gave Sandra weak smile. By the circles underneath her eyes, I could tell she hadn't gotten much sleep. I peeked behind me and saw Monique had gone back to playing the game on her tablet.

"She's going to be okay. It looks like a cold that just needs to run its course. You know the drill, keep an eye on it. Make sure she gets her fluids and is eating. Keep an eye on her insulin. She should be back to her normal self in no time."

"Yes!" Monique yelled at the game, smiling.

Her mother and I both peered over at her. I giggled. "If she's not there already."

"Monique, stop yelling."

"Sorry, Mama."

I smiled. "Sometimes sickness is worse for the parents than it is for the kids."

Sandra blew out a breath, slumping back into her chair. "Tell me about it."

"I remember the looks in the eyes of my mom and dad as they tried to keep up a front for me when I was in the hospital."

Sandra turned to me.

"I had type 1 diabetes at Monique's age, too."

Her eyebrows dipped. "Had? I thought it was incurable."

I nodded. "It is. Usually. But by my freshman year of college my kidneys had started to fail under the strain of my illness. I had a kidney-pancreas transplant. Not only did it save my life but my new pancreas cured the diabetes."

"Wow!" Her eyes widened. "I can't imagine seeing Monique go through all of that." The ghosted look in her eye told me of her fear.

I placed my hand on her knee. "Thankfully, you don't have to worry about all of it. We're just taking things one day at a time. Right now Monique's health is fine. Her diabetes is being managed very well by her loving mama." I smiled. "Whatever comes up in the future, we'll deal with it."

Sandra blew out a breath. "Okay." She nodded.

"One thing at a time." I hesitated, not knowing if I really should say the next words that were coming to mind but I felt I needed to say something. "And how are you doing?" I moved to the other side of the examination room, and glanced over at Monique, happy to see she had a pair of headphones in as she stared down at the screen of her tablet.

Sandra inched closer and shrugged. "Managing. My job is going well and I'm scheduled for my annual review in a couple of weeks. I'm in line for a raise."

I smiled. "That's great, Sandra. I hear good paralegals are hard to come by."

"You didn't hear this from me, but we're the real stars of the firm." She giggled.

I joined in, adding, "I won't tell a soul. Dr. Carlson showed me your blood test results. Everything came back well. Have those techniques I told you helped with managing your stress levels?"

"They have. I've been trying to incorporate more self-care into my days like we discussed."

"That's excellent. A healthy mom is important to take care of the little one." I glanced over at Monique who peered up from her tablet and gave her a wink. She giggled before turning her attention back to the screen.

"Thank you, Dr. Reyes," Sandra said as she gathered her purse.

"Kayla, please."

She smiled, and not for the first time I noticed how beautiful Sandra was.

"Okay, I'll see you in a couple of weeks."

She nodded.

We both stood and I gave her one last look as she left out of the office. I gave Monique a smile and wave when she glanced back at me. Her smile beamed as she took her mother's hand.

I stared at Monique's retreating back, feeling like a total hypocrite. I'd told her in a previous conversation that I wouldn't bring up counseling, and I hadn't, but I'd wanted to. I, of all people, knew how difficult discussing something as horrific as sexual assault could be—ever since I went out one night with some friends from med school and woke up the next morning, naked in a stranger's bed, with only hazy recollections of the night before. Unfortunately for me, the guy whose bed I woke up in happened to be a police officer. One who made it his personal mission to make my life a living hell after I'd attempted to report his crimes.

A buzzing sound from my pocket, pulled my attention from those ugly memories. I took a deep inhale when I saw the text was from Joshua. I'd almost forgotten about going out that night with some colleagues. I'd told Joshua about it that morning, but had told him I didn't really want to go.

If you really didn't want to go you wouldn't have mentioned it, was his reply. Right before he pried the information out of me on where we were going to meet us there. Turns out, the bar my colleagues had picked was owned by the wife of one of Carter's co-workers.

Josh: *I'll see you in an hour.*

While I wasn't thrilled about the idea of going out with co-workers to a bar, a sense of calmness knowing Josh would be there overcame me.

* * *

Kayla

"There're a lot of firefighters in here," I commented, looking around, skeptically. I didn't have an issue with firefighters but I some-times associated firefighters with police. If firefighters were all over this bar, chances were high police officers would be as well. That made me fidgety.

"They're hot, right?" Andrea, one of our office's physician assis-tants, grinned as she leaned over to whisper in my ear.

"Yeah, I guess," I mumbled, ignoring Andrea to glance around at the patrons. Andrea, myself, and another colleague had left the office just after five since we were finished seeing patients for the day. The rest of our colleagues would be straggling in over the next thirty minutes. And so would Josh. Thank goodness. I honestly hadn't planned on going out with my coworkers, at least I thought I hadn't. But he was right. If I really didn't want to attend I would've never brought it up. A piece of me did want to go out and get to socialize more, but after the last time I'd tried to be carefree …

Just then a buzzing from my phone alerted me of a text.

Darla: *I found two more locations for you. Let's schedule a time to visit them.*

It was my realtor. I hesitated to respond. I'd all but forgotten about my supposed search for a permanent home. The thought of leaving Joshua's place weighed heavily on me. But it probably was the right thing to do. I sent a quick text in response, requesting we go visit the places sometime the following week.

"Oh my goodness, he's coming over!" Andrea squealed next to me like a high schooler.

"Who? What?" I turned, staring at her, putting my phone down.

She expertly flipped her long, shiny dark hair over her shoulder, giving whoever she was attempting to attract a sultry look.

It must've worked because while I was still staring at Andrea, to my right I heard, "Is this seat taken?"

The male voice was smooth, almost like a caress. Before even looking I could tell he was the type women swooned over.

I turned my head to see a man looming over our table. His dark eyes sparkled mischievously as they penetrated Andrea's own gaze. He was handsome—dark hair, dark brown eyes, fit physique that reached over six feet.

"Sure thing, Don," Andrea commented.

His brows wrinkled for a second and he glanced down at his own shirt. "Department just changed our uniforms. I forgot my name's now prominently displayed. Not fair you know my name and I don't know yours." He grinned.

"Andrea."

I blinked at Andrea. The woman was literally swaying in her seat a little. I grinned. I understood the feeling as I picked up my phone to check the time.

"This is my colleague, Dr. Reyes," Andrea introduced.

I glanced up from my phone, meeting Don's gaze.

"A doctor? You might have to get my heart restarted since Andrea here's giving me palpitations," Don slyly stated, covering his heart with his right hand.

"I'm off the clock. I'm sure one of your fellow brothers in here will be happy to get your heart restarted," I teased, starting to feel a little more at ease. Don seemed harmless, and the fact that Joshua would be there in ten minutes gave me a sense of comfort. He was never late.

"I'm offended, Doc." Don's face turned to one of mock hurt.

"Give it a rest, Donnie. The beautiful doctor doesn't want to be worried about your bullshit," another deep voice entered the conversation.

Holy moly! I thought as my eyes landed on a pair of green-hazel eyes, framed by the longest natural eyelashes I'd ever seen on a man or woman. This man was a few inches taller than Don, and was a little broader, but he adorned the same dark blue, short sleeve top that Don had on. My eyes lowered, reading the name emblazoned on his shirt. Emmanuel.

"Screw you, Emmanuel. Fucking newbies," Don grumbled.

"New my ass. Anyway, Doc, please don't let Donnie here get to you. He's an acquired taste. Encantada de conocerte." His eyes languished on my face, wrinkling at the sides as he smiled.

"Mucho gusto." I nodded.

His smile grew.

I shifted in my seat when Emmanuel pulled out the chair directly across from me. He was nice to look at, and charming, but he wasn't the man I wanted sitting across from me.

"Speak English. Andrea here is feeling left out," Don stated.

Emmanuel never broke his gaze from me.

"Hablas espanol. De donde eres?"

"Mi mama es Puertorriqueño y mi papa es de La Republica Dominicana," I answered in my parents' native tongue. While my mother grew up in New York City, she was originally born in Puerto Rico and my father came over from the Dominican Republic when he was a teen.

"Interesante."

I nodded. I could tell Emmanuel wasn't from either country. By his Spanish accent, I guessed that he was actually Spanish.

"You're not even from Spain."

I giggled lightly at Don's ribbing of Emmanuel. He merely gave Don a passing glance.

"I'm still new to Rescue Four so Don makes it his personal mission to give me shit."

"Damn right!" Don added, causing Andrea to giggle.

"Y tu, bonita? Where do you work?"

"That's a personal question, isn't it?" a hard voice came from behind Emmanuel, startling the entire table.

The way my body instantly reacted to the deep timbre of Josh's voice, I didn't need to look up to know it was him. But like a moth to a flame, my eyes traveled upward from Emmanuel to the man I'd wanted to see all day, standing behind him. A smile unlike the one I'd given Don or Emmanuel earlier touched my lips. It was a smile only reserved for Joshua Townsend. My relief at seeing him there wasn't even tamped out by the dour expression on his face as he eyed Emmanuel.

"You're in my seat," Josh stated firmly.

Emmanuel, an alpha in his own right, stared unflinchingly at Joshua. "Didn't see your name on it."

Oh shit.

Joshua's face morphed into a scowl that reminded me so much of his older brother for a second that I had to do a double take. He bent low, getting in Emmanuel's face. "You've got two options. Get your ass up or get your ass up."

I'll be damned if the underlying steel I heard in his command didn't have my nipples hardening in response. But the tension between the two men caused me to grow nervous.

"Josh, I—"

My interruption was cut off by the loud scraping of the wooden chair against the floor as Emmanuel stood. The two men stared at one another for a long while, faces hard.

I held my breath.

Finally, a sly grin spread over Emmanuel's face. "Fucking Townsends."

"Fucking Rescue Four jocks."

"Your brother's one of us jocks."

"Don't I know it."

"If I would've known she was your woman, I wouldn't have stepped to her."

Josh leveled a look at Emmanuel. "Now you know."

Emmanuel held up his beer and tipped his head in acquiescence before giving me one last wink and sauntering off.

Joshua turned to me, his eyes going from dark to sparkling in seconds. "I'm not late, am I?"

"Right on time."

A sly grin formed on Joshua's lips and I found myself swallowing, remembering how those lips felt on my skin. His green eyes darkened, silently making promises I damn near wanted to beg him to keep.

"You want a drink?"

I shook my head and held up the seltzer water with lime I'd ordered as soon as Andrea and I arrived.

"I'm going to grab a beer."

Minutes later, the table began filling out as more of my coworkers arrived. Joshua had switched from sitting across the table, to sitting next to me, his thick, strong thigh pressed up against mine. His arm rested draped over my shoulders. His thumb sent chills through my body as it grazed tiny circles over my bare shoulder.

"Are you cold?" His deep voice rang low in my ear. He must've felt the shiver that ran through my body at our instant contact.

"Not anymore."

Our eyes locked and I could feel the warmth spreading throughout my veins. My eyes dropped to his bobbing Adam's apple and my mouth watered.

He moved closer, bringing our faces within an inch of one another's. "Tenga cuidado, sweetheart." A warning.

If I was a lighter color, I'm sure I would've been blushing. I always found it endearing when Joshua spoke his mixture of Spanish and English or "Spanglish" as it was more commonly referred to.

"I'm always careful, Mr. Townsend," I retorted.

"There's my girl."

I lifted my brows, wondering what that was supposed to mean, but was interrupted by the loud conversation taking place by my coworkers.

"What do you think, Reyes?"

Reluctantly, I broke away from Joshua's gaze to glance across the table. I placed a comforting hand on Joshua's thigh upon hearing his grunt of disapproval. He hadn't liked our interruption either.

"Think about what, Dr. Carlson?" I asked, leaning in.

"This whole police brutality mess. That incident that was caught on film last week in Williamsport Park."

My body stiffened. I hadn't been expecting that and I'd gone out of my way a number of times over the previous few days to avoid conversations on the topic. The prior week a group of teenage boys had been hanging out in Williamsport Park and an altercation of a uniformed officer striking one of the young boys, who was Latino, in the face had been captured. The video made me physically sick to watch so I avoided it at all costs.

"Uh, well—"

"I mean, you know how these young kids are today. Punks, always talking back to the police, disrespecting authority figures. I think that's the real epidemic."

"Seriously?" I asked, angling my head to stare at my colleague. Dr. Carlson was a man of color, who'd grown up in a not so great area of Williamsport himself. I, for one, would've thought this made him a little more sympathetic to the plight of those young boys, but apparently not.

"Absolutely. I'm sure if they would've just given the officer their names and told him what they were doing in the park, the issue wouldn't have risen to the level that it did."

I was speechless. I wanted to respond but couldn't string together the words I wanted to say. My brain became fraught with indignation. My heart rate began skyrocketing. I opened my mouth to speak but I knew nothing coherent would come out, so I clammed up.

"And why did the officer specifically ask those teenagers what they were doing in the park?"

I turned to Joshua, who was sitting up, leaning into the table, his eyes intent on Dr. Carlson.

"They weren't the only teens in the park that day. It was the middle of the day on a summer afternoon. There were teens, nannies, young children, and more in the park, but that officer chose to stop the group of teens that were mostly non-white. From my understanding there weren't any reports of them doing anything out of the ordinary."

"Please, you know how loud groups of teenagers can be."

"Right, *any* group of teens."

"Well, we don't know all of the facts. The video was less than a minute and does not give a full picture of what happened before or after recording started. I just think we need to give officers more credit..."

Dr. Carlson continued, Joshua and a few other colleagues interjecting with their comments, but I couldn't listen any longer. I'd heard so many attitudes regarding the same issue over the last few years. At first, I found it surprising how many people, of all races, were quick to defend the police, but then it just became borderline sickening. I recognized that my own personal experience clouded my judgement. It was hard maintaining the same level of respect for police officers after what happened to me. Unfortunately, my mind began to flashback to that horrible night two years ago. It'd started with me being in a place much like the bar I was in at that moment.

My head began to spin and even taking a long sip of my seltzer water didn't help the spinning or the way it began to feel like the walls were closing in on me.

"I just want to know what happened to the police being the good guys." I heard in the midst of my near panic attack. That was the final straw.

I stood up on shaky legs, and looking at no one in particular, I said, "I-I need to go to the restroom. I'll be back."

"Kay," Josh's voice rang out but I didn't answer. I didn't want anyone, especially him, to see me in this vulnerable state. I didn't even want to see myself like this. That was evident when I arrived in the bathroom, locking the door, and wrapped my fingers around the porcelain sink, lowering my head to avoid looking at myself in the mirror. I sealed my eyes shut and began counting backwards from one hundred.

Thankfully, that did the trick. Once I got to the mid-eighties, my breathing began to stabilize. I felt my body temperature returning to normal, but I continued to avoid looking in the mirror. Grabbing a few paper towels, I patted off the sweat around my forehead and neck. I took another minute to gather myself and fluff my hair a little. I peeked up into the mirror and for a second I caught a glimpse of the girl I used to be. The girl I'd been before leaving Williamsport.

Taking a step back from the mirror, I tossed the wadded up paper towels in the trash. I didn't need to think about that girl I'd left behind. She was young, foolish, and naïve. I grabbed for the door, swinging it open, and jumped when Joshua's tall figure stood inches from me, eyeing me with concern.

He barreled through the door, forcing me to step back or be run over.

I watched as he fully moved into the bathroom, shutting and locking the door behind him.

He tilted his head, eyeing me carefully, sizing me up. "Want to tell me what happened out there?"

I wrinkled my brows, frowning, but avoided his eyes. "What are you talking about?" I was proud of myself for managing to keep the stutter out of my words.

He pushed out a heavy breath before advancing on me again. I backed up until my back hit the wall of the bathroom stall. He placed both of his palms at either side of my head.

"Trust isn't something I give readily, especially not the second time around."

I frowned, wondering where the hell this was going.

"But I gave it to you … twice. I trusted you as a friend and you left for seven years. I trusted you again and allowed you to move into my home. All I'm asking is for you to return the favor."

"Wh—"

"What happened out there?" he questioned again, his tone brokering no room for bullshit.

I sighed and looked out over his shoulder to the corner of the bathroom, remembering the conversation that'd sent me spiraling into a near panic attack. Then I started to get angry.

"It just pisses me off," I blurted out, turning my eyes to meet Joshua's, "how people vigorously defend one group of people without knowing the full truth. They automatically assume the police were right and those boys were wrong. It's bullshit."

Joshua pulled back, lowering his hands but still eyeing me carefully. "The police? That's what had you so upset you had to get up from the table?"

I nodded. "Yes … and no. It's the adamant defense of them. As if they can do no wrong. He wasn't there." I pointed angrily at the door.

"He?"

"Carlson. He wasn't there to see what happened but he was so damn sure those kids were wrong. It's not right. Police are people just like the rest of us. They can be wrong sometimes, but this freaking hero worship that's …" I trailed off knowing that I was too irate to continue without spilling my secrets. "It's just not right. Sometimes the people we turn to be our saviors are the very ones we need protection from."

I pushed out another hard breath; my chest was heaving but I'd felt as if I'd gotten a little bit of the weight off of it. That was, until I looked into Joshua's storm-clouded eyes.

"The poli—" Whatever he'd been about to say was silenced by a loud knocking on the door.

"Hey, you still in there?" someone called through the door.

"Wait a fucking minute!" Joshua growled back before turning back to me. "Tell me what happened," he demanded, his chest heaving.

"I—"

Another knock. "Come on, buddy. My lady's really gotta go!"

Pissed, Joshua turned from me, stomping over to the bathroom door, yanking it open. "Look, motherfucker, I told you—"

"No!" I chimed in, placing my hand on Joshua's shoulder. "I'm sorry, we've been in here a long time. Please," I begged, taking Joshua's hand in mine, pulling him from the bathroom entrance.

After another tug of the arm, Joshua finally looked from the guy at the bathroom doorway to me, silently agreeing and moving out of the bathroom.

"Dance with me," I insisted, pulling him in the direction of the dance floor.

Somehow, Joshua took the lead, escorting us to the middle of the dance floor. A slow song just happened to be playing. We weren't the only pair out there. In fact, it was almost difficult to find enough space for us, but as always, it seemed Joshua was able to bend those around him to his will. A space opened up for us, and his muscled arm moved around my waist, pulling me into him. My body immediately heated with the closeness. Comfort and the feeling of safety, I hadn't even realized I was longing for, filled my entire body.

I leaned my head on his shoulder and let his strength wrap itself up in me, making me forget everything except his embrace.

"Whoever it was that hurt you, I will kill them."

My body went rigid at the deadly tone in his voice. But Joshua kept dancing right in time with the music.

"I've never killed anyone before, but once I find the person who put that fear in your eyes, there's nowhere they'll be able to hide from me to keep safe. I want you to understand that."

I lifted my head to stare into his eyes. The coldness I saw in his penetrating gaze struck me to my core. I shook my head. "Joshua, you can't—"

He took my chin in between his thumb and forefinger, lowering his lips to mine. The kiss was short, but there was a promise in it. "It's already done, Kay."

Any protest I would've made died on my lips. I should be ashamed at how his words turned me on. But I wasn't. I'd never felt safer than in that moment. My body began to heat up and it wasn't a result of the dancing.

A shiver ran through me from the brush of his warm breath against the sensitive skin of my neck, from his whispered words.

"Take me home." My voice was breathless.

* * *

JOSHUA

A coldness I'd never felt before settled over me in that bathroom. It wasn't Kay's words, it was the insistence with which she had stated her disdain for Carlson's defense of police. The way her eyes went wild when talking about how unfair it was. How I could tell she wasn't just referring to those boys in that video but about her own self. The nagging thoughts I'd had ever since I'd first laid eyes on her at the fundraiser some close to two months earlier were starting to make sense. The self-defense lessons she requested, the change in her attire, the way she'd worn her hair when she first got back. All spoke to the need to protect herself from someone or something.

I should've picked up on it sooner. I would have if I hadn't been distracted like I was at that very moment.

"Shit, Kay!" I cursed when she moaned deeply as I ran my teeth down the column of her neck. I pressed her back against my closed bedroom door. "Tonight, I'm going to taste you," I groaned in her ear. I smirked at the rise of goosebumps I felt along her arms.

"Please," she begged.

My cock twitched in my pants.

I used my hands to make quick work of unbuttoning her shirt, exposing the black silk bra she'd worn underneath. My mouth watered and I dipped my head to run my tongue along the soft tops of her mounds. Another loud moan broke free of her lips, spurring me on. I tugged at the sides of the top she wore, ripping it free from her body.

"Be careful!" she insisted.

I growled, reaching up to nip at her bottom lip. "We both know you don't want me to be careful."

A confirming smile crossed her lips and she leaned in, nipping my bottom lip. The bite of pain had my groin tightening and my already growing erection pressing against my pants. I kissed my way down the center of her chest, stopping to reach around and undo the offending barrier that stood in the way of my mouth on Kayla's full breasts. Once they were free, I stood back, taking my fill of her round, cinnamon globes and milk chocolate nipples.

"Touch them for me." I needed her to be as much a part of this experience as I was. She needed that, too.

She looked at me, tilting her head to the side.

"Touch your breasts for me, Kay."

Her hands tentatively lifted to her breasts, covering them before squeezing them. A tiny moan fell from her full lips.

"Pinch your nipples."

"Mmm." Her head fell back against the door, her hips thrusting in my direction.

"That feel good, baby?"

"Yes," she hissed.

"Good. Let me make you feel even better." I pushed her hands away and covered her right nipple with my mouth while kneading her left one with my hands. I'll be damned if she didn't taste just as good as the chocolate color her nipples were.

"Josh, I need more," she panted.

"Be careful what you wish for," I growled, ignoring her yelp of surprise when I picked her up over my shoulder and strolled over to my bed.

"Joshua, what the he—" Her final word was cut short as I planted her body at the center of my bed, not giving her time to orient herself before I was stripping her of the rest of her clothing.

I covered her body with my own, needing to feel her lips on mine again. My kiss was returned just as hungrily as it was given. Somehow, I found the power to break free from her lips and let my mouth travel down her body to her breasts and lower to her abdomen. There I caught the long, running scar that was a testament to all she'd endured in the first two decades of her life. I kissed along the scar, committing its outline to memory before going lower.

"I-I haven't shaved in a few days," she informed me.

I lifted my head, staring at her. "I'm a grown ass man. Pussy hair doesn't scare me."

Her eyes widened in disbelief. I didn't give her much time for a response to my declaration before I was lifting her up by the hips and nudging her legs apart with my shoulders.

I lowered my head and had my first taste of her sweet nectar. Kay was wet as fuck. I savored the flavor of her, licking and sucking at her labia, teasing her before moving to engulf her clit with my mouth.

Somewhere along the line, my moans got lost in the sounds of her moans. The room filled with the sweet sounds of her enjoyment which was fucking music to my ears. My erection painfully strained against the mattress, but I couldn't and wouldn't let my mouth off of Kay's pussy until I felt the evidence of her orgasm on my tongue.

With my tongue lashing, I demanded that she come for me.

Another loud moan followed by a rolling of her hips, and seconds later my bottom lip and chin were met with her bodily response to my ministrations.

"Fuck!" she gasped, sitting up. "If I'd known you were that skilled with your mouth, I wouldn't have been gone for so long."

"Your loss, sweetheart," I chided, pressing a kiss to her mouth, letting her taste herself on my lips. "Now we've gotta make up for lost time."

"We sure do." Kay's soft hands went to my belt buckle, undoing it before unbuttoning my pants.

"Damn," I hissed, throwing my head back when she reached in and began stroking my cock. "You're going to have me coming in my pants like a fucking adolescent."

She grinned. "That's the goal."

I shook my head. "Not tonight. The goal is to hear you yelling my name while you come, again and again." I stole another kiss, and removed her hand to fully undress myself. "Turnover." My voice was strained, thick with need.

Kayla moved, turning over on all fours.

My jaw tightened and my dick strained even more at the sight of her exposed ass. I always loved the sight of her bare ass when she was in this position.

"Condom."

I stopped, my hands inches from her flesh. "What?" I understood the word she was saying but my brain had only one thought at that moment.

"We need to use condoms, Josh. We have to be more consistent with protection."

"Are you on birth control?" The words were instinctive. Spat out before I could even fully comprehend what I was asking. I'd never, not once, not used protection with a woman. The fact that I hadn't even realized it until Kayla brought it up would be something I'd have to beat myself up about later.

"No," she answered, shaking her head.

Fuck. "I'll pull out," came my immediate response. My hands went to her hips, pulling her to me.

"Josh …" Her voice had both need and a warning.

"I've never not used protection and my last test was clean."

"M-mine too."

It probably was a little late in the game for this particular conversation but I needed her to be clear. I waited for any more protests from her. When none came, I gripped my erection and placed it at her entrance, sliding in.

Her back immediately arched and a groan escaped her lips. The breath was stolen from my lungs and replaced by the most euphoric feeling ever.

"Goddamn," her whispered cry came out.

I grunted, unable to mutter a verbal response beyond that. The feel of Kay's tight pussy gripping my cock made talking impossible. The only thing I could do was move. So, I did. I pulled back, almost pulling completely out of her before forging back into her, forcefully.

"Shit, Jooosh!" she moaned.

Her cries only caused me to want to bury myself so deeply inside of her, that I wouldn't know where I ended and she began. When she began bouncing her full ass on my cock, I just about lost my fucking mind.

I leaned over, moving my hands from her hips to her breasts that were bouncing, as well to the rhythm we'd set together. I squeezed and plucked at her nipples while using my knee to nudge hers apart even farther. I leaned in, pressing the top half of her body down against the mattress and thrusting even deeper into her core. The squishy sounds of our lovemaking filled the room, as did our moans.

I moved my hand from her breasts to her hair, loving the way my hand sank and almost disappeared in her mass of curls. I grabbed a handful of her auburn hair, turning her head to the side and leaning over to bite and suck at her earlobe. Pulling back, I said, "You're mine, Kay. You were always meant to be mine!" I growled, pounding into her more.

Her mouth parted but all that escaped was a silent cry as she came around my thrusting dick. The squeezing and tightening of her muscles around mine was almost too much. I didn't want this to end just yet. My body pushed me to come right there and then, but I was a man of my word. I rode her through her own orgasm before pulling out of her.

Disregarding my own body's need for a release, I flipped Kayla onto her back. Her hazy eyes widened in shock, then hungry need. I pressed both of her breasts together, lining my cock up in between them. I thrust in and out, continuing to squeeze her breasts together, titty fucking her. Within seconds, the stimulation proved just what I needed to get off. My come came out, soaking the skin of her chest, neck, and chin. For the first and only time in my life I regretted not coming inside of a woman. I brushed that feeling to the side and struggled for air after my release.

I growled in Kay's ear as I rolled us over, so she laid on top of me, my back against the mattress.

"Shit just got real complicated between you and me."

CHAPTER 14

*K*ayla

What the hell did that mean? *Shit just got compli-cated.* As far as I was concerned, this thing between Josh and I had *always* been complicated.

"And the kitchen has the granite countertops and tile backsplash that you love," Darla's voice interrupted my thoughts.

I welcomed the distraction. It'd been a few days since that night at the bar and afterwards. Joshua and I were growing closer, with me spending every night in his bed, in his arms, my drifting off to sleep after yet another spine tingling orgasm. It felt like a dream. I woke up and felt safer than I had in a long time. I'd all but forgotten about my appointment with Darla that evening after work, until my phone's calendar reminded me of it on my schedule. To not be rude, I kept the appointment although my heart wasn't in it.

"I love it," I told her, giving her a half-hearted smile. "And you said this place has two bedrooms, right?"

"Right," Darla confirmed, stepping around me toward the long hallway.

After a second of me examining the large kitchen space, I followed the sound of Darla's heels against the hardwood floors, down the hall toward one of the bedrooms. The master bedroom was huge and allowed for lots of sunlight. This place was the second one we'd looked at and it fit the criteria I'd given Darla for what I wanted. On paper, it was perfect, but in my head, I was steadily comparing the place to Joshua's. This place had hardwood floors, something I'd thought I wanted but now I was partial to marble flooring. The granite countertops in the kitchen were a dull grey whereas I loved the way light reflected off the white countertops in Joshua's home. I pulled myself from my ruminating, realizing what I was doing. Besides, Joshua never said he'd wanted me to move in long-term. Sure, he'd made no mention of me moving out at all, and yes, the previous night he'd even declared he'd take another man's life for me, but that didn't mean ...

"And as owner in this particular building, you will be in part ownership with Townsend Real Estate ..."

I spun on my heels, turning to Darla. "Townsend Real Estate owns the building?"

"Well, technically them, and the owners of the units, which you will be once you purchase."

"I—" My response was cut off by a loud banging noise that came from the front door.

"What the hell?" Darla questioned.

"Oh my God!" I yelled as a masked man barged into the room. My sights narrowed in on the barrel of his gun that was pointed in my direction. My flight or fight response immediately kicked in and I looked around for a place to run but we were trapped.

"Get on the fucking ground!" he yelled. "Now!" He pushed the gun in Darla's face first and then shoved me by the shoulder to the floor.

In my peripheral I saw a second figure move to the doorway.

"Give me this!"

I felt my shoulder bag being snatched from my hand.

"Hey!" Darla yelled as her bag was taken.

"Shut up, bitch!" the second voice yelled.

What the hell is happening?

"You find it?" the first man that'd burst into the room questioned.

"What's the code to the safe?"

"Ahh!" Darla screamed when one of the men grabbed her by the hair, demanding some combination code.

"What safe? I don't know about any safe!" she insisted.

"Stop lying to me, bitch!"

"She's telling the truth," I spoke up, fearing he would become even more violent. "She's my real estate agent. She doesn't work in this building. We don't know about any safe or combination."

Through the eye cutouts of his mask, I saw dark eyes turned on me. I shivered at the lack of empathy I saw there. It wasn't the first time I'd seen such a look. Terror mixed with anger began to rise up in me. Who the fuck did these assholes think they were to interrupt our day like this and steal our belongings?

"What the fuck are you doing?" I called out, sitting up on my knees, finding a strength I hadn't even known I possessed.

"Get down on the floor, bitch!" the second guy called out, moving to my side to raise the gun.

On pure adrenaline, fear, and instinct, I bent my arm, and with all of the strength I could muster I elbowed the guy right in his crotch.

He crumpled immediately, yelling, "Argh!"

"Ahh!" Darla and I both screamed when he dropped his gun, causing it to shoot off a round.

That must've spooked the hell out of the first guy because he yelled, "Oh shit!" and ran out of the room.

The would-be robber laid on the ground, moaning in pain.

"Wh-what are you doing?" Darla questioned as I moved to pick up the gun.

I had no idea how to handle a gun but I kept it trained on our assailant and ordered, "Call 911!" to Darla instead of answering her question. I scrambled from the floor and shut the door of the bedroom we were in, not knowing if the other guy was still in the condo or not.

"Let me out of here!" The guy I'd dropped with an elbow, groaned, trying to get up.

"Oh God!" Darla shouted into the phone, fearing the man.

"Take one step in this direction and I'll blow your fucking head off." There wasn't even the most minute trace of a tremor in my voice. I didn't even know how to shoot the gun I held but I would figure it out to make good on my word. That's how pissed I was.

"Please hurry!" Darla implored to the 911 operator.

I ignored the realization that soon police officers would be swarming the apartment. I had to remind myself that, in this case, the police were needed.

It felt like forever but I nearly jumped out of my skin when a loud voice rang through the condo.

"It's the police," Darla whispered.

I moved from in front of the door and slowly lowered the gun before opening it.

"Thank God!" Darla blurted out upon seeing the uniformed officers. She quickly re-explained what happened to the officers, as they'd also been told by the 911 operators.

I stared on as the officers handcuffed the masked man. I hadn't even thought to remove his face mask.

"Ma'am?"

"Don't touch me!" I jumped when one of the officers reached for my arm. I stepped back, shaking. "I-I'm sorry." I had to remind myself that they were there to help us.

Minutes later, a police detective entered the room, also requesting that we tell him our stories of what happened.

I'd hoped as soon as we finished answering his questions, we'd be given the green light to leave. But minutes after arriving, the detective received a phone call and as soon as he hung up, he insisted that Darla and I be brought down to the station. He informed us that it was for our safety. My knees felt weak at the idea of going to a police station. The strength I'd mustered until then was all but whittling away.

* * *

JOSHUA

"Where is she?" I demanded as soon as I pushed my way through the double doors of the police station and saw Brutus standing there, waiting.

"Calm do—"

"Don't fucking tell me to calm down! She could've been fucking hurt. Who the hell is behind this? What the hell was she doing there in the first place?" I demanded.

"Looking at one of the units. She was with her real estate agent."

That answer only added fuel to my anger. Not only had I been called out of a meeting to be told not one, but two Townsend Real Estate properties had been burglarized, but that Kayla, *my Kayla*, had been at one of the locations when it happened.

"Someone's going to lose their fucking head," I growled as I passed Brutus, walking straight to the police captain's office.

As soon as my security learned of the attempted robberies, they were on the phone with the police commissioner who happened to be a friend of my father's.

"Mr. Townsend."

I glanced around his office. "Kay," I blurted out, grabbing her in my arms.

She fell into my hug, burying her head into my shoulder. I felt her trembling body mold into my arms. "It's okay," I whispered into her ear, consoling her. *I'm going to kill whoever is behind this.*

"Were you hurt?" I questioned, pulling back and cupping her chin, my eyes roving over her face and body, examining her for any bruising.

She shook her head. "No, I'm fine." She inhaled deeply and gave me a crooked smile. But I could see the fear in her eyes. I pressed a kiss to her forehead and wrapped my arm around her waist, before turning to the captain.

"Hurt? She damn near castrated one of guy's that tried rob them."

I glanced over at the police captain who'd had the nerve to fucking chuckle, before I returned my gaze to Kay.

She shrugged. "He pissed me off," she stated, a smirk touching her lips.

I pressed a kiss to her lips. "That's my girl." I moved closer to her ear so only she could hear my next statement. "Though we're going to talk about what you were doing there in the first place."

I moved back to turn and give my attention to the police captain.

"Who was it?" My voice was eerily calm, overshadowing the anger rolling around in my body.

"Thanks to Miss Reyes here, we have one of the men in custody—"

"I need to see him."

A scowl covered my face when the captain began shaking his head. "I'm sorry, that's just not possible. We have our best detectives on the case—"

I turned from the captain, feeling my anger rise. I didn't want Kay seeing me get this pissed off. "Brutus, have Patrick take Kay and Ms. …" I paused, looking to the woman who I knew was Kay's realtor.

"McDaniels," she answered.

"Ms. McDaniels home." I moved closer to Brutus so only he could hear me. "He is not to let Kay out of his sight. Understood?"

Brutus nodded and left.

"Go ahead. I'll be in later," I told Kay in the most soothing voice I could muster in the moment.

"You're not coming?"

"Not yet. I need to discuss some things with the captain first."

She gave me a wary look but eventually followed Darla out of the captain's office. I watched for another few seconds until she disappeared around the corner toward the front entrance.

"You may have rules to follow, Captain, but this—"

"Not rules, Mr. Townsend, the law. We have to follow the law. I cannot have a civilian questioning a suspect in an ongoing criminal investigation. We will do everything in our ability to bring the other person behind this break-in to justice."

I glared at the captain. "What's his name?"

His eyes shifted around the room. He finally shrugged. "I guess it wouldn't hurt to tell you his name. James Cunningham."

I narrowed my eyes and peered over at Brutus who gave me a quizzical look. I knew the name but I wasn't about to inform the captain of that. I eyed the captain carefully. His department was in over their heads. This was a set-up. Townsend Industries had experienced two break-ins that day. One at the condo where Kay had been, while the other was at one of my luxury developments, outside of this department's jurisdiction. And the name he'd just given me was that of an employee I'd fired a few months prior.

I talked with the captain some more but knew I needed to go over his head.

"We need to head to the office," I told Brutus as soon as we stepped out of the police station, after he assured me that Kay was home safe and being watched by one of his best on staff. While I wanted nothing more than to get back to her, I needed to be all over this situation first. Whoever was behind this had not only fucked with my company and family name, but they'd endangered her life and that wasn't something I could easily walk away from.

* * *

"How the hell did this happen?" I was pissed as I glared at the screen of the robbery that'd taken place the evening before at one of my sales offices. It'd been hours since I'd left the police station. It'd taken that long to get the camera footage from the robberies. Myself, Aaron, and Brutus, stood in Brutus' office on the bottom floor of Townsend Industries, watching the footage.

The night before, while the break-in where Kay was, was taking place, another robbery occurred. As the sales agent who was on duty was getting ready to close up the model homes, two masked gunman bum rushed the door, knocking her down and tying her up. They raided the model home, breaking furniture and stealing some of the art pieces they could carry.

"This was supposed to be a robbery?" I questioned Brutus but kept staring at the screen.

"Supposed to. She said they kept asking her where they kept the money."

"She?" I turned to Brutus, squinting. "The sales agent in that

163

office's name is Jackson. Last time I fucking checked, Jackson was the name for a *he* not a *she*."

"He's on vacation."

"How convenient," Aaron interjected, reading my mind as well.

"Who's the she on the video?"

"Temp worker we got through the agency we work with."

I glanced between Aaron and our head of security, turning my attention back to the screen. "Play it again."

I watched with folded arms as the temp worker prepped to leave for the evening, shutting down her laptop and gathering her belongings. She turned out the lights and opened the door just as a man appeared, his face and head covered, pushing the door open forcefully, causing her to stumble back before falling. Soon enough, a second man appeared, shutting the door behind him and locking it. The first man lunged for the woman, pulling her up by her hair and pulling out what looked like some sort of twine from his back pocket. He dragged her into one of the smaller offices. That's where the camera cut out since there were no cameras in the smaller, inner offices.

"Was she injured?" My tone was clipped.

"Some rope burns on her wrist but nothing beyond that."

I squinted as I glared at the frozen screen.

"Shit!" Aaron growled, pulling his phone from his pocket. "Mark, what is it?" He was silent for a minute as he listened to his assistant's response. "I'm on my way."

"What's going on?"

"A meeting I already had scheduled. You need to handle this shit." He narrowed his gaze on me, pointing his phone in my direction.

I turned back to the screen. "I'm all over it." I turned back to Brutus after the door slammed shut behind Aaron. "Where is she now?"

Brutus, who towered above me by five inches, turned. "Where do you think?"

I nodded and followed behind Brutus out his door, across the hallway, through a set of heavy double doors that led to another closed door. He opened and I entered behind him to see the woman from the video sitting on the side of a long table, looking up at me, bewildered.

"Ms. ..." I waited.

"Alyssa Hawkins."

"Is it all right if I call you Alyssa?"

She nodded.

"Good. Do you know who I am?" My voice was a smooth as silk.

"Joshua Townsend, of course."

"Great. Then we can skip the formalities." The scraping of the wooden chair sounded along the concrete floor. "Alyssa, I'm sure you're aware that my security brought you here so that you could recount all of the details of what happened last night."

She visibly swallowed, her eyes ping ponging between myself and Brutus, who still stood, arms folded behind me.

"Don't look at him," I snapped, the charming façade I'd first had upon entering the room slipping just a little. "Brutus is our head of security, but I am the one who runs Townsend Real Estate. Everything that happens with this business, happens to me. It's my name on the line and I don't take that lightly. What happened to you last night, concerns me a great deal. You can understand that, right, Alyssa?"

Her brown eyes enlarged with worry but she nodded. "Yes, Mr. Townsend. And I told the police everything that happened."

"Tell me." Sitting up, I placed my arms on the table, clasping my hands, signaling that I was all ears. I listened intently as Alyssa recounted the events of the proceeding evening. She told of how they ransacked the home for approximately fifteen minutes, demanding to know where the money was.

"See, Alyssa, that's what I find so confusing. It's a model home. You were the acting sales agent, not even an employee of Townsend. You work for us through a temp agency. Why would two criminals be asking you for money? That doesn't make sense to me at all. Can you explain that?"

She shook her head, brunette locs moving around her shoulders. "I have no idea, Mr. Townsend."

I sat back, crossing my legs, and just stared at her for a minute. She began squirming in her chair.

"Look, Mr. Townsend, I don't know what you're thinking, but I came down here after hours of questioning at the police station—"

"You were brought down here."

She paused.

"There's a difference, Alyssa. One of our security staff picked you up from your home and brought you here. You didn't volunteer to come down all on your own."

She shook her head. "Yes, but what I meant was, I came willingly. Because I have nothing to hide."

"Are you sure?" I angled my head.

"Yes, of course."

"Then why were you taking pictures the last time you temped for us?"

Her mouth fell open. Out of the corner of my eye I watched as Brutus lowered his tablet, angling it so Alyssa could view the screen. I already knew it was footage of her taking pictures on her phone of the model home. The video was from a month ago, when she'd last temped in that same office.

"Those were for a friend."

"A friend?"

"Yes. We were texting and I'd told her I was covering for the sales agent in one of the Townsend model homes. She wanted to see what it looked like. So I took some pictures to send them to her. See, look …" Without any prompting, Alyssa pulled her phone from her shoulder bag and scrolled through until she found what she was looking for. She turned the phone so that I could read the exchange between her friend and herself.

Indeed, her friend had requested a look inside of the model homes. But until I had verification that this friend was even real, I would suspend my analysis on the truth of her statements.

"Okay, Alyssa. I just have one more question I wanted to see if you could help me with. Why would two people think the sales office in our model homes had any money?" I narrowed my gaze on her.

She shrugged, giving Brutus and I a wary look. "I have no idea. I never told them there was any money in the office. All I know is any money they got came out of my purse, from what I saw. They stole from me, too."

I nodded. "I understand, and trust me, if we find out you had nothing to do with this, you will be justly compensated for all of this hassle. You have my word on that." With that, I pushed away from the table, standing. "My security will see to it that you arrive home safely. We will be in touch."

I gave her a tilt of my head and turned to leave. I heard Brutus mutter a few words into his cell. He was ordering one of his team to take Alyssa home.

"This makes no sense!" I spat out, about an hour later, standing in the middle of Aaron's office.

"Did she have something to do with this?" Aaron's tone was clipped, his usual scowl marring his face.

I gave a shrug. "My gut tells me no but I'm having Brutus check in on the friend story, as well as running a background check."

"Didn't she already have a background run?"

I nodded. "All temps who work for us do via the temp agency but Brutus' check is much more in depth."

"And you still think this is connected to the other shit?"

"I told you over the phone this morning it is," I retorted sharply. "I know it is. It's the only reasoning that fits."

"How so?" he questioned, leaning back against his desk, crossing his legs at the ankles.

"It's definitely connected to the other break-in. Both Kay and Darla stated the men demanded some type of combination code for a safe. These guys were looking for money. Someone either told them money was there or they're just that fucking stupid to think an empty model home and condo unit would have money in them. And the guy they have at the police station, the one Kayla fucked up? I fired him from one of my crews just a few months ago."

Aaron sat up, scowling. "You get to speak with him?"

"Working on some back channels to make that happen." I ground my teeth, impatient for the opportunity to speak with James Cunningham face-to-face. The police captain might've wanted to play by the rules but sometimes it was necessary to make my own rules.

"Someone led these fuckers on," I mused out loud. "Set up Townsend Real Estate, likely for some bad press. The same person who's been behind Townsend Real Estate's troubles over the last few months."

"You'll handle this."

"Of course I wi—"

"I mean it, Joshua. I've got too much other shit to worry about. I don't need any of this coming back to bite my family in—"

"I said I fucking got it handled," I answered sharply. "You're not the only one with a family on the line." A muscle in my jaw ticked upon remembering that Kay had been in danger due to all of this.

Aaron's hazel eyes narrowed on me but I was done talking.

I started to head out of the office.

"Mother and Father will be back in a few weeks. Mother is insisting that we all get together for one of her Sunday dinners the same day she returns," Aaron called behind me.

I rolled my eyes. "I got the email. It's on my schedule," I confirmed as I twisted the doorknob to pull his office door open.

"See that it is."

I didn't respond to my brother's comment. I exited his office and made my way down to my own, calling Brutus.

"I'm working on getting you a meeting with James."

"The sooner the better. Look, I also need you to do a background on Kay." I hadn't forgotten what happened the night before. My hands were tied with what was happening with Townsend Real Estate but I wasn't going to let the ball drop where Kayla's past was concerned, either.

"You think she's in on this?"

I pushed down the anger that filled me at such a preposterous thought. "Don't even fucking suggest that ever again." I paused and inhaled, trying to get my thoughts back on track so I wouldn't hang up the phone and head down to Brutus' office to beat the shit out of him at even stating those words out loud. "I need to know what happened to her before she moved back to Williamsport when she was living in Portland."

"What type of information are you looking for?"

"Was she hurt or injured in some way. I want to know who the fuck did it and fast. I know you've got a lot of shit on your plate, but—"

"It's not a problem."

I nodded although he couldn't see me. "And start with the police in Portland. Instances of police misconduct," I instructed. I had a gut feeling.

"Will do."

I hung up with Brutus and packed up my desk to take work home with me. I was fucking toasted after the long night and early morning. And there was only one person I had intentions on seeing.

CHAPTER 15

K *ayla*
    I awakened the moment he climbed into bed with me. I attempted to reach for him, but his long arms were already bracketing my body, pulling me closer to him. I blinked my eyes open and found myself staring into those eyes that I was always getting lost in. They were red-rimmed. He'd been up all night.

"Are you okay?" His voice was so tender. It betrayed the storm that raged in his eyes.

I nodded and leaned forward so that my head laid on his broad chest. "I am now."

"I'm going to take care of this, Kay. Those men that broke in, they won't get away with this. You know that, right?"

His conviction was evident in the rigidity in his body, in the sternness I heard in his voice, and the far off look I saw in his eyes when I lifted my head.

I leaned in, pressing a kiss to his lips. "You got one of them already."

His face hardened and he took my chin between his fingers. "That was dumb going after a man holding a gun.

My eyes ballooned. "Last night you said—"

"I know what I said. It was still dumb. You could've been shot and ki—" He broke off, looking to a far off corner of the room.

I felt his heart beating rapidly underneath the hand I had splayed on his chest.

"Don't ever do that shit again," he commanded, tightening the hold on my chin.

"What good is self-defense if I can't use it?" I sat up farther, growing angry.

"There's a time and place for everything, Kay. A man has a gun in your fucking face is not the time to get fancy with the little bit I've taught you."

"It worked, didn't it?" I sat up, crossing my legs and folding my arms over my chest. I was growing pissed. I'd been scared shitless with that gun in my face but in spite of my fear, I'd acted. I'd thwarted one of the robbers and taken control of situation. I'd been able to regain a part of me that I thought I'd lost forever. And now Josh was trying to take my victory away.

I started to get up from the bed. "I'm going to—"

"Nowhere!" he growled in my ear after tackling me to the bed. "You're not going anywhere. I've spent the last twelve hours in police stations and my offices working on this shit. You're not getting out of my sight." He bit my earlobe.

As much as I didn't want it to, my anger began to recede. I could see his point. It was pretty stupid to attack a man holding a gun on me. But still.

"Who says I want to sleep with you?"

"The way your nipples are perking up through that thin top of yours."

He was right. My nipples were aching to be touched. My body's reaction to his nearness was always instant.

"Trust me, Kay," were his last whispered words before he pressed a kiss to my lips, and then my nose, and cheeks.

I didn't respond verbally, instead opening up to him, wrapping my legs around his waist and allowing his body to sink into mine. The feeling of safety that I'd been craving all night began to replace the fear.

* * *

"THANK YOU FOR MEETING ME," Sandra greeted, a wary look in her eyes.

It'd been about a week since the break-in. While I'd taken off the day after, I was glad to have work to keep me distracted. Joshua, of course, checked in with me daily, keeping me updated on the progress they were making on the investigation. Every night he reassured me that the bastards would be caught. I didn't need his promises, however. I knew he was doing everything he could, and I knew that it wasn't just because this was beyond just business to him. He was working to reassure me. I couldn't put into words how comforting that knowledge was.

But as I sat there on the bench, staring at Sandra, I wondered who she had to comfort her. I took her hand in mine, just because I could tell she needed it.

"Of course. Let's sit down." I gestured with a nod of my head to one of the benches. We were in Williamsport City Park. The park had miles of paved trails, stretches of neatly trimmed grass for sitting in the sun or under a tree, and benches for park dwellers as well. I swallowed when the thought occurred to me that this was the same park in which those teens had been stopped and brutalized by those police officers. A sense of dread welled up in the pit of my stomach.

"I'm sorry to take you away from the office," Sandra's soft words floated to my ears.

This isn't about you right now, I reminded myself. I'd come to meet Sandra because she sounded so distraught over the phone when I'd spoken with her earlier. She'd called to make a follow-up appointment for Monique, but the tremor in her voice led me to ask how she was doing. She could barely get out the "Everything's fine" lie she'd tried to use to conceal her angst.

"Please don't apologize. I could tell something was wrong over the phone." I turned fully to her, clasping her hands in mine. "Do you want to talk about it?"

Sandra lowered her head and nodded.

I didn't miss the tears that welled up in her eyes before she did.

"I s-saw him ... my ex."

It took me a moment to understand why that was such an issue, but then I remembered what she'd revealed about her ex. "You mean, the one that ..."

"Drugged and raped me with a few of his friends." She nodded. "Him."

"How? When?"

She paused, swallowing. "He's the newest lawyer at the law firm I work f-for." She could hardly get out the last words as tears began streaming down her cheeks. Sandra was a paralegal at a law firm in the city.

"Oh, sweetie," I cooed, pulling her into a hug. I felt her body shiver as she cried on my shoulder.

After only a minute or two, I released her from the hug and Sandra began wiping away tears in an attempt to get herself together. I handed her a tissue, to which she gratefully accepted.

"I should be over this. He shouldn't have this much damn control over me after nine years," she declared, another tear slipping.

I swallowed. "What happened to you isn't something you just get over."

"Yeah, but ... it's been so long. This shouldn't reduce me to crying like this in the middle of the day."

I bit back the response that it was a natural reaction due to not dealing with what happened to her. But I couldn't say those words without being a hypocrite in my own right so I held back.

"He works at the same firm you do?" I carefully asked, instead.

She nodded. "Not the same department but he was brought past my area as part of the new employee tour guide of the office. Thankfully, he didn't see me because I was away from my desk." She pushed out a harsh breath. "I stood there, cowering behind a wall while he passed passed with one of the firm's partners."

I wrinkled my brows. I wanted to be as sensitive as possible when asking the next question. "Is this the first time you've seen him since that night?"

Again, Sandra dabbed at her eyes while nodding. "Well, the next morning. He dropped me off at my place and pulled off like nothing ever happened. He broke up with me via text the next day saying he couldn't trust me after what I'd done with his friends."

"What?" Pure rage rolled through my body. How could that bastard be so goddamn cruel?

She shook her head and shrugged. "He went off to college on a football scholarship a few weeks later and has been gone ever since ... or so I thought. I've never seen his friends since that night." Sandra sighed heavily, and her shoulders sank. "I took the rest of the day off. Told my boss I wasn't feeling well. I am going to work from home tomorrow but what am I going to do? I can't work from home for forever."

Her voice was so full of angst and fear, that pissed me off even more. That slime ball shouldn't have the right to make Sandra feel like she has to run away from her job or completely turn her whole life around. This shit wasn't fair.

"He's a son of a bitch!"

Sandra let out a chuckle through her tears. "That, I know."

"I'm sorry. I didn't mean to say that out loud." An idea popped into my head but it infuriated me to even think about. Still. It might be Sandra's only alternative to avoiding working around the person who'd violated her. "Have you considered looking for new employment?"

Sandra lifted her head, her wide brown eyes pinned to mine. "Finding a new job could take weeks or months. In the meantime ..."

In the meantime, she'd still have to work with that rapist. Not if I could do anything about it. "Maybe not. I might know someone who could help. Can you email me your resume? You have a resume, right?"

"Yes, of course." She nodded. "Who do you think could help?"

"I don't want to say just yet. Just know it's someone I trust."

Someone with very powerful connections throughout the city of Williamsport.

She nodded.

"Okay, I've got to get back to the office, but send me your resume and a good cover letter within the next hour, all right?"

"S-sure." Sandra looked startled, as if she hadn't expected this.

I hadn't either but it was the only way I knew I could be of help to her, outside of my normal responsibilities as her ND.

"It will work out," I told her, placing my hand on her shoulder, as we rose.

"Thank you, Kayla. I didn't come here expecting this. I just needed to tell someone."

I nodded in understanding. "Venting can be very therapeutic."

She nodded slightly. "I just want to put the past behind me and raise my daughter in peace."

Don't we all. Oh how much I understood the desire to forget such things ever happened to you.

"Okay." It came out in a whisper, barely audible to my own ears.

"Thank you for meeting me."

"Here." I handed her my business card just after writing my personal email address on the back. "Don't forget to send what I asked. I'll contact you as soon as possible with any follow up information I have."

She nodded and we embraced for a second before both departing. The whole time as I took the subway back to my office the anger I'd felt while listening to Sandra, combined with the flashbacks of my own memories of assault, continued to piss me off.

CHAPTER 16

*J*oshua

"It's been a long fucking day," I grumbled into the phone to Aaron. He'd called just as I was getting out of my car to head inside of the house.

"Any news?"

"I spoke with the officers who took the temp's statement."

"Off the record, right?"

"Who do you think I am?" I knew, legally, there were things the police couldn't tell me about the investigation, but … well, let's just say the Townsend sway was enough to get things done when we needed to. "And I put a call in to a friend of mine I think can get us some information sooner."

"Who?"

"You don't think I can handle this without you micromanaging?" I stopped just short of the door, back going ramrod straight. I didn't like being questioned, even if it was by my own brother. He of all people knew how capable I was of getting shit done.

"Fine. Just don't fuck this up. If you need any help, don't be a—"

"Yeah, yeah. Don't be a bitch and not ask," I retorted snidely, finishing the statement I knew was just itching to spill from his lips. "Go spend the evening with your family."

Aaron grunted and disconnected the call. I pulled mine from my ear before turning the knob to enter into the mudroom. There, I placed my briefcase and removed my suit jacket before entering the main part of the house. Movement in the kitchen caught my attention, pulling me forward.

"Complete bullshit!" Kayla mumbled, angrily, as she slammed something on the counter. From behind I could see her arms moving quickly as she slammed a red bell pepper onto the wooden cutting board. She picked up a knife and began slicing through the tender skin of the pepper as if it'd just called her mother a bitch. The entire time she mumbled, angry curse words, many of which I couldn't make out.

I stood far enough back, my back pressed against the kitchen's island, arms folded, just watching her.

"Ow, shit!" She abruptly dropped the knife and lifted her finger to her face for inspection.

The drop of crimson red I saw from my viewpoint had me in motion. "Jesus, Kay!" I shouted, startling her. I grabbed her hand and brought her to the sink. I turned on the water and moved her finger under the stream to wash the blood away. "Doesn't look too deep. Don't move. I've got a first aid kit in the bathroom."

I moved from the kitchen and was down the hall to the half bathroom in a handful of footsteps. Pulling open the cabinet, I reached for the first aid kit and opened it to make sure it was fully stocked. Once I returned to the kitchen, I frowned at the sight of Kayla standing by the counter with a paper towel wrapped around her finger, water turned off.

"I told you not to move."

"Whatever," she grumbled.

I lifted my brows but took her wrist in my hand, pulling her to me. Again, I inspected the cut on her finger. It was small and probably wouldn't need stitches or anything. The bleeding had just about stopped. I rubbed some of the antibacterial ointment from the first aid kit on it, before using a small piece of gauze and wrapping tape around it.

"You know I'm a doctor, right?"

I tilted my head. "What's your point?"

She rolled her eyes before turning back to the counter where she'd been cutting. "Dammit! There's blood on the board. I just ruined the lentil loaf I was making. Shit!" she cursed, frustrated.

"Hey." I halted her movement toward the garbage can, wrapping my hands around her upper arms. "First of all, lentil loaf *should* be ruined so let's thank the Man upstairs for that. Secondly, what's got you so upset?"

She blew out a breath, causing a curl that'd fallen into her face to blow outward, but landing back in the same spot, just over her eye. "My lentil loaf is very good," she mumbled.

"I'll take your word for it, sweetheart."

Another eye roll. "Whatever." She turned, stepping out of my embrace and slamming the chopping board back onto the counter.

I frowned, not liking at all that something was weighing so heavily on her. "Kayla," I called, turning her to face me again. "Tell me what's going on. Why're you treating my cutting board like it ate your lunch?"

"I'll replace the cutting board."

"I don't give a shit about that cutting board, Kay. And you know it. Tell me what's going on," I demanded. I was working to control my own anger at that point.

"It's just not right!" she finally answered, her hands waving in the air.

I continued holding her by the arms. "What's not?"

"Life. This world," she replied as if I should've known what she meant. "All of this shit happens and people walk away like it's nothing. And assholes who hurt others get to go on and live their pathetic little lives as if they've never done anything wrong."

Heat rose in my chest, and not the good kind of heat either. "Who, Kayla?" My voice was low.

"N-not me. Someone else."

I narrowed my gaze. "Who?"

Her eyes shut and she inhaled deeply before pushing out the breath. "A patient of mine." She opened her eyes. They bored into mine, as if pleading. "I can't give you more information. It's private. I just …" she sighed. "She's a good person. Just wants to raise her daughter and live her life."

"A patient?" This was about more than a patient.

"And the asshole that—" She broke off, briefly covering her lips with her hand. "I can't say." She looked at me, as if begging me not to ask for more information than she could give.

I ground my teeth together, clenching my jaw. "Kay, I solve problems for a fucking living."

Her forehead wrinkled as she looked quizzically at me.

"You keep talking in circles when you could just be upfront with me and I can solve this problem." I was growing pissed.

"It's not my problem to solve." She hesitated. "Not all of it anyway. But I do need to ask you something … for a favor."

"So ask," I urged, my hands moving from her arms to her waist.

"My patient needs a new job." She hummed, her hands going to my arms, pulling me into her body. "She's a paralegal."

I reached up behind Kayla with my right hand and took her loose hair into it, tugging lightly, pulling her head back to peer up at me.

"You want me to get her a job?"

Her eyes widened slightly. "If you could just ask around. I know you probably know a ton of lawyers or firms. They might need a new paralegal."

I worked my lower jaw, staring at her intently. Her eyes never left mine. "This is the patient you were just mumbling about?"

She tried to nod but then remembered I had her hair in my hand. "Yes."

"I'd need her information. Like a resume, credentials—"

"I already emailed you her resume, cover letter, and references."

I paused, staring down into those brown eyes. The hand that wasn't tangled up in her hair reached down to cup her ass. "I could ask around for your friend, if you answer something for me." I spun us around so her back was to the kitchen island.

"What's that?"

"Why the hell were you looking at condos the other night?"

Her lips formed into a thin line. "I was looking for my own place."

A muscle in my jaw ticked. "For what?" I pressed my body against hers.

"To live."

"You live here." I reached down and licked the outside of her ear.

"Y-yes but this is temporary ... r-right?" she questioned.

I pulled back and stared down at her, my eyes dropping to her full lips. I captured her lips with my own, planting an unforgiving kiss on her mouth. The words to answer her question wouldn't come, so I was left with action. My hands roamed all over her body, squeezing and massaging her ass before moving up to her breasts.

"Fuck!" I growled when my cell in my pocket began ringing. "Shit!" I cursed once I saw who the caller was. I turned to Kayla "I have to take this."

Kay nodded, biting her kiss-swollen bottom lip

I suppressed the groan that welled up from my very core.

"You couldn't have waited ten minutes to call me back?" I hissed into the phone as I moved from the kitchen down the stairs to my office. I shut the door behind me.

Damon's deep chuckle moved through the line. "My mistake. Did I call while you were in the middle of something?"

"Asshole," I grumbled. "Anyway, I'll make this quick since you're out of town and we both have shit to do."

"What's up?"

"I've got trouble at Townsend. My security's looking into it but I thought you might've heard something or know someone who has."

"I haven't seen anything in the news, so that means you've worked hard to keep it hush, hush. What's going on?"

I gave Damon the rundown on the trouble that'd been happening at Townsend Real Estate, including the robberies, the previous week.

"Shit."

"Tell me about it. But it doesn't make any fucking sense. Robbers looking for cash in a real estate development and a safe in an empty unit? That's the last place there'd be any cash lying around."

"Right," he agreed. "So, you want to know if any of my, ahem, *associates* have heard anything."

"Yes," I answered directly. Damon was a successful, self-made real estate mogul who'd started out on the not so legal side of this business. And he still had those connections.

"I'll put some feelers out around town as soon as I hang up with you. I should hear something within the next few days."

"I appreciate it."

"No problem at all. After all you've done for me, this is just a small token of my appreciation. I gotta go. Catch you when I get back."

"Yeah, make sure you work on the left jab beforehand."

Another chuckle. "No doubt."

We hung up. Between Damon and Brutus working on this thing from both ends, I knew I'd hear something soon. That still didn't allay my anxieties in the meantime. I had to be patient and I hated that shit more than anything. It made me want to punch something. I yanked my office door open to see a startled Kayla.

"Hey, I wasn't eavesdropping," she stated. She held up a stack of takeout menus. "Since I ruined dinner, I thought maybe you'd want to have something delivered."

I took her by the wrist and pulled her in for a quick kiss. "You didn't ruin dinner because I wasn't eating a damn lentil loaf anyway. Let's go out instead of ordering in." I stepped forward, pulling the door closed behind me.

She gave me a sideways glance. "Out where?"

"You still love Thai?"

"Of course. Who doesn't love Thai food?" She poked out her bottom lip as if seriously contemplating that question.

"Good. I need about fifteen minutes to change and I'll be ready."

"Me too."

* * *

Wow. That was my first thought when I exited my bedroom, about fifteen minutes later to see Kayla coming out of the guest room in a new outfit. She still hadn't moved all of her belongings into the master bedroom, a fact I planned on changing soon. But that thought was placed on the back burner as I stared at Kayla in a white frilly skirt that stopped at middle of her thighs. She paired the skirt with a tucked in black and white polka dotted top that was sheer and sleeveless. The outfit showed off both her long, toned legs and arms. The kicker of the entire outfit were the six-inch, strappy heels she wore with it.

"There she is," I stated as my eyes reached hers.

The timid look in her eyes was evident as she frowned. "Who?"

"*My* Kay." The one I was used to, had grown up with. The one who didn't hide her beautiful figure and hair behind buns and boring clothes.

Her eyelids fluttered. "You say that as if you mean it."

"I say it because it's the fucking truth." I stepped forward. "You ready?"

"As I'll ever be."

"After you." I held out my arm to allow her to pass. As she did, I let my eyes roam over her entire backside—loving the way her skirt hiked up another inch in the back, due to the roundness of her ass. The smooth cinnamon silk that posed as skin, covered her legs, curving around each muscle that bunched and revealed itself as she walked.

She paused, looking back at me over her shoulder when she heard my groan. "Are you in pain, Mr. Townsend?" The airy note in her voice sent tiny shockwaves directly to my cock.

"I might be, Doc. You got a remedy for it?"

Those full lips turned crooked on a mischievous grin of her own. "I just might."

"Just what the doctor ordered," I mumbled as I held the door open for her to pass through, my eyes once again stuck on her. The tension I'd felt throughout the day had ebbed just enough that my concentration was on nothing but Kayla Reyes.

* * *

Kayla

That night, I didn't want to think about the past or even my patients and their problems. I wanted to feel as carefree as I'd always claimed to be in my youth.

"Seriously?" Josh bellowed, glaring at me across the table as I chewed.

I'd just swiped another shrimp from his plate and popped it into my mouth with my chopsticks. I giggled, covering my mouth as I chewed.

"You have shrimp on your own plate."

"I know," I said after swallowing. "But it tastes so much better when it comes from yours." I moved to reach for a piece of his eggplant that was included in the shrimp curry dish he'd ordered, but was stopped by his hand covering my wrist.

He pulled my arm, bringing me closer to him across the table. "Eat up, sweetheart, because you *will* be paying me back for every bite you steal from my plate." The deep promise held in those green eyes caused a shiver to run down my spine, and my mouth to water.

Although I tried to keep the feelings at bay, my body remembered all of the ways in which Joshua could bring it pleasure. My nipples hardened and I thanked my earlier self for wearing a padded bra with this sheer top.

Slowly, Joshua released my wrist, and sat back in his chair, almost daring me to take another bite from his plate. Feeling daring myself, I did.

With my eyes trained on him, I parted my lips and planted the eggplant into my mouth, and closed my eyes as the flavor of the coconut milk and curry seasonings hit my tongue. A sound from across the table had me opening my eyes again. When I did, Joshua's eyes were watching me so intently it was as if they were burrowing in to my very soul.

He tilted his head to the side. "Why'd you choose that outfit to wear tonight?" he finally asked.

I lifted my eyebrows. I totally wasn't expecting that question. I saw the hungry look in his eyes when I first emerged from the guest bedroom.

"What? You don't like it?" I held my arms out to my sides.

He leaned in, placing an arm on the table. "You damn well know the answer to that question," he growled.

A chill ran through me. I relished it when he used that tone, especially when he was looking at me the way he was.

"I love it on you and I'm pretty sure you do, too. So why haven't I seen it before now?"

I wrinkled my brows and shrugged. "I don't know. Maybe you just weren't paying attention." I lowered my eyes to the table.

"Bullshit."

I pushed out a breath knowing he wouldn't fall for that lame excuse.

"You've been living with me for two months. This outfit is new."

He was right. I'd purchased it on a shopping trip I'd gone on with Patience and Michelle a few days earlier. I was tired of the clothes in my closet.

"Because I want to start feeling like the old me. The Kayla who didn't put so much thought into what others thought of me, or how something as simple as wearing a skirt could get me into trouble." I couldn't look up at Josh but I continued. "I wasn't as carefree as everyone thought when I was younger. I cared about a lot. I cared the time I saw my mother cry and leave out of the doctor's office because she couldn't bear the sight of me sticking myself with a needle to test my insulin, for the first time. I was only nine. I cared when I heard both of my parents up late at night in heated discussions because of the medical costs for my treatments and hospital stays. I cared every time I went to bed and wasn't sure I was going to wake up because I couldn't get my insulin levels to moderate. And I damn sure cared when my best friend came to me and told me she was diagnosed with stage four ovarian cancer."

"Kayla, I know—"

I held my hand up, letting my eyes meet his. "I cared, Josh, but I wasn't going to let any of it stop me from living my damn life. Even at nine years old when I was first diagnosed with diabetes, I remember the first emotion I felt was anger. I didn't want my life to change but I knew it would and that made me angry. So I made a decision that I wouldn't let my illness or life's problems stop me from being exactly who I wanted to." I sat back in my chair. "And somewhere I lost that, and tonight, I wanted it back." The last part came out just above a whisper.

That was the whole truth. Hearing Sandra speak of having to see her rapist at work, and now helping her look for a new job, made something well up in me. People shouldn't have to change who they were because of the selfish, harmful actions of others.

"Not somewhere." His voice was rigid with anger.

I looked up, almost afraid to ask but I had to. "What?"

Joshua's dark head shook. "You said somewhere you lost that. Not somewhere but someone or something caused you to lose yourself." His mouth snapped shut.

"No." Shaking my head, I reached across the table, covering his strong hand with mine. I grew warmer when he moved his hand to cover mine, squeezing it. "*I* caused me to lose it. I gave my power away by believing bullshit and caring what others thought. I'm done with that."

His eyes narrowed on me, assessing.

"Let's go dancing," I suggested. Not only did I want to move my body, and put this outfit to use, but I also wanted to change the subject. The past was the past and it deserved to remain there.

"Kay—"

"I'm serious. I want to dance. Please," I begged, jumping up and down a little in my seat.

Josh's jaw softened and a small smirk broke free on his lips. I knew I'd won.

"As long as you save some of that energy for later on. You still owe me for my stolen shrimp." He nodded at the plate in front of him.

I grinned. "We'll see how the night ends, Mr. Townsend."

I watched as Josh placed a few bills on the table, covering the cost of dinner and a generous tip. He took my hand into his and led us out of the restaurant. We were in a section of downtown Williamsport where there were plenty of restaurants and bars, many of which had dance floors. I gladly followed Josh as we entered into one of the bars. The fast pumping, pop music mix instantly had my shoulders swaying from side to side.

"Dance with me!" I shouted in Joshua's ear so he could hear me over the bass.

"You thought I was letting you get away from me?" He wrapped his hands around my waist and led us out to the dance floor in the middle of the throngs of dancing patrons. I began swaying my hips from side to side, letting myself feel the rhythm of the music. I lifted my arms high in the air, still feeling Joshua's strong arms holding me. It was as if his hold alone, not the music, gave me the freedom to let loose. I was safe with him.

I shimmied and wiggled my hips, eventually turning and letting my backside brush up against his front. Giggling, I leaned my head against his shoulder when I felt the bulge in his pants.

"I hope that's for me."

"As long as you know what to do with it." His lips hovered just above mine.

"I can think of something."

His lips met mine and before I knew it we were full on making out on the dance floor. One song melted into the next, and then the next, and we continued dancing. I couldn't remember the last time I'd felt as free and uninhibited. Even before what happened to me on the West Coast, I wasn't as free spirited as I'd been in my youth. Losing both of my best friends, albeit in different ways, had made everything seem less exciting, more dull. But that night, as I danced in Joshua's arms, feeling his lips on mine before they began slowly trailing down my neck, all of that reticence was gone. And I craved more of it, and that called for us to be alone.

"Take me home," I whispered in his ear.

"About fucking time."

I think we hadn't even been at the bar for an hour when Joshua's tight grip around my hand was leading me out the door.

"Joshua, slow down," I giggled, almost stumbling in my high heels. I had to get used to walking in six-inch stilettos again. "Oh, excuse me," I stopped short to apologize to a woman I bumped into on account of Josh's rushing. However, my heart caught in my throat when I glanced up and saw who the woman was.

"Mrs. Armstrong." My eyes widened as I glanced next to her to see her husband staring between Joshua and I.

"Mr. and Mrs. Armstrong," Joshua greeted the pair with a calm familiarity.

I couldn't wrap my mind around it. These were Chelsea's parents. I hadn't seen them since I'd left town. That, among other things, left a thick feeling of guilt rolling around in my chest. I attempted to tug my hand free from Joshua's hold but he held firm. Out of the corner of my eye I saw him look down at me.

"H-how are you two? It's been so long."

Mrs. Armstrong's mouth dropped open and tears formed in her eyes. Blue eyes that reminded me so much of her daughter's. Her mouth snapped shut when she glanced down and zeroed in on Joshua's hand wrapped around mine. Again, I tried pulling away, but it was a no go with the hold he had on me.

"Kayla, we heard you moved away. Good to see you back in town," Mr. Armstrong stated just before clearing his throat.

"Finally, decided to bring her practice back to the city that raised her," Joshua stated with pride filling his words.

"Practice? You stuck to the plan, going into medicine?"

I nodded. "Yes, ma'am. Naturopathy."

"That's great. It's a growing field."

My heart squeezed at the sadness that was in her tone. Chelsea's mother knew of my and her daughter's plans to become doctors together.

"It was great to see you. We hope to see you around again. If you'll excuse us," Mr. Armstrong spoke up, taking his wife by the waist to leave us.

I lowered my head, not wanting to meet those emerald green eyes I could feel pinning me.

"It's great to see them again." I nearly choked on the lie and the shame.

Though he studied me for another few heartbeats, eventually we began walking toward the garage where he'd parked his car. The ride home was silent, mainly because I was in my own head about Chelsea's parents and what they must be thinking of me. The one night I decide to let my hair down a little, literally and figuratively, I was reminded why it wasn't such a great idea.

"I think I'm going to sleep in the guest room tonight," I mumbled as soon as I crossed the threshold behind Joshua. I didn't even bother to wait for his response, instead heading toward the staircase, when a firm arm snaked around my middle, pulling me back into what felt like a brick wall.

"I knew you were going to try and pull this shit," he growled into my ear.

CHAPTER 17

*J*oshua

"What the? Joshua, put me down! What the hell are you doing?" Kay wailed as I slung her over my shoulder like she weighed nothing. I proceeded up the stairs to my bedroom.

"Lunatic!" Kayla yelled once I plopped her ass on the bed. She stared up at me, eyes dripping with anger and confusion. Her mouth was turned up into an angry pout, which looked so damn good I had to restrain myself from tasting those lips. "I told you I'm sleeping in the guest room."

"Like hell you are. You're not running away again."

"I'm still in the same house. How is that running?" She threw her hands up in frustration and I swore that in a matter of minutes those same hands were going to be locked in my grasp, over her head as my hips pistoned in and out of her.

I moved closer to the bed, crowding her space. "You know damn well sleeping in the guest room is an effort to put space between us. Why?"

"You didn't see what just happened? Mr. and Mrs. Armstrong. The expressions on their faces?"

I furrowed my brows, bending even closer. "The only looks I saw were of surprise and some grief."

"What about when Mrs. Armstrong saw you holding my hand? Even if she didn't give us a funny look, how do you think that made them feel?"

"I don't really give a shit how it made them feel," I growled.

Kayla gasped and pulled back.

I ignored the twinge of guilt in my chest. "Look, Mr. and Mrs. Armstrong are great people. I love them still. I feel for the pain they suffered and must still be suffering from losing Chelsea, but that's where it ends. I grieved long and hard after Chelsea died." I snapped my mouth shut to prevent my telling her she would've known it'd taken me close to two years after Chelsea died to entertain a woman beyond a one-night stand. But she'd left. She wasn't there to witness any of that. I knew in my heart of hearts, if she had been there, things would've been different. For the both of us.

"She was my first real love. But she's gone and I had to accept that. It was the only way I could move on with my life. They've seen me date other women before."

Kayla parted her lips to respond but then sucked her bottom lip in between her teeth. The anger that'd been present in her eyes trailed away and became replaced by reticence.

"Tell me what you're thinking," I demanded, moving closer.

She shook her head.

"Don't," I snapped sharply. "Don't shut me out like that."

"I ..." She pushed out a breath, running her hand through her hair.

Goddamn that move always made me wild with want for her. A vision of that auburn hair spread across my silk pillowcase, her biting her lower lip just as she was doing but for entirely different reasons seized me.

"I guess I just have to get used to seeing them. I wasn't expecting it," she finally stated. Her brown eyes rose to meet mine and I needed more contact. The need for words ceased. It was time for some action.

"You'll have time to adjust." I moved over her, my hand going underneath her skirt and cupping her mound. "In the meantime, you owe me for those shrimps you stole off my plate."

Her eyes widened.

"Oh, you think I forgot?"

"Forgot?" she moaned, eyelids fluttering. She shook her head. "No, I just thought you'd be a gentleman and not make me pay up."

"Oh, sweetheart." I placed a kiss to her nose, her lips, and then her earlobe, before moving to whisper in her ear, "Not only are you going to pay, you're paying extra for making me carry you up those damn stairs."

* * *

Kayla

Though I protested a little, this was a debt I was more than willing to pay. I gasped and moaned, arching my back off the bed as Joshua had both of my hands raised above my head. He licked his way from my neck to my lips, offering me a taste of his mouth. A taste I couldn't refuse. I sucked his tongue into my mouth, garnering him free reign to taste all of me. I shivered all the way down to my core when his tongue snaked out, licking the roof of my mouth.

I struggled to break my hands free of his hold but he tightened his grip. I wasn't satisfied with that. I wanted to feel him.

"J-Josh," I panted, breaking free of his lips. "I want to taste you tonight."

He pulled back just slightly to stare down at me.

This was the first time I'd offered to pleasure him with my mouth. It wasn't something I was terribly comfortable with but just the idea of doing it for him, made my mouth water.

His nostrils flared as his eyes penetrated me with his gaze. "You sure?"

My heart squeezed. I nodded.

His hold on my wrists loosened and I didn't hesitate in moving from underneath him. I pressed against his shoulder so that he was flat on his back before I moved down to his waist, undoing the button of his jeans and belt. He helped me, pushing his pants all the way down, kicking them off along with his shoes.

I ran my tongue across my bottom lip at the sight of his thick, veiny erection staring angrily at me. I lowered my head, licking the precum that had seeped out. Joshua's sharp intake of air filled me with a sense of empowerment. One that I needed to push away the final remnants of hesitation I had. I cupped the bottom half of his cock with my left hand and continued licking the tip. The salty, tangy taste filled me with a hunger I'd never experienced before. Joshua's groans grew louder and I wanted more of him. I'd hesitated putting all of him in my mouth at first, not knowing if he'd even fit. He was thicker than most.

"Don't stop now," he grunted.

I raised my gaze to meet his. His eyes had darkened considerably. I knew exactly what that look meant. I had better make this quick or I was about to find myself flat on my back. Grinning, I lowered my head and wrapped my mouth around his hard-on. A muffled moan moved up my throat. Joshua's hips rose, pushing him farther into the cavern of my mouth. Up and down, I bobbed on his cock, hoping to deliver even a piece of the paradise he brought to me whenever he performed oral.

"Shit, baby," he growled deeply, raising his hips again.

His words demanded I pick up the pace, which I did, raising and lowering my head in quick succession. Goddamn, he tasted like heaven. I chided myself for not doing this before. My mouth watered, hungry to taste his come. I ran my tongue over the tip again and again, anxiously slurping up any little bit that seeped out. Joshua's large hand went to the back of my head. He dug his fingers into my hair. I grinned inwardly. He loved running his hands through my hair. Of course, he'd seize this opportunity to do it.

I removed my own hand from the stem of his cock, allowing myself more room to take him in as far as he could go. I ran my tongue over the veins that ran along the underside of his shaft. I hungrily anticipated the release of his semen onto my tongue.

Unfortunately, before that could happen Joshua lifted me away from him, forcing him from my mouth.

"I want your legs wrapped around me when I come." His voice was so thick with emotion and need I could barely make his words out, as he feverishly ran his hands over my body, removing each piece of clothing he found along the way.

I yelped in surprise when I found myself flat on my back, Joshua hovering over me, eyes eating me up as he pushed himself in me as deep as he could go. My mouth fell open and my back arched off the bed, my body greedily begging for more. I felt every ridge and vein of him as he slowly, torturously, eased in and out of my sopping wet pussy.

"And you were going to sleep in the guest room tonight," he taunted as he picked up the pace.

"Shut up," I panted, pulling him by the shoulders, fusing our mouths together. I blinked my eyes closed and blocked out everything that wasn't this, right now. Joshua and I, our bodies gliding against one another. Him taking me to higher and higher levels of pleasure. His tongue exploring my mouth while his cock pulsed in and out of my body. Never had I ever been made love to like this. Just when I was sure I couldn't take anymore, the sensation that told me I was going over started in my toes. It moved up my legs until reaching my core, exploding through the rest of my body. My words were incoherent but I was sure the way my pussy muscles spasmed around his cock Joshua got the message.

His hands moved underneath me, cupping my ass, and he pumped vigorously into me. Lowering his face into the crook of my next, he tightened his hold on me. He was coming. I wrapped my arms even tighter around him, squeezing my thighs around his back. I wanted everything he released. I'd have to think about the implications of my actions later, but right then, I wanted all of him. And he gave it to me, over and over as he let every drop of his semen seep into my greedy canal.

By the time he finished, we were both exhausted. Or so I thought.

I inhaled sharply at finding myself turned over on my belly, my waist being lifted so I was on all fours. Before I could even comprehend what was happening, I threw my head back, arching my back at the feel of Joshua's hot mouth on my pussy lips.

"Shit!" I cursed. My hips began moving wildly against his face. My thighs began trembling.

"You taste too fucking good," he mumbled against my core. He quickly buried his face between my legs again, sucking my clit into his mouth, bringing me to another spine tingling, toe curling orgasm.

"You're insatiable," I panted.

"And you love it."

That I did.

CHAPTER 18

*J*oshua

"Don't give me that look," Kayla stated, sternly glaring at me through the bathroom mirror.

I glared right back, reaching up to grab for the ends of the braided pigtails she'd put her hair in. The style was adorable on her, but I preferred the curly, wild mane to be free, mostly so I could run my hands through it.

"Your hair's tied up." I frowned deeply into the mirror. I moved closer, pressing my front against her backside. I also admired the way the spandex shorts she wore outlined the tops of her thighs.

"First time I'm seeing these," I stated pointedly, staring at her shorts.

"Got them while shopping with Patience and Michelle."

I nodded, happy at the growing friendship between my sisters-in-law and Kay.

"We're going for a run. There's no way I'm wearing my hair down while I run. It's too hot."

"I have something to cool you off." I pressed a kiss just beneath her ear.

"N-no!" she shivered at the same time she protested. "None of that." She dodged the next kiss I went to place on her neck, turning to me and putting her arms around my neck. "We're leaving the house today. It's much too beautiful out to remain cooped up indoors."

The playful smile at her lips was enough to make me give her anything she wanted. "Fine. I'll be getting my hands in your hair at some point today."

"Ouch!" she yelped after I slapped her ass.

I grinned and laughed as she slapped me on the arm. "Careful, don't hurt yourself on those biceps."

She rolled her eyes. "Oh, thank you for what you did for Sandra," she beamed.

I frowned, not remembering what she was even referring to at first. "No big deal," I answered when the memory finally surfaced.

"It *is* a big deal. She called the office so happy yesterday to have gotten the job at the new firm. And she's making more money which she's happy about."

"That's great." It really hadn't been an imposition. I passed the woman's resume along to an attorney friend of mine whose firm was looking for a new paralegal. "She had an impressive resume."

"Yeah, she'd said at one point she was on the track to go to law school." Kayla bit her lip and shifted her gaze in a way that told me there was more to the story than that. But since I knew she wasn't going to offer up anymore details about her patient, I took her by the arm.

"Let's go. It takes about an hour to get to where the trail is."

She squinted her eyes in a way that damn near had me growling. All of her facial expressions got under my skin. Which made me want to get under *her* clothes. "You never said we were going out so far. I thought we were going for a run around here."

I raised an eyebrow. "You don't trust me?" I reached out and smacked her ass again just because.

She giggled. "Of course I do." She shrugged. "Just wondering."

"You have any other plans today?"

She gave me a deadpan expression. "You know what I'm doing with the rest of my damn day."

I smirked. She was spending the day with me. I would've preferred if it were naked in my bed but that wasn't the case. My parents had arrived home after their two week vacation, so that meant dinner at Townsend Manor.

"What the hell are you smirking about?" Kay questioned, hand on her hip, breaking into my thoughts.

"Just remembering how I got you to agree to accompanying me to Mother's dinner."

She ducked her head, bashfully.

"Let's go." I held the door open for her and again watched her ass in the spandex shorts as she walked past me. It was going to be a great day.

* * *

Kayla

"I thought we were going for a run but it's a perfect day for a hike," I commented, my eyes raised to the crisp blue sky. There wasn't a cloud in sight and the trees along the trail we walked provided just enough shade to keep the sun from beating off our backs. *Chelsea would've loved this,* I thought. That thought actually brought a smile to my lips. The guilt was still there, but I swallowed it down.

"Reminds me of this tiny community right outside of Portland. I lived there for a little bit."

"How long?" Josh glanced over his shoulder to ask.

"Few months," I answered carelessly, still looking around at the sights. If I had been paying attention I would've spotted the fact that Joshua had stopped walking to stare at me curiously. "Oops!" I yelped just after bumping into him.

"Why'd you leave?" His eyes were narrowed in a way that led me to believe the question was more layered than a simple inquiry.

I shrugged, peering over his shoulder. "I missed home, I guess."

"You guess?"

I pushed out a breath, my shoulders slumping. I didn't want to go there. "I *know*. Okay? I enjoyed the community for the short period of time I was there, but I missed home. I'd been away for long enough and I was ready to come back." That was at least partly truthful.

He gave me another long stare. "We're still working on finding out who is behind the robbery."

I frowned. "I know that. I don't blame you for wh—"

"You should. It was my company. My place, security should've been tighter and it wasn't. That's on me to fix. We'll get the son of a bitch that dared to fuck with what's mine."

I tilted my head. I didn't know if he was referring to the property or me. Or both? Either way, I hated the look of guilt that crossed his face. I stepped in closer, taking his face in between mine. I pressed a kiss to his lips. "I trust you, Josh. You'll figure it out and whoever is behind all the bullshit that's been happening at Townsend Real Estate will regret the day they ever tried to cross you." I meant every word with everything I had in me.

"Then you trust me?"

My head shot backwards at the unexpected question. "Of course."

A muscle in his jaw ticked. "Okay." He turned and continued up the trail but something was off about his "okay."

I frowned but proceeded behind him. Whatever had just happened I was determined not to let it get us off track. It was much too beautiful a day and there really wasn't anywhere I'd rather be.

We continued walking in companionable silence when I began hearing the sounds of water in the distance. My head perked up at the same time Joshua took me by the left hand.

"We're almost there. About another half a mile." He looked over at me, grinning. "Think you can make it?" I saw the challenge in his eye and had the urge to reciprocate.

"Can I make it? The *real* question is can you keep up?" I broke free from his hold and pushed him a few steps backwards, surprising him, and took off running, laughing as I went. This feeling, the lightness I was feeling at that moment was what I'd missed most of all about being away from home. Away from him. The trail, though lined with some brush and stones along the way, was fairly easy to navigate as long as I watched out where I was going. Within seconds I heard

Josh's chuckle turn into heavier breathing as he began jogging to keep up pace with me.

I quickly glanced over my shoulder to see he was just about a half a step behind me, barely breaking a sweat. He was choosing not to pass me. Taunting me with those long, muscular legs that could've easily overtaken my shorter strides.

"Eyes on the trail and not my ass!" I called over my shoulder.

"I can easily do both."

I giggled and pushed myself to pick up my steps, the sounds of water growing slightly louder. I inhaled deeply, filling my lungs with the fresh summer air, closing my eyes.

"Oh wow," I breathed out as soon as my eyes opened. I stared around at the beauty that surrounded us. We'd come to an opening in the trail that led to an embankment on a lake. The lake contained small waterfalls within it. "This is ..."

"Beautiful, right?" Josh finished my thoughts.

I nodded, swallowing as I worked to catch my breath.

"I found this place about two years ago. Came out for a hike and discovered this. Other hikers visit but it's somewhat isolated, so there's not as many visitors as there are at the old waterfall."

A smile touched my lips. The waterfall had been Josh and Chelsea's place, at first. I hadn't got a chance to see it, in person, until we released Chels' ashes. But it was also the first place Josh and I made love.

I nodded, still looking around. A bird sitting high up in the trees, squawking, caught my attention. When it flew off an involuntary laugh fell from my lips. Its wings were the most beautiful shade of indigo I'd ever seen. Without giving it another thought, I began toeing off my sneakers and socks and walking closer to the edge of the embankment.

"What the hell are you doing?" Joshua called, following closely behind me.

I glanced over my shoulder, giving him a saucy grin. "You promise to save me if I fall in?" I laughed, not expecting a serious answer.

"Don't play like that, Kay!" he growled, tugging me backward to his hard chest.

I felt the tension coiled through his body as I turned to him. "It's okay—"

"It's not okay! This lake is deeper than it looks."

"Josh, I'm a great swimmer. Besides, I wasn't getting all the way in. Just my feet."

He gave me a hard glare; his jaw was rigid.

I pressed my lips to the corner of his mouth. "Dip your toes in with me," I whispered in his ear.

He pulled back, still eyeing me warily.

"Please."

He finally relented, nodding.

I watched as he toed off his sneakers and socks, then took me by the hand, guiding us both to the water's edge.

"Oooh, that's cooold!" I shivered but waded in a little farther, just up to my ankles. I tugged Josh's hand to bring him closer.

"Mid-August and the water's still cool."

"Large bodies of water usually don't warm up until late August, early September around here. Just in time for summer to end and everyone to pack up their beach bags."

"What're you, encyclopedia britannica?" he asked, moving behind me and wrapping his arms around my waist. Needless to say, my body instinctively reacted by melting against his chest.

I laughed, shaking my head. "Learned it in my fifth grade social studies class. That lesson stuck with me for some reason." I shrugged. "Most of the lessons on things I wanted to explore as a kid but couldn't because I was sick, did. I wanted so bad to go camping as a kid, hike, swim in a lake like this. But my parents were so over-whelmed with my hospital visits, doctors' appointments, and hovering just to make sure I was okay, we didn't get to do a lot of that stuff.

"Which was why you never were able to go out to the waterfall with Chels and I."

I swallowed and nodded. "Right. My parents biggest fear was that

I'd be out somewhere and not have the insulin I needed or a snack to even out my sugar levels. There was one time we did go on a hike, my mom, dad, and I. It turned into an absolute disaster. My mother had brought food and snacks for me to eat to help keep my blood sugar stabilized but she forgot the insulin in the car. I had to eat and take the insulin at the same time to keep my levels just right. My dad had to hike back the two miles we'd walked to get the insulin. I ended up being fine but after that, but they were done. My father insisted we pack it up for the day and head back to the car. Though he never said it out loud, in front of me at least, he was pissed at my mom for forgetting. And my mom was just as pissed at herself."

I wiped a bit of sweat from my forehead.

"Sometimes I don't know how their marriage survived all of that." I leaned my head against Josh's shoulder and lifted one of my legs, splashing the water with my foot.

"Having a sick kid isn't something I'd wish on any parent." His voice was so sincere and heavy.

I turned in his arms, placing my arms around his shoulders. And just because his lips looked so delicious I gave him a peck on them. "I imagine it was a lot for them, but you want to know the truth? I think it helped make their marriage stronger."

He gave me a curious look.

"The way I see it, the illness or death of a child can either do one of two things, bring people closer together or tear them apart. I think my parents got lucky, or were blessed, or something because my being ill allowed them to learn to have to rely on one another. And faith. My mother started going back to church. 'Til this day she swears it was prayer and her long talks with God that healed me."

"And you? What do you think?"

I shrugged. "I think whatever someone needs to get them through the day. I know it was a lot of medical research and science that healed me but nothing's wrong with a little bit of faith."

"Faith, huh?"

I lifted up on my tiptoes to get closer to his eye level. Our faces were just inches apart. "Yeah, faith and good science," I added.

A darkness moved through his eyes. He was warring with something but his lips wouldn't reveal what exactly. Instead, he lowered his head and took my lips in a kiss that stole my breath. Just like they always did.

Just as Joshua deepened the kiss, a noise behind us caught his attention. His hold tightened around my waist and he turned to glance over his shoulder.

"Hi." A young girl who appeared to be about seven waved.

"Suzzie, leave those nice people alone," a woman I assumed was the girl's mother scolded. She looked up at us and smiled bashfully before taking her daughter by the hand and moving past us.

"Kid almost got a peep show," Josh chuckled.

I swatted his chest.

"You hungry?"

"Always."

"Good, c'mere." He pulled me by the waist toward the embankment edge where a few large boulders sat. Perfect for sitting and the lunch that he'd packed for us.

We ate and talked about work. Though Josh kept up a good front, I knew the situation with Townsend Real Estate was getting to him. It was his baby, so to know someone was essentially running a smear campaign against it was hard to watch. It pissed me off just to see how much it weighed on him. Changing the conversation, Joshua asked me about work and I told him about why I loved working with families.

"I always imagined doing exactly what I'm doing right now. It's a little different than what I'd originally thought it would be, but I love it just the same." I turned to face Josh. We remained silent for a minute, staring at one another. He knew I was referring to not having Chelsea there to share the dream we'd dreamt together.

He took my hand in his and kissed my knuckles just as his phone rang.

"Yeah," he answered gruffly.

I wrinkled my brows, watching as his eyes darkened while he silently listened to whoever was on the other end of the phone.

"I'll be there in an hour and a half," he stated before abruptly ending the call.

"What's up?"

"Work," he answered shortly.

"You have to go?" I didn't even let him answer the question before I began packing up our half-eaten lunch.

"I wouldn't end this if it wasn't important." I heard the apology in his tone.

"I know."

"I'll make it quick. We still have a date for tonight."

The way Josh's demeanor went from laid back and casual to rigid was almost scary. I watched his determined steps as we descended back down the trail we'd come. I knew something big was happening concerning his business.

* * *

JOSHUA

"It's about fucking time," I declared, pushing past Brutus and the police officer that was accompanying him, into the concrete basement at Townsend Industries. We were on the ground floor of the Townsend building and Brutus had finally secured a meet between me and James fucking Cunningham.

"What the hell is going on? I was supposed to be taken to a different facility. What is this?" James demanded as soon as he saw me push through the door. His eyes shifted nervously to the officer behind me.

As soon as my gaze landed on his fucking face, an anger like no other rose from the pit of my stomach. The expression on Kay's face when I first saw her in the police station came to mind. She'd had a wide-eyed terror stricken look in her face, but was doing her best to keep her composure. I wouldn't let that slide.

Without saying a word, I charged over to James who stood about two inches taller than I. I slammed my open palm into his neck, causing him to immediately go down, gasping for air.

"Hey! You said this was just going to be a talk!"

"Shut him the fuck up!" I growled to Brutus behind me, directing him to take care of the officer. "Get out!"

"I-I can't leave you alone with—"

"Come with me, Officer Venetti. Don't worry …" I heard Brutus tell the officer as he pushed him out of the door, closing it behind him.

I held my glare on James who was still trying desperatcly to breathe. Moving closer, I stooped low. "You're not dying … yet."

He struggled to speak, still barely able to suck in are as he clutched his hands to his neck. His eyes were wide and tear filled, a look of terror in them. The same one Kay had in her eyes that night. The look in James' eyes, however, brought me a sense of satisfaction, instead of rage.

"That hit wasn't for trying to rob my place or set my company up. That was for scaring the hell out of my lady. For holding a gun on her." I clenched my fists at the thought of a gun being pointed at Kay. But I had to control my anger in order to get the information I needed. "You know I could make it so your body would never be found."

His eyes, which were already wide, doubled in size.

"I'm a fighter, James. But not a killer. Not most of the time, anyway. Only a few things would make me end a man's life. You fuck with my family, my business, or my woman. Even in business I can tolerate a lot more than if you were to fuck with my woman. You did that by holding a gun to her face. I just want you to understand it when I say, I have no problems taking your life here and now, before I ask you these next few questions. Are we clear?"

I paused, waiting for him to agree. Once he nodded, I continued.

"Good. Who is behind the set-up?" I got straight to the point.

"I don't kn—" He couldn't finish his sentence before my hand was wrapped around his neck, squeezing, tightly.

"Remember my warning," I seethed through clenched teeth. "Please do, test me on it. Please do," I taunted, squeezing his neck tighter.

"Okay, okay," he wheezed out, holding his hands up. "A g-guy came to me a few days after you f-fired me."

"What guy, James?"

"He said his name was Tim. He showed up out of nowhere on my doorstep. Said he was with the Better Business Bureau, at first, and they were doing research on Townsend Real Estate's unfair treatment of employees. I told him how I'd just been fired."

"Which he undoubtedly knew already. Keep going."

"He just wanted to know my story. I told him. Then a week or so later, he calls, says he has a proposition for me."

"To rob my damn company?"

James nodded.

"And your stupid ass believed someone working for the Better Business Bureau would have you rob Townsend Real Estate?"

"No." He shook his head vigorously. "No, but then he said he wasn't with the BBB but that he worked for a man who had a vested interest in seeing Townsend fall. He said there'd be something in it for me if I robbed the condominium that was for sale. Said the former owners had a safe in it that they hadn't emptied out."

"That makes absolutely no fucking sense, James!" I growled, grabbing him by the collar of the orange jumpsuit he wore.

"I know! But the guy told me I'd make an easy ten grand out of the deal. I was broke. It sounded like a bargain to me. So I took it."

I rose to my feet, standing over James who still laid on the floor. I eyed him, looking for any signs of deception.

"What was this Tim's last name?"

"McDonald or Mc something or other. Ouch!" he bellowed when he received a sharp kick to his abdomen.

"Give me a straight fucking answer, James."

"McKellen. He said his last name was McKellen."

"Tim McKellen," I sounded out loud, running the name through my mental rolodex. It didn't ring any bells but I felt this was connected to someone I knew. I stooped low in front of James again. "I'm leaving now. You will be taken back to jail by the officer that brought you here. You will never mention this meeting to anyone or you will find yourself in a very ugly scenario behind bars. You won't have to worry about ever making it to the end of your ten year sentence for armed robbery. You understand what I'm saying to you?" I glared at James.

"Yesss," he drew out.

"Good." I nodded and stood, turning my back on him to move to the door. James was as good as dead behind those prison walls. I'd already saw to that, but I wouldn't reveal that to him. That'd be a little surprise he'd learn in the next few months. Since he'd pleaded guilty to the armed robbery, there would be no trial. He was going straight to jail where he wouldn't live out the next six months. That was his real punishment for pulling a gun on Kayla. This minor beating was just to get some information. Now that I had it, I had no use for him.

"You can take him now. Thank you, Officer Venetti." I held out my hand for the officer to shake. When he gripped it, I said, "As promised, your son will get the medical treatment he needs at no financial cost to your family. Anonymously, of course." A smile I'd perfected over the years in the course of business dealings touched my lips.

"Th-thank you," the officer stated, his gaze bouncing between Brutus and I.

I gave Brutus one last nod before turning and heading home. I needed to get changed so Kay and I could make it to my parents' for dinner.

CHAPTER 19

*J*oshua

Silently, I watched as Kayla wrestled with how to wear her hair for the dinner at my parents' house. The tension of my earlier meeting began to recede as I noted the half up, half down hairstyle she'd chosen for the night. My fingers itched to get tangled up in those auburn strands.

I licked my lips as she dropped the towel from her lithe body. Moving into the bedroom, I observed her. When she put a little more sway into her hips, sauntering over to the dresser where her panties and bras rested, I knew she was now putting on a show. My groin tightened and a groan moved up my throat, spilling out of my mouth when she bent completely over, exposing all of her hidden treasures, just to step into the lace panties she opted to wear that night.

Fuck, Kay!

"My mother's going to be pissed as hell at you for causing us to miss her dinner tonight," I growled, moving closer.

"You stay your ass right there!" she chided. "Mrs. Townsend will not blame me for being the scallywag that kept her son from visiting."

Her cautioning fell on deaf ears as I moved closer, wrapping my arms around her anyway. "Scallywag?" I repeated, nipping at her earlobe.

"You heard me." She slapped my hands but that didn't stop me from planting a kiss on her neck.

"Do you know what I want to do to you right now?"

She turned to face me, now wearing a black bra and panty lace set. The dark fabric against the brownness of her skin had my vision blurring for a second.

"Stop," she yelped, swatting my hands again. "I'm serious, Joshua."

I growled, taking a step back.

Kayla went over to the chair that sat across my bedroom where her dress for the evening was laid out. At least, she was going to wear the shimmery dark blue dress I'd picked out for her.

"I still can't believe you went into my closet and picked this for me to wear tonight."

I grinned as I watched her step into the dress, shaking her hips a little to help pull the dress up. I'd finally moved all of her clothing in from the guest room and even made room in my walk-in closet for her dresses and pants suits. As soon as I saw that dress hanging in the closet, I knew I wanted to see her in it as soon as possible. Mother's dinner was the perfect event for such an occasion.

"It'll be even better the moment it's pooled on my bedroom floor."

Her eyes lifted to mine, a smile apparent in them. "Can you help me with this?" She turned, exposing her back to me.

I let my eyes trail down her naked back but I frowned at the thought of helping with the zipper, thereby obstructing my view.

"If I must." Begrudgingly, I sauntered closer and slowly raised the zipper, securing the dress to her body. I kissed the nape of her neck and inhaled deeply to ingest the scent of coconut and lavender that was in her hair.

"The sooner we get this over with the sooner I can have that dress on my floor. Let's go," I growled, taking her by the hand.

Kayla sucked her teeth. "Such impatience. How do I look?"

"Good enough to eat," I stated without turning back to look at her. If I did, we weren't going to be leaving the house. "Which I plan on doing, over and over again once we return home," I finished saying as I held the door open for her.

Another grin was cast on her pink tinted lips and I had to remind myself of how much I loved my mother.

It took approximately ten minutes to arrive at Townsend Manor. While my parents' home wasn't in the same community as my brothers and I, we were close enough that we could reach their place in no time.

"God, I forgot how big this place is."

Kayla's voice pulled at my insides. I shut off the car in the semi-round driveway and turned to face her. I viewed her profile as she stared up at the house, taking in its expansiveness.

"It's just a house, Kay."

"Pssh." She looked at me as if I were crazy.

To others, it was *the* Townsend Manor. Many a business deal, gala, and high society event had been hosted at this place.

"You spent plenty of time here when we were teens," I reminded her. "You're no stranger around here." I opened the car door and exited, quickly moving around to hold the door open for her. I was satisfied when she took my hand.

As we got to the door, it opened before I was able to ring the bell.

"Joshua," my mother greeted, her eyes glinting with pride.

"Hello, Mother." I leaned down and kissed her cheek, wrapping my arms around her waist for a hug. She clung on, as usual, which I always allowed.

"I missed you."

"You were only gone for two weeks," I chided.

"Two long weeks. I had to force your father not to do any work. And you know how stubborn that man can be," she tutted.

I raised an eyebrow at my mother. The truth was, my mother was just as stubborn as my father but I would never say those words out loud.

"Kayla!" my mother squealed, ignoring the look I gave her.

"Mrs. Townsend. Thank you for inviting me tonight."

My mother waved her off. "You're family. Please, come in. Robert!

Joshua has arrived," my mother called out. "Come, Kayla." She pulled Kay toward the back of the house by the hand, leaving me alone.

"Nice to see you, too, Mother!" I called sarcastically.

"Leave my wife alone. She always loved that girl."

Me too.

My eyes bulged as that brand new thought crossed my mind. It had been an instant response to my father's words. I shook my head, breaking free of the thought that would obviously need to be scrutinized at a later time.

"Looking good, old man," I joked with my father. He had definitely gotten a tan while in Greece. It contrasted nicely with his greying hair and beard.

My father's handshake was firm as he tugged me in closer to him. "We need to talk."

I nodded, knowing exactly what he was referring to. "You heard about the robberies?"

He gave me a deadpan look. Of course he'd heard.

"You want to know what's happening?" I didn't bother waiting for an answer. "Brutus is on it and I've got a friend of mine digging in some background channels for me, also. Had a meeting today."

"And the police?"

"I've got it covered, Father."

Before he could respond, my father's head rose and turned toward the door. The doorbell had interrupted him. "We'll discuss this later." His hand dropped from my shoulder and he strolled to the door, opening it to a grinning Carter and Michelle, with their kids in tow.

"Hey, Grandfather! Hey, Uncle Josh!" nine-year-old Diego chimed, a huge grin on his face.

"Diego." I lowered my hand for my nephew to clasp and pulled him in for a hug. "What's up, bro?" I greeted Carter. "Michelle, beautiful as always." I pressed a kiss to her cheek. "And the little one." I glanced down to the sleeping baby in her arms. Baby Samuel was a little over two months old and the light of his parents' eyes.

I wonder what our kids will look like.

Holy shit. Another stray thought. I needed to get a grip before I started saying shit like that out loud.

"Hey, Josh," Michelle greeted, pulling me from my silent freak out.

I tossed her a smile, taking a step back to allow them entryway into the house.

The baby started to squirm and make noises in Michelle's arms.

"I knew he'd wake as soon as we got here. I need to change and feed him," she stated, looking to Carter then to my father.

"Linda's with Kayla in the kitchen. I'll take you." My father took Michelle by the waist and directed her to the kitchen.

"You better be careful before the old man tries to steal your woman," I teased Carter, poking him in the ribs with my elbow.

"Who's an old man?" Diego interjected.

Carter frowned, looking down at his son. "Nobody. Your uncle's just a sh— He's just trying to be funny." My oldest brother gave me a sideways glance.

I folded my lips, to prevent the laugh that wanted to escape.

Carter, Diego, and I caught up for a few minutes until Diego headed back to one of the play rooms my mother had set up for all of the children. He demanded that we notify him the moment his cousins, Kennedy and Kyle, arrived.

"Sure thing, bud," Carter responded, ruffling his son's hair before he went running off. "So," he turned to me, "Kayla, huh?"

My lips firmed into a straight line. I didn't like the smile playing at his lips.

"She still living with you?"

"Mind your business," I tossed back just as our father returned.

"What's up?" Tyler's loud ass voice interjected. He'd obviously opted to use the code to open the door. We all had keys or access codes to enter my parents' home but rarely used them when they were there.

"Perfect timing," Carter welcomed our youngest brother but continued to eye me.

"The party can't start without me," Ty added just after hugging my father. He gave Carter and I a handshake. "So, what'd I miss?"

"Nothing."

"You haven't been around to meet Kayla, have you?"

Carter and I both spoke up at the same time.

Tyler lifted an eyebrow at our brother. "No, I haven't, but from what I remember she was fucking hot!"

"Tyler Joseph Townsend, I don't give a damn how big you get, you are not too old for me to put you over my knee!" my mother chided out of nowhere.

Thank goodness for my mother's interruption because I felt myself readying to take a swing at my kid brother. I didn't like the mischievous glint in his eyes.

I turned to find all three women staring at us. I was sure my mother's blue irises were burning a hole through my youngest brother's head, but my eyes were trained on a different redhead. Instinctively, like a moth to a flame, I walked over, wrapping my arm around her waist.

"I was just kidding, Mother," I heard Ty answer in the background.

"Hey," I said low in Kayla's ear as if it'd been hours since we'd seen one another instead of a handful of minutes.

"Hey. Your parents' kitchen is insane," she stated, eyes going wide. "The recipes I could make in there …"

"My mother's not letting you make a damn lentil loaf in her kitchen."

Kay's giggle warmed every part of my insides.

"Hey, Red," Tyler bum rushed the conversation. He extended his arms as if moving in for a hug.

"The hell do you think you're doing?" I growled.

Tyler stood back, staring at me. "My, my. Touchy, aren't we?"

It was on the tip of my tongue to tell my brother to fuck off, but then Kayla had to go and make things worse, by stepping out of my hold.

"Hey, Ty," she greeted, a warm smile on her face.

"I see you haven't forgotten the most important Townsend in the room. How's it going, Red?" Ty questioned, pulling her in for a hug. Ty and Kayla were very familiar with one another, or at least had been. As the youngest, Ty was around when Kayla would come over or we'd hang out. He was a few years behind me in school, but he'd been at Excelor at the same time Kayla, Chelsea, and I had.

"How could I forget you, Ty?"

My brother gave me a superior look. "I always knew you had a thing for me. You know younger men are in these days. I'm just putting that out there." He shrugged.

"Ty, I will f—"

"And I'd like to put out there that you better learn to use your offensive line more effectively before you're sidelined." Kay's words cut off my angry rant to my brother, causing everyone except Ty to laugh.

"She's got a point there, bro!" Carter slapped Tyler on the back.

Ty put his hand to his chest. "You wound me, Red. Us redheads gotta stick together."

Kayla nodded. "We do, which is why I'm offering some friendly advice."

Another round of laughter from all of us. I placed my hand on Kay's waist and kissed her temple.

Gone was the unsure, bashful Kayla that had returned from the West Coast. This confident, quick witted, laughter loving, and at times daring to say whatever came to mind, Kayla was the one I knew and loved.

* * *

Aaron, Patience, and their children arrived just as we were all sitting down to dinner.

"Sorry, we're so late. *Someone* had to take a business call," Patience apologized, giving Aaron the eye.

"Everything all right?" my father spoke up.

"No!" My mother cut off Aaron's response. "Robert, you know we do not discuss business at the table. I haven't seen my children or my grandchildren in weeks. We absolutely will not spend this time discussing Townsend Industries. Do that at the office." Everyone at the table knew my mother's word was final. She loathed talk about business at the table. If it were up to my father, we'd discuss business twenty-four seven. Though he'd retired as CEO years earlier, leaving Aaron to run the company, with me in tow, he still sat on the board and was very familiar with the happenings within the business.

"My apologies, Mother," Aaron stated and pulled out a chair for Patience to sit.

The children were sitting at a smaller, nearby table, giggling and chatting with one another. I couldn't help but watch them. An unfamiliar tug pulled at my insides. I turned and my eyes connected with a pair of doe brown eyes that also tugged at my heartstrings. I couldn't fully describe that moment even if I'd wanted to but there was a decision made in my subconscious. One I wouldn't be able to put into words until later, but something was solidified in that moment. Under the table, I took Kayla's left hand in mine, bringing it to my lap. I needed to touch her, to make sure she was real.

"Joshua, did you hear me?" I turned to the far end of the table where my mother sat next to my father.

"No, Mother. What was that?"

"I said, I'm glad to see you've been slowing down with all that fighting. I was just reading—"

"Fighting? So you do fight?"

My back straightened and I tightened my hand around Kayla's.

"You haven't told Kayla yet?" my mother inquired.

I gritted my teeth, hating being put on the spot like this.

"I thought it was just practicing in your basement."

The table went silent. *Shit.* This certainly was not how I wanted her to find out.

"I'll tell you more about it later. Can we discuss something else?" I said to no one in particular.

"Kyle did well on his spelling test this week," Patience spoke up, shifting the conversation. Kyle doing well on his spelling was a big deal to the family. My mother chimed in next with what great news that was, and eventually baby Samuel began cooing and everyone directed their attention toward the baby. Everyone except myself and Kayla.

My eyes were pinned to Kayla's profile as she stiffly ate her meal with her right hand while trying to tug her left hand from my grasp. I held firmly and eventually she stopped trying. Like I said, we'd talk about it all later.

* * *

"Looks like another one bit the dust."

I turned, narrowing my eyes on my youngest brother who was grinning like the fool he was. He was flanked by my two eldest brothers.

"The hell is this fool talking about?" I grumbled, looking at the other two.

Aaron shrugged. "I don't try to decipher what our youngest sibling is talking about anymore."

"Anymore?" Ty chimed in, "You never did, big bro."

Ty turned to me, eyes gleaming in delight. That look got under my skin. As a kid, Tyler was always the one who was up to something. The most mischievous out of the four of us. I guessed it was to be expected seeing as how he was the youngest and all. His antics on and off the football field proved he still hadn't grown out of his mischievous ways.

"Anyway," he stated, "I'm referring to the fact that all three of my older brothers have gone ahead and taken the big plunge."

I tilted my head.

"Fallen in love. Gotten married. Started families. The whole shebang."

I rolled my eyes. "Get the fuck outta here, Ty."

"Hey now! Mother would not be happy with such language," he chided.

"Fucking clown," I grumbled under my breath, looking between Carter and Aaron.

Carter smirked and chuckled but then said, "He does have a point."

"Thank you, Carter. You were always my favorite older brother," Tyler added snidely.

Aaron grunted.

"Don't sweat it, Aaron. You were in the running for the top two, top three spot." Ty shrugged.

"He's an ass but he's got a point."

I rocked back on my heels, not believing Aaron of all people would be agreeing with our younger brother.

"Don't give me that look," he added.

My gaze bounced between the three of my brothers. While Aaron's expression remained serious, I could see the hint of laughter in his eyes, along with Carter and Tyler's. The latter twos lips began twitching until they finally burst out laughing, obviously at the dismay written all over my face.

"Fuck both of you and you too!" I growled in Aaron's direction. "Fucking in love. Not me. Not ever," I retorted at their increased laughter. I had made that vow seven years ago and intended to keep to it. I cared for Kayla, sure. A great deal. And I wasn't sure I could see my life without her in it anymore, but did that mean I was *in love*? Maybe …

"Fuck off. I don't have time for love and family and all that shit. I've got work to tend to."

"And fighting?" Tyler questioned in between guffaws. "Forgot to mention that to her, huh?"

"That's because he's been spending less time at the gym and more time with someone else," Carter added.

"You know what? Fuck all three of you. I need to speak with Father, anyway." I ground my teeth as I brushed past the three of them and moved down the hall to my father's study. He was in there and I spent the next ten minutes updating him on the situation with Townsend Real Estate.

"I have a feeling I'll be hearing something very soon," I finished telling him. It'd been a little over two weeks since I'd first contacted Damon. He'd gotten to me through text message, giving me little tidbits of information he'd heard from the feelers he'd put out. With the information I'd gotten from James earlier in the day, I knew Brutus would be able to find something soon. I needed to wrap this shit up. The mere thought of the scared look on Kayla's face after the robbery had my fists twisting at my sides. In an instant I was ready to hit something. Hard.

Ordinarily, that feeling would've sent me to gym to get into the ring with the biggest motherfucker I could find. But when my father placed a firm hand on my shoulder and said, "Go home. Spend time with your woman," I stared up at him and nodded. The very thought of taking Kayla home and holding her writhing body in my arms as we made love in my bed was enough to ease the tension that had coiled in me. Somewhat, at least. It wouldn't fully be alleviated until the bastard behind all of this was caught.

But my father was right. Right then, I needed Kayla in my arms. So I took his advice. Within the next twenty minutes, the two of us were making our good-byes to my family.

"Ty is still a character, I see." She gave out a little laugh in the car on the way home.

I grunted. "He's a jackass. But his season starts in a few weeks. I'll get you a season pass to the family's private skybox." I made a mental note to call my assistant in the morning to do just that.

"That'll be fun," she said as we pulled up to my driveway. She tossed me a smile but something was amiss in her eyes. She looked away before I could quite make out whether or not it was me or if there really was something off.

Either way, I needed to touch her. Cutting off my car's engine, I climbed out and made it to the passenger side door in record time. I reached for Kay's arm to help her out of the car, but as soon as she was upright, my lips met hers in a searing kiss. She moaned into my mouth instantly, and my dick grew harder than it ever had. There was no waiting this time. We were in my private driveway, which wasn't visible to any neighbors. I'm not entirely sure that even in that moment I would've cared, either way. I slammed the door closed and pressed Kayla's back to it.

"Ever since you put this fucking dress on, I've been waiting to take it off," I groaned against her plump lips.

She sighed contentedly, running her hands up and down my sides.

"I need you," I ground out.

"You already have me," she answered in the sexiest voice that I knew was used only with me.

"Fuck, Kay!" I growled, running my hands underneath her dress. I squeezed and massaged her ass until her moans grew louder and louder. Eventually I couldn't take it anymore and I pulled at the fabric, needing to get to the treasure they hid. With my left hand I cupped her hot core and felt her wetness spilling into my hand. "You're so wet, baby."

"Joshua, I—" She broke off on a moan when I ran my index finger along her labia, slowly.

"You what?" I urged at the same time I pushed one of my long fingers into her core. She was so fucking wet and tight as her muscles gripped my finger. God, she was beyond beautiful, the way she tossed her head back, her hair spilling over her shoulders. Her hips began rocking against my finger.

"You like that?" I taunted.

"Mmm," came her reply.

"Show me. Show me how much you enjoy it, baby!" I demanded, entering a second finger. I massaged her clit with my thumb while reaching for her g-spot. My cock was hard as a brick, begging to be released from my pants to enter into the tight little pussy of hers, but I wanted to savor this. I needed to watch her as she derived pleasure from me. I gave and she took.

Her hands tightened around my shoulders at the same time her inner muscles tightened around my probing fingers.

"Come for me, baby," I encouraged, knowing she was close.

Her head lolled back against the roof of my car, her chest heaved and her pussy squeezed tightly around my fingers as she came. My mouth watered and I fell to my knees, hoisting her leg over my shoulder, putting my mouth on her weeping pussy. I licked up every drop that I could wring out of her, essentially sending her into another orgasm. By the time I finished, the shaved hairs of my beard were saturated with her essence, and I couldn't have been more pleased. Save for the fact that my cock was demanding its own release. It was time for me to give my body what it was demanding.

Quickly, I rose to my feet, unbuttoned my pants and belt. Before I knew it, Kay's hand was on my rod, pulling me free of my pants. I looked up and stared into her hazy eyes. She was as far gone as I was.

"Guide me inside your sweet spot, baby," I urged just before I bit her bottom lip and sucked it into my mouth.

We both sighed and groaned when the tip of my cock first breached her entrance. My hips sank into her body and a dizzying feeling overcame me. I reached for the top of my car to brace myself, and began pistoning my hips rapidly. Kay's body responded in kind, pumping against mine, her arms around my shoulders tightened and our lips scrambled to suck and taste one another's. I was completely lost in the experience of just the two of us. I had no regard for the fact that we were outside, in my front driveway, going at it like rabbits. I wouldn't have given a shit if someone saw us either. I'd never felt like this about anyone. Ever.

As the heaviness of that realization began to settle on my shoulders, I felt my body stiffen and my orgasm started in the soles of my feet.

"Come with me!" I grunted. I ran my thumb along Kayla's distended button, running circles over it. Her thighs tightened around my hips and a strangling noise came from her throat.

I sank my teeth in the exposed skin of her neck, suckling the sweet taste of her skin as we came together. I emptied everything I had in me, into her, figuratively and literally.

Mine.

That was the only word that repeated itself over and over in my head. This woman was mine. I squeezed my eyes tightly, remembering the stupid shit I'd said to Tyler's ribbing earlier. I didn't mean it. I knew at the time I hadn't meant it. I just hadn't been prepared to deal with the reality that I was deeply, utterly, and yes, hopelessly in love with my best friend from high school. Maybe I had been for a while.

"Shit!" I cursed when I picked up my head from Kay's shoulder to realize the noise I heard in the background wasn't just my own soul coming back to my body, but my cell phone. Fuck it. Whoever it was could wait.

"Y-you should get that." Kay's voice was low and held a tremble as I pulled out of her. She dipped her head, avoiding my gaze, as she worked to fix her now crumpled dress.

"Are you hurt?" I questioned looking at her for signs that I'd been too rough against the car. Fuck. I should've waited until we were inside, but my need for her had been all consuming.

"No." She shook her head, again avoiding eye contact.

"Kay—" My phone began ringing again. "Fuck!" I cursed and pulled my phone free from my pocket, checking to see who was calling. It was Damon. I knew whatever it was, was important. *Shit.*

"Yeah," I answered, in an urgent and annoyed tone.

"Apologies for being MIA for a little bit. But I got that information you were asking about, and if you want to get this shit handled, I suggest you jump on it now," he began without preamble.

Damn.

This would be happening right now. "Give me a sec," I stated, grabbing my keys from the ground. Apparently, they'd fallen out of my pocket or my hand in my rush to get to Kayla.

"I got it," she insisted, taking the keys from me and moving toward the door.

I narrowed my gaze at her retreating back. Something wasn't right. I couldn't put my finger on it, but we obviously needed to talk.

"Josh?" Damon called into the phone.

"Yeah, yeah, I'm here," I answered just as the door closed behind Kayla. I made the decision to deal with the information Damon was about to tell me and then get back to handle whatever was the issue between Kayla and I.

Unfortunately, things would turn out a hell of a lot more complicated than I'd anticipated. The heat level of my body rose the more Damon talked. He'd been able to find out some information through his contacts. Apparently, whoever it was that was at the bottom of all the shit that was happening with Townsend Real Estate had been asking around for a few guys to set up the robberies.

"Someone from the Better Business Bureau had been looking for fired employees of yours," Damon stated.

I lifted an eyebrow. James had been telling the truth.

"Go on."

"Guy named Rich McCloud had tried to hire a runner who used to work for me back before I went legit. Well, mostly legit. Anyway, he was told there'd be money in the model home and empty condo."

"In a safe, right?"

"Yeah. My guy didn't fall for it but he remembered the name."

"Rich McCloud. McCloud," I repeated, being familiar with the last name.

"McCloud is the name of—"

"Yup," I grunted into the phone. He was a real estate developer in the city as well. At least, he used to be. "I gotta go. Thanks for the intel."

"Not a problem. Handle your business."

"I always do," I responded before hanging up with Damon. I immediately dialed Brutus to inform him of the information I'd just learned. Within an hour his team had gotten the names and locations of the other three robberies as well as the names of who had hired them. All fingers pointed to Rich McCloud, who was the cousin of one Wallace McCloud, the formerly well-known real estate developer in Williamsport. One my family had a not so nice history with. The more I found out, the more the pieces started falling into place as to why this person had it out for my company. His business had gone under and he blamed Townsend Real Estate for his troubles. Too bad for him, his pathetic life was about to get much worse.

CHAPTER 20

*K*ayla

"I was surprised you called. Especially after what happened the last time we tried to view a place," Darla commented, mumbling the last part.

I turned to her in the empty loft apartment we were standing in and nodded, giving her a half smile. "How're you doing after that?" I asked.

She shrugged. "Better. I took off for a couple of weeks but Townsend Real Estate has been more than generous, paying me handsomely for time lost. It was way more than I expected." She smiled brightly.

I simply nodded, not knowing that information. But I was sure Joshua was behind making sure Darla was taken care of after the robbery.

"I'm sorry about not calling more to check in with you."

She waved my comment off. "Don't even worry about it. I'm sure the experience was as traumatic for you as it was for me. I haven't seen any news outlets talking about it and the police only reached out to me that one time after it happened."

"I haven't heard much but I know Joshua has been working his butt off to figure it out. I think that's what had him leaving town in such a rush the other day." Which, for me, was the perfect opportunity to meet up with Darla. I needed to find a new place to stay.

I'd overheard Tyler, Carter, and Aaron teasing Joshua that night at his parents' house. What's more, is that I heard Joshua's response. *I don't have time for love or anything that comes with it.* My chest ached with the memory of his harsh words. I rubbed my hand along my chest to attempt to ease the pain, but that didn't work. I'd tried over and over to push his declaration from my mind but it kept coming back, reminding me that something I wanted so desperately, was the very thing I couldn't have. His heart.

That's why I was there with Darla. I had to make a clean break and I needed to do it while he was away. Sure, it was the coward's way out, but the way I'd given myself to him in his driveway right after hearing his grim words was a testament to how much of my heart was wrapped up in this. He had my heart, but I didn't have his.

"This place is great because of its open floor plan and the natural lighting that it receives from the fact that it faces the west side. I'm pretty sure that was done on purpose."

I barely listened as Darla went on about the condo's amenities. I was there, but my heart wasn't in it.

"Excuse me," I told Darla as my phone buzzed. I pulled it out of my bag and rolled my eyes when I saw Joshua's name appear on the screen. After hitting ignore, I stuffed my phone back into my bag before turning back to Darla.

"Let's put in the offer."

* * *

Joshua

I pulled the phone away from my ear, frowning. That was the third unanswered call I'd made to Kayla in the last two days I'd been gone. Immediately, I began dialing Carter's number.

"Hey, what's up?" he answered.

I heard a lot of bustling in the background.

"Are you on shift?"

"Yup. Twenty-four hours."

"Fuck."

"What's up?" Carter asked, his voice turning serious.

"I need you to check on Kay for me when you get a chance. She's not answering her phone."

"Hm, since when?"

"Since I left the other night. I just need you to check in on her, make sure she's all right. I'm handling things with Townsend Real Estate."

"The other night? Well, I know Michelle's spoken with her since that night. They made plans just yesterday to have lunch sometime this weekend."

My head jerked back and I pulled the phone from my ear. He couldn't be talking about the same Kayla I was referring to. Not *my* Kayla. Since when did she and Michelle become such good friends yet she can't even pick up the phone for me.

"I don't know, bro, but it sounds like you fucked up."

My head snapped up. I hadn't noticed I'd said that last part out loud. "I didn't fuck up," I mumbled.

Carter fucking chuckled into the phone. "That's what we all say. Anyway, I'll check on her to make sure she's fine when I get off."

"Thanks." I tossed the phone onto the black leather seat of the town car I was riding in.

"Woman problems?"

My eyes rolled over to Brutus who sat at my right. "The only problem with my woman you need to concern yourself with is the information I requested."

"I had to pull my staff from Kayla's background search to work on McCloud."

"Well, this is almost over. I want that information as soon as I return to Williamsport."

"Noted," Brutus replied before stating, "We're here."

"Let's get this shit over with." We were going to confront Wallace McCloud. And by confront I meant eviscerate him.

Through some more questioning and digging, Brutus was able to confirm the information that we received from Damon and James Cunningham. The man, Tim, turned out to be one of McCloud's cousins, who he'd blackmailed into doing his dirty work for him.

Now, we were sitting outside of the house where that chicken shit, Wallace McCloud, had been in hiding. The building that Kay had been looking through with her realtor that day had been purchased from McCloud's once-thriving realty company by Townsend for much less than its asking price. While we purchased it for about ten million, with the work we'd put into it, we nearly doubled the building's resale price. McCloud's lack of business savvy had led him to a series of poor business decisions, which had forced him to sell the building at a discount. Apparently, now he was blaming Townsend Real Estate for the demise of his company.

"This is where he lives?" I questioned with disgust. The house we were sitting outside of was a small two-story home that had seen better days. The once blue siding was in need of replacement. The roof obviously needed fixing and part of the white gutters hung inches below where they were supposed to be attached to the roof. We were a couple of hours outside of the city of Chicago.

"His grandmother's house," Brutus answered. "He decided to hide out here after his wife divorced him, taking more than half of his assets. He'd moved the rest of his money to the Cayman Islands, thinking that'd keep it safe until everything with Townsend blew over. He knew we were looking for whoever was behind this mess."

"He has money in the Cayman's but leaves his grandmother to live like this?" I lifted an eyebrow. "Let's go." I pushed the car door open, waving the driver off.

I pounded the door with my knuckles, not caring whether or not I'd push the damn thing off its hinges. I stepped back when it sounded like footsteps were moving toward the door. Out of the blue, an image of a frightened Kayla pushed to the surface of my mind. I instantaneously cracked my knuckles. As soon as the door opened and I saw Wallace's stupid fucking face, I reacted.

"Ahh!" he yelled as a result of the right jab I sent to his jaw.

I was far from done. The jab was to stun him; it was my left hook that sent him crumbling to the ground. But just before his six-foot even body buckled completely, I caught him by the collar of the green T-shirt he wore, keeping him on his feet. I pushed inside of the house.

"Wallace? Who's at the door?"

I couldn't see the woman who called out, as my gaze was still trained on Wallace. But I realized it was his grandmother.

"We're just some business partners of Wallace's, ma'am. Go back upstairs," Brutus, responded, blocking his grandmother's view from the stairs into the living room.

"Business? Oh that's a good thing, right? My Wally has been so concerned about business for weeks now," she responded, a light cheer in her voice.

I paused and waited to hear her receding footsteps before turning back to Wallace.

"Sit!" I growled, pushing him down onto a beat up loveseat.

"What the hell is this about?" he groaned. "I'm calling the damn police!"

"Please fucking do, you shit for brains moron. Call them and have them arrest me for assault. I'll be out in an hour and come back to beat your stupid ass again for the inconvenience. Then, I'll have the police here connected with the Williamsport police department so they can arrest your ass for setting up the two robberies. And then, let's get the FBI on the damn phone for the blackmail you attempted with my West Coast deal."

His eyes widened. Wallace was obviously a lot dumber than he looked. The surprised expression on his face revealed he hadn't expected me to find out all of the ways in which he'd been trying to sabotage my company.

"I'm not even going to ask why you did it. The answer is obvious. Your business went to hell in a handbasket under your direction. You had to sell your building to us at a loss. Your company folded and you blame me ... because you're a fucking idiot," I snarled at him as I stated the last part. This dumbass really blamed me for his failures.

"And that arrogant brother of yours!" he spat back

I sat up, raising my eyebrows. "I have three arrogant brothers. Which one?" I cracked my neck, ready to punch the shit out of Wallace again.

"Aaron, that shithead— Ah!" His head snapped backwards, when another jab to his nose caused a cracking sound. "Fuck!"

"Shut up," I growled, not wanting his grandmother to come back down the stairs. I'd hate for her to watch her grandson get his ass beat. "It's impolite to call people names," I stated low, close to his ear.

He was still holding his nose in agony.

"What's my brother got to do with this?"

"I know he was behind you buying the company. He wanted to make me look bad for my kid teasing his. It was just kid stuff and he embarrassed me in that principal's office, then stole my business!"

I took a step back, glaring down hard at Wallace. *This fucking idiot.* "You really believe that, huh?"

He looked up at me in bemusement. "I know it."

I shook my head, clicking my tongue before rolling my eyes. I crouched down low. "Let's get a few things straight. Aaron doesn't run Townsend Real Estate. *I do.* Anything that has to do with Townsend Real Estate needs my okay as the final word. Not his. Secondly, Aaron's not the type who would go through his business to seek revenge for a personal vendetta." I moved closer to his face, pulling him to me by the collar of his shirt. "He, like the rest of us Townsends, are more than willing to get directly in your face over personal shit. And third, I want this to be very clear, so there's no confusion. Most of what you've done to Townsend is business, but you robbed the wrong fucking building while my woman was there. *That* makes this shit personal."

"Unff!" He curled over, grabbing his belly and falling off the loveseat due to the right elbow I'd sent to his abdomen.

"You doing this here?" Brutus questioned, his eyes going from me and then to look up the steps.

I shook my head. "I know a place not too far from here." I peered down at Wallace, my anger rising at the pathetic look in his eyes as he glanced up at me. Seeing red, I grabbed him by the back of his neck, lifting him to his feet and moving toward the door, using the rag Brutus passed me to stuff his mouth, quieting his screams.

Hours later, as I wiped my hands free of blood, Brutus strolled over to me.

"He'll have a few less teeth but he'll survive."

I grunted, looking over at Wallace being dragged from the ring by two members of my security team. We were at one of my underground fighting spots in the heart of Chicago. I had my security bound and gag Wallace to drag him here so I could beat his ass without his grandmother being present. Brutus had instructions to deliver Wallace back to Williamsport, right into the hands of the police department. They'd conveniently been given all of the evidence that linked Wallace to his crimes. The FBI had also been contacted, anonymously, of course. Not only was Wallace financially ruined but he'd be able to spend the next fifteen to twenty years in jail, thinking over all of his dumb mistakes. By the way he fought, I'd be surprised if he survived the first year locked up.

"Carter's on the line for you."

I looked up at Brutus who was thrusting his cell in my face.

"Why aren't you calling my phone?"

"I did. It went straight to voicemail. I knew Brutus was with you."

"What's up?"

"I found your woman. By my guess, you're not going to like where, though."

CHAPTER 21

*K*ayla   I checked the time on my wrist watch as I pushed through the double doors toward my office building's parking lot. It was just after seven. I'd stayed late at work, to take a few late patient appointments and get through some paperwork. At least, that's what I'd told myself. The real reason was because I just didn't want to go home. I'd decided to rent an apartment since for some reason I just couldn't go through with the actual purchasing of a condo. While I liked the apartment it didn't feel like home. I tried to convince myself it was just because I hadn't moved my furniture in yet but in the back of my mind, I knew that wasn't the truth either.

I pushed my hair back with my hand, sighing and looking up to stop short in my tracks. Right outside of the office building stood a huge, burly man dressed in all black. He was leaning against a dark Lincoln town car. I wouldn't have paid him too much attention save for the fact that he looked familiar. Like I'd seen him before.

"Ms. Reyes?" he questioned as I moved closer.

"Who's asking?" My gaze shifted around the mostly empty parking lot. This guy and his car were in between me and my own vehicle. I eyed him wondering if I could outrun him.

"Ms. Reyes, my name is Brutus. I work as head of security for the Townsend family. Mr. Townsend has asked me—"

"Which Mr. Townsend?" I questioned with narrowed eyes.

"Joshua," he answered without hesitation, "has asked that I escort you to his location."

I took a step back, eyeing this Brutus person warily. "How do I even know you're telling the truth?"

Unperturbed, Brutus nodded. "Mr. Townsend thought you would ask that." Without answering my question, Brutus pulled a cell phone out and dialed. "I'm calling him." He put the phone to his ear. "Yes. Yup, just as you said. Okay." He held the phone out to me. "It's Joshua."

I refused to reach for the phone, still not wanting to get too close. Though, I did remember seeing this guy at the police station with Joshua the night of the robbery.

Brutus nodded again, turning the phone to him and pressing another button. "You're on speaker."

"Get in the damn car, Kay," Joshua's angry sounding voice reverberated through the phone.

I shook off the chill that ran down my spine at hearing his voice for the first time in days. I had to remember to be strong. "No."

"Kayla Reyes, if you don't get in the car—"

"You'll what? I mean, you couldn't even show up yourself? And where the hell is this Brutus supposed to be taking me? I don't know this big scary looking guy. This could be considered kidnapping." I turned my gaze up to Brutus. "No offense."

He shrugged. "None taken."

I heard Josh's telltale grunt through the line.

"Kay, I know you moved out and I know why. I'm asking you to trust me. Please get in the car with Brutus. You're perfectly safe with him."

I didn't want the sincerity in his voice to penetrate my anger but it did. My shoulders sank a little. "What about my car?"

"It'll be fine at the office parking lot. We'll get it tomorrow."

"Tomorrow? Wh—"

"Get in the goddamn car," he growled.

I bit back a laugh. "Fine."

I heard a few hushed words between Brutus on the phone before I stepped closer to the door he now held open. I climbed in, wondering what the hell I was even doing. Twenty-four hours ago I was certain I wanted a clean break from Joshua Townsend and one simple gesture on his part and I'm riding to God knows where to see him.

I spun the different possibilities of where we could be going around in my mind. Going to Joshua's home seemed the most obvious choice but then again this felt like he had something else up his sleeve. I wanted to question Brutus as he silently drove but I figured I'd get no answers there. From the stern look in his eye when he glanced back at me through the rearview mirror every so often, I figured he wasn't the type of give up information easily. Call it a hunch. While Brutus didn't come off as the friendliest, I wasn't particularly nervous or frightened. Though, I was wary of trusting Josh with my heart, I completely trusted him with my safety and well-being. If he sent this Brutus to pick me up, then I was safe.

After about twenty minutes of driving I began to second guess myself when we parked outside of what looked like an abandoned building.

"Where are we?"

"You're safe, Ms. Reyes," Brutus responded as he held the door open for me to get out.

I exited the vehicle and stood, looking up the total height of the building. It appeared to be about ten stories high.

Brutus moved past me to knock on the door. First two knocks with his knuckles followed by a short pause and then three quick knocks.

I jumped a little when the door suddenly opened. I was even more stunned to see Josh appear, dressed in a pair of workout shorts and a T-shirt.

I frowned. "If this is your idea of a dinner date, you've really gotta do something about your romantic gestures."

A wrinkling around his eyes occurred as he smirked but it was quickly replaced by a narrowing of his eyes and a frown. "You haven't answered my calls in five days. You moved out without one word. You thought I was going to let you run this time?"

My mouth opened but any response I might've had caught in my throat.

"I know why you left this time around. Now, I think it's time to show you all of me." He stepped aside, allowing me entrance.

I entered the darkened room and noticed the crowd of men and chairs that sat around a large fighting-style cage. *The hell?* Inside a man was being helped out and down the stairs by another man, while a large man stood in the middle of the ring, looking around.

"Josh, what the hell is this?" I spun around, jumping a little when the heavy door slammed shut behind Brutus.

"This is my fight club, Kay."

"Your what?"

"You asked the other night at my parents about my fighting." He lifted a hand gesturing toward the cage. "This is it. This is where I come to decompress at the end of a hard day or week."

I turned to look at the cage then back to Josh. "How long have you been doing this?"

"Seven years."

My eyes bulged. "Since ..."

"Chelsea died and you left. Come with me." He took me by the hand, pulling me closer to the crowd.

"You're not fighting, are you?"

"I said I'd show you all of me. So yes, I'll be fighting tonight."

My stomach muscles tightened in fear. I knew Josh was a formidable opponent to anyone who tried him but that didn't mean I needed to see it.

"Relax, sweetheart," he cooed in my ear and pressed a kiss to my temple. "It'll be over before you know it. Damon," he called over my shoulder.

I turned to see a man who looked somewhat familiar approaching us.

I swooned just a little when his mahogany cheeks bunched as he smiled. "You must be Kay."

"Kayla," Josh corrected. "I'm the only one who calls her Kay."

I tossed him a look. He simply gave me an arrogant stare back, daring me to say he was wrong. He wasn't. In fact, I'd always hated that nickname until he started calling me it. Most others couldn't get away with it but he could.

"Anyway, I need you to watch my woman while I'm in the ring."

"Where're you going?" I questioned, tugging Josh's hand.

"Up there." He nodded toward the ring. He moved closer, pressing a kiss to my knuckles. "Don't worry. I'll make it quick."

I watched as he sauntered off toward the cage, a lump forming in my throat.

"It's all good, Kayla. I've got you covered. Your first time viewing a fight club, I assume?" Damon's voice was laced with velvet and silk. He could probably win over even the iciest of attitudes with that smooth, deep voice.

"Yes." I nodded. "You're used to this, I guess, huh?" I looked over at him.

"In more ways than one. Here, sit." He motioned to a folding chair that was in the front row of a line of chairs.

"Are all of these guys fighters?" I glanced around at the men who filled the seats. Some wore typical fighting style clothing, shorts and no top, while others looked like they'd just come from work or home relaxing with their families.

"Everyone here is a fighter but some are just spectators tonight."

I looked at Damon, and for the first time realized he was dressed in a three piece suit. A very nice suit, at that. "Are you fighting tonight?"

"Don't let the suit fool you. I can take anyone in here, suit or no suit. But to answer your question, no. Not tonight. Business ran a little late so I missed my time slot. They're getting started."

I turned straight ahead and saw Josh entering the cage. He'd removed his shoes and the pair of shorts he had on. Now he was only dressed in a pair of tight, spandex shorts, and wraps around his hands.

"Where're the gloves?" I whispered over to Damon, not taking my eyes off of Joshua as he climbed in the ring.

"We don't wear gloves down here."

I briefly glanced at Damon whose eyes were front and center. I turned back to the ring, swallowing down my nervous tension. Joshua knew what he was doing. I allowed my eyes to glide over his glistening body. Had he put on baby oil? He seemed larger than life under that spotlight. I mean, to me he always seemed larger than life, but when he circled around again and I got another glimpse of his eyes, I inhaled sharply. His usually emerald eyes had darkened to nearly black and they were focused on the guy across from him in the ring.

"What's this guy's name? The one he's fighting," I added for clarification.

"Brick."

I jumped back. "Brick?"

Damon shrugged. "Got his name because hitting him is like hitting a goddamn brick wall. I dislocated a knuckle the first time I got in the ring with him." Damon winced, seemingly at the memory of that fight.

Oh God! I thought as a buzzer sounded and Brick moved in on Josh taking a swing. I pushed out a sigh of relief when Joshua ducked, easily dodging the punch. Not only was he able to get out of the way, but before I could blink again Josh had landed a punch of his own right to the guy's ribs.

"He's fast," I stated in awe, remembering that from the many mornings he spent teaching me some of these very same moves.

"That's his talent down here. No one can really keep up with him in the ring."

"Even you?" I joked.

Damon shrugged arrogantly, adjusting the collar of his suit. "I hold my own."

I grinned, turning back to the ring just in time to see Brick land an elbow to Josh's chin. "Hey!" I stood, yelling angrily.

"It's all right, little mama. He pivoted his head just in time. Just barely nicked him. Look," Damon consoled, urging me to look up.

When I did, my eyes bulged as I saw my man hammering away at Brick's midsection before stepping back to land a side kick to his ribs. I sucked in air. I grabbed my own ribs, as it looked like it hurt, badly.

234

Brick stumbled backwards, falling against the caged wall of the ring. Joshua took a couple of steps back, obviously letting him regroup. What was he doing?

"Finish him!" I growled, loudly, causing a few stares to turn my way. I ignored them all but I did give Damon a look when I heard him chuckling to my right. Rolling my eyes, I turned back to the cage to see Joshua circling Brick, narrowly missing another punch and then a kick. Suddenly, Joshua made a move that looked like he was falling, but it took Brick off of his feet, landing him on his back. Josh was on top of him in nanoseconds, rolling him over and twisting his arm painfully.

I could hear Brick's groans of pain until finally with his free hand he tapped against the ring's floor. Josh let out a breath and released his arm.

"Your man won." Damon nudged me with his elbow.

"I never doubted him for a second," I stated coolly, falling back into my chair.

Damon's chuckle made me laugh.

"So that's what he does down here, huh?" I said out loud but to no one in particular.

"That's what we *all* do down here."

I looked to Damon who was staring ahead at the ring. I squinted, wondering what was behind his need to fight. And a whole world of questions for Joshua came to mind. I needed to see him.

"Is that the changing room?" I asked Damon, pointing to the double doors.

He nodded. "Hey, women aren't supposed to go back there!" he called behind me.

I looked over my shoulder. "Watch me."

I turned and kept going, the sound of his laughter fading the farther I moved away.

CHAPTER 22

*J*oshua

"You're going to be sore as hell in the morning. You were putting on for your woman," Buddy called me out, mirth filling his brown eyes.

"You saying I didn't fight well?" I questioned, holding my hands out as he unwrapped them.

"You know that ain't what I'm saying. But we don't call Leo Brick for no damn reason. You're supposed to leave something off of those punches when you fight him. Your ass got ahead of you tonight. You'll be paying for it in the morning."

"It's okay, I know a good doctor."

My head popped up at the sound of her voice.

"Get out." I gave Buddy a stern look.

"Geez, no introductions."

"Get out," I said again through gritted teeth.

He chuckled before tossing my hand wraps on the bench next to me and heading for the door. "Ma'am." He tipped his head at Kay before exiting.

I silently watched as the bottom of the flowy dress she wore skimmed the skin of her brown thighs. I licked my lips as she came to stand in front of me.

Rising to my feet, I advanced on her until her back bumped up against the wood paneled locker that lined the back wall.

"It's fancy in here," she said breathlessly looking round, doing her best to avoid eye contact.

"Look at me."

"Why did you bring me here?" she asked when her eyes finally landed on me.

"Because I love you."

Her mouth dropped open.

"I know you overheard me that night at Mother's dinner. What I said to Ty about not having time for love. It was bullshit. I wasn't ready to admit to anyone, especially my shithead kid brother the truth."

"Wh-why?"

I lowered my head and gritted my teeth, hating to admit my own cowardice. Lifting my hands, I bracketed them around Kay's head. "After Chelsea died and you left I felt broken, hurt, and alone. I never wanted to experience that type of pain again so I closed myself off to even the possibility of love." I pushed out a heavy breath. "And then you came back. And though I was still pissed at you for leaving, I couldn't stay away."

She shook her head, lowering her gaze. "I never wanted to leave. I just … I couldn't face the fact that I was in love with you. I felt like I was betraying my best friend. But even after all these years, it's like the feelings never left. When I heard you say that the other night I was crushed."

I bit back my anger at myself, hating that I'd made her feel like she was anything less than the most important person in the world to me. Pushing off the lockers, I moved back to the bench where my gym bag sat. I felt around on the inside for the ring box I'd carried in it. When my fingers wrapped around the box I pulled it free and turned to face Kayla.

"Wh-what're you do—"

"I know you probably would've wanted me to have done this the *right* way by asking your father for permission and all of that first. But, I'll get to that." I flipped the box open, revealing the three karat diamond. "Kayla Daniella Reyes, say you'll never leave me again, and you'll be my wife?"

Her mouth gaped as she peered at me through misted eyes. "I— Are you crazy?"

I chuckled. "Yes. About you. Answer the question, Kay."

"Yes." She nodded vigorously.

I ripped the ring out of the box and had it on her ring finger in less than two seconds flat. "Perfect," I stated, looking down at the ring on her finger. It fit perfectly.

I lowered my lips to capture hers. She moaned into my mouth, sending a warm current through my entire body.

"You're mine forever, Kay," I whispered against her lips. "I've shown you all of me. Now it's your turn … after you pay up for trying to run out on me again."

Her forehead wrinkled. "What's that mean?"

"You'll find out.

* * *

"Joooosh!" Kay whined my name, only causing my dick to grow stiffer as I pistoned in and out of her.

Smack!

The sound of my hand clapping against her ass as I smacked it reverberated around my bedroom.

"I need to come!" Kayla demanded not for the first time as I plunged in and out of her wetness.

"Hell no!" I growled again, refusing to let her off the hook so easily. "You only come on my say so."

Kayla tossed me a glare over her shoulder, her eyes squinted in anger and pure ecstasy. I could see the moment she decided to challenge me. She began pushing her hips back against me, pumping wildly, causing her ass to bounce and jiggle every time she made contact with my hips.

Fuck.

I tossed my head back and groaned when she tightened her pussy muscles, performing a kegel around my thrusting cock.

"You're paying for that as well," I grunted and pulled completely out of her.

"Jo—" Her yell ceased when I turned her over, grabbing her underneath her thighs and pressing her legs back as far as I could while sinking balls deep inside of her.

"Oh God!" she called out.

"That's right, baby. Call my name," I arrogantly declared, moving my hips in a circle, hitting her insides from every angle.

"Shit, Kay! I love you," I called out, feeling free to finally express the truth of my feelings for her. Those three words no longer scared me. I loved this woman beyond reason. Always had in one form or another.

"Come with me, Kay!" I shouted at the same time my orgasm took over. My eyesight blurred and the only thing I felt was Kay's walls clamping around me. Milking me of everything. I willingly gave it all. We came together, both calling out one another's name. The next thing I remember was pulling out and rolling over, taking Kay with me so that her sweaty frame was sprawled on top of mine. I drifted off to sleep with my arms tightly sealed around her waist. Even in sleep she wasn't getting away from me. Not ever again.

CHAPTER 23

*J*oshua

"What, Aaron?" I growled into my phone, early the next morning.

"This is Mark, Mr. Townsend."

I frowned. "Mark? What're you calling so early about? And why are you calling me Mr. Townsend?" I blinked and rubbed the sleep from my eyes, rising carefully, trying not to wake Kayla.

"Just thought it was a good idea to keep it formal."

I pushed out a breath. "I really don't need this shit right now, Mark. What are you calling about?"

"I'm calling to inform you that Mr. Townsend, your brother, would like to speak with you before his first meeting at nine-thirty."

"And he couldn't call me to tell me this?"

"Mr. Townsend is not in the office yet. He's running a little late. He requested that I call you to be here as soon as he arrives."

I pulled the phone from my ear, checking the name on my screen to make sure I was still talking to the right person. "Aaron's coming in the office late? Interesting. Tell him I'll be there when I get there." I hung up the phone and looked to Kay, who was now awake, staring at me. Those big, brown eyes and pouty lips were too inviting for me not to taste, so I did.

Leaning in, I ran a trail of kisses over the outline of her jaw until met her lips, morning breath be damned.

I moved closer, but she put her hands to my chest. "You have to go."

"Aaron can wait."

She shook her head. "We'll talk later."

I pulled back, staring at her. "I know what you're doing and I don't forget anything." Kay was finally going to come clean about what'd happened to her in Portland. I'd told her she'd either tell me everything or I'd look into the file I'd been given by Brutus. I'd at least give her the chance to tell me before I found out on my own.

She worried her bottom lip before saying, "I figured."

I pressed a kiss to her lips. "You and me, we're in this thing together. There is no backing out of this for you. Understood?"

She nodded.

"Good. I'll be back soon."

* * *

"Mark," I greeted as I breezed through the double doors of Townsend's top offices.

Mark lifted his head and gave me a curt nod. "Mr. Townsend."

I blew out a breath. "Will you cut the shit, Mark?"

He blinked, tilting his head coolly. "Mr. Townsend, I don't understand what you mean."

"You know damn well what I'm referring to. All this Mr. Townsend bullshit. Only Aaron requires that amount of formality."

He lifted and dropped his shoulders. "I wasn't sure the protocol. I didn't want anyone to think I obtained this job through anything but my own merit."

"Oh for fuck's sake," I growled, rolling my eyes to the ceiling. I heard the gasp of one of Aaron's lower level assistants. I glanced over at her, giving her a curt smile, and she immediately put her eyes on her computer screen. "Is the boardroom open?"

"Yes."

"Good. Boardroom. Now!" I pivoted on my heels and headed toward the boardroom that was on the other side of the hallway. I glanced over my shoulder to ensure Mark was following. He was but with a frown on his face.

I held the door open, shutting it once he moved past me. "All right, let's get this shit settled. First of all, I don't want to be in the middle of shit between your brother and you. I know all too well how messy family entanglements can be. Connor is still pissed because I let you fight that night."

"Because he—"

I held up my hand. "Not my business. You work that out with him. I've got three of my own headstrong and stubborn ass brothers to deal with. And on top of that, a headstrong woman."

"Headstrong women can be a lot of fun."

My eyebrows rose and head shot back as I stared down at Mark.

He shrugged. "Or so I heard."

I gave him a genuine grin. His eyes darted from mine as he looked to the corner of the room. Not avoiding my eyes but his mind had drifted off to something or *someone* else.

"You heard?"

He turned back to me with angry eyes. "Heard. Experienced. What? You don't think a woman would be interested in me?"

I wrinkled my brows at the anger in his tone. I stared down at him. "You mean because of your wheelchair?"

He nodded.

I rolled my eyes. "You're O'Brien's kid brother. If you have half the charm of your brother, I'm sure you get more than enough pu— women," I corrected the last part of my sentence, remembering I was at work and not the fighting gym. "Anyway, I never apologized to you for what you overheard that night at the gym. Like I said, whatever is between you and Connor is between you two. But yeah, he did ask me to help his brother out. And it just so happened that Aaron had fired yet another one of his assistants making that position available. Aaron knew you were Connor's brother but that was only after he'd made the decision to hire you. You got hired based on your resume, experience, and stellar interviews. You've *remained* at Townsend for well over a year because of your hard work and your uncanny ability to put up with my crazy ass brother."

Mark gave me a wary look. "So Aaron didn't know I was related to Connor until after he chose me?"

I nodded. "In fact, I had to do some fast talking to keep him from going back on his decision. He didn't want it to appear as if he hired you because of your brother's and my business connection. And honestly, while he hasn't told me this, I think he was surprised that you even wanted to work."

Mark look surprised.

"Considering Connor's business endeavors and all. I know for a fact that you're part owner of his businesses, making you wealthy in your own right. You don't have to work a day in your life."

"I work because I choose to. I have my own goals and ambitions outside of what my brother's built." His tone was firm, serious.

"And that's why Aaron hired you and why you've been such an asset to his team. Trust me, my brother would've had no hesitation firing you the minute you fucked up. And he would've had zero guilt about doing it. Nor would I, to be honest. We don't pity you. You've got great skills and work ethic to offer Townsend. We appreciate great employees. Got it?"

Mark narrowed his eyes, still skeptical. "Connor tell you to say all this?"

I tilted my head. "What do you think?"

A brief moment of silence was followed by a grin spreading across his face. "All right, then. Thanks, Josh."

Sighing, I took his proffered hand into mine, shaking it. Mark was a great employee and Connor was my friend. Yes, I'd done him a favor by passing along his kid brother's resume to Aaron but, as I'd just told Mark, it was he alone that won himself the job.

I held the door open for Mark, and as we crossed the hallway back to the main office, the elevator doors opened. Aaron stepped out of the elevator first, his hand holding onto Patience's as she exited behind him, her ever-expanding belly leading the way.

"Josh," she greeted, slightly out of breath.

My smile grew. "Still won't let you out of his sight, huh?" I pulled her into a hug, chuckling when I heard Aaron's growl behind me.

"Not hardly," Patience answered. "How's Kayla?" she questioned over her shoulder as she and Aaron continued walking down the hall toward his office.

I followed the pair, entering behind them into his office.

"She was being stubborn for a minute there but we've worked it out," I answered, not thinking about my response. Only once I glanced up at Patience did I realize I just gave my sister-in-law an opening to get all in my private affairs.

"How so?" she asked, stepping closer.

"She agreed to move back in with you, I assume."

I looked over Patience's shoulder to see Aaron, behind his desk staring at me. "How'd you know?"

He shrugged. "I have my ways."

"Carter," I mumbled.

"She moved out?" Patience spoke up.

"Sort of," I answered Patience while narrowing my gaze on my brother.

"You could always get her pregnant and then force her hand by threatening to take her kid away to get her to marry you," Patience stated in a nonchalant voice.

Aaron's scowl deepened when he slammed a file on his desk, eyeing his wife with a narrowed gaze. To most, that look would've made them cower in a corner, but when I looked back at my sister-in-law a smile played at the sides of her lips and her eyes held laughter as she stared at her husband.

These two.

"I'd considered that. Thankfully, it won't be necessary since she agreed to be my wife."

Patience gasped. "Oh my goodness! Congratulations! I knew it was coming." She jumped up and down, happily, coming over to hug me.

"I haven't told anyone else yet, so keep it to yourselves for now."

Patience nodded, smiling, already pulling out her phone. "Will do, but I need to text Kayla and congratulate her. Oh, this will give me something to do." She turned from me, phone in hand, fingers moving over the keys as she texted Kayla I assumed.

"Congratulations," Aaron's deep voice rang out from behind his desk.

"Thanks." I glanced back over my shoulder to make sure Patience's attention was still on her phone before turning back to Aaron. "There're still some things she and I need to work out."

Aaron's forehead wrinkled.

"Something happened to her back in Oregon. I have a feeling it's going to be something I need to handle."

Aaron eyed me for a long minute, his eyes darkening ever so slightly. He wasn't one to play when it came to the safety of the women in our life. "Anything you ne—"

I held up my hand. "I won't hesitate to ask if I need help."

"Good thing this Wallace McCloud nonsense is out of the way."

"And we didn't take much of a hit even with all of his scheming."

My brother nodded. "Tell me about Illinois," Aaron finally spoke up.

I filled Aaron in on the happenings in Illinois over the previous week.

"The police question you about how you came across all of this evidence?"

I lifted a shoulder, shrugging. "Of course. But some quick talking on my part satisfied them. Wallace should be in a jail cell for the rest of his life."

"However long that will be," Aaron growled.

I glanced over my shoulder upon hearing Patience's intake of air. Her eyes were narrowed at Aaron. I returned my gaze to my brother who was giving a blank stare to his wife. They were silently communicating something but I opted to remain out of it. Wallace would be taken care of, in or outside of prison.

"He was pretty pissed at you. Thought I'd purchased his building under your orders."

"Did he?"

I shook my head, rolling my eyes. "Dumbass. Had no concept of how to run a company and blamed everyone else for his fucking failures."

Aaron snorted. "Typical. And his kid's an a—"

"Aaron!" Patience snapped.

I lowered my head, grinning when Aaron's mouth snapped shut. Whatever he'd been about to call Wallace's kid he was still thinking it but his wife, acting as his conscience, stopped him.

"Nicely done, Josh. Our board will be happy to know all of this mess is behind us and Townsend Real Estate is still thriving."

"Damn straight. Anyway, I need to go. Got to make some visits and I have a shit ton of meetings."

I turned and walked over to Patience to give her a parting hug.

"Oh," she stated, startled.

"You okay?"

"What's wrong?" Aaron's voice was full of worry.

Patience giggled, covering her belly with her hand. "Nothing's wrong. The babies are just moving like crazy. Feel them." She took my hand, placing it on her belly. I looked over my shoulder at Aaron who was frowning deeply.

"Stop it! You were up half the night feeling them move," Patience chided Aaron.

"Oh shit!" I cursed when something moved across her belly. I lifted my hand, staring at it before placing it back on her stomach.

Patience beamed. "That's Baby A."

I wrinkled my forehead. "How do you know?" I was completely in awe, feeling another movement under my hand.

"Their placement. Baby A's right here and B is ..." she moved my hand over more and lower until I felt more moment, "right there."

I want this.

246

That thought crossed my mind and was quickly followed by an image of Kayla with a swollen belly. I briefly wondered if, given her health problems in the past, being pregnant would pose a problem for her. However, that thought was quickly dismissed when I felt another movement under my hand. I stood, my eyes still transfixed on the way Patience's belly moved and bubbled up as if the twins were fighting to stretch out in there.

"Does it hurt?" I asked, frowning.

She laughed. "He asked the same thing." She jutted her head in Aaron's direction. "No, it doesn't hurt when they move. Well, not usually. Baby A kicked me in the kidneys once or twice, and they love banging on my bladder. Speaking of which," she began to rise and Aaron nearly knocked me over to move to her side to help her stand, "I need to go now."

"See ya later, sis," I called to her as I watched her exit the door Aaron held for her. He nodded to a security guard that was in the hallway. The security guard followed Patience down the hall to Aaron's private bathroom.

"You're lucky, bro."

I didn't expect an answer so I was surprised when Aaron retorted with, "I'm very aware of that." His response was full of sincerity.

I walked past him and he surprised me yet again when his hand clasped around my arm. "I remember that look you gave me that night."

I frowned, angling my head in confusion.

"After I'd told Patience I loved her for the first time and she didn't say it back. I said—"

"She was the missing piece to the puzzle," I finished his sentence. One I'd repeated over and over in my head since that night, especially since Kayla came back to me.

"I remember your face that night. When you said you understood." He paused, looking me in the eye. "If she's your puzzle piece do whatever you need to do to keep her safe. Most won't understand the lengths I went to to keep my wife. I don't give a fuck about what they don't understand. What I do give a fuck about is the fact that I breathe easier when she's in bed next to me at night. If it's the same for you, then do what you have to."

I stared at my brother for a long while, ingesting his words. He was right. Some things were just meant to be. I'd finally accepted that Kay and I were one of those things. I nodded at him and moved through the doors.

The rest of the day felt like it dragged by, even with meeting after meeting. Aaron's words rang over and over in my head. The more I thought about it the more I wanted to kick myself. I could've gotten to the bottom of this thing sooner had it not been for Wallace McCloud and his bullshit. I needed to figure out what had happened to Kay before she moved back to Williamsport so we could finally put it to bed and move on to focus on planning our wedding.

Finally, at five o'clock I couldn't take it anymore. I made a beeline for the door, focused on only one thing—speaking with my soon-to-be wife.

CHAPTER 24

*K*ayla

How am I supposed to say these words out loud? That was the question that had been rolling around in my mind as soon as I'd woken up that morning. Joshua had given me a short reprieve the night before. We'd spent the night too wrapped up in each other's arms to do much talking; however, the next morning was a different story. But throughout the day, the events that happened close to two years earlier in Portland kept replaying. I found myself twisting the beautiful diamond on my ring finger as I watched the clock, counting down the seconds until I had to confront the memories I'd been running from, head on.

Now, it was after five, and I was home with my fiancé sitting across from me, his eyes transfixed on me. My eyes drifted from his to the manila envelope that sat next to his left elbow on the kitchen island.

"What's that?" I questioned, hoping it was work related and would therefore cause him to forget about this impending conversation. Not surprisingly, it didn't work.

"*This*," he began, holding up the envelope, "is everything you don't want to tell me."

My head lifted and I nearly spilled my glass of water onto the table as my hand trembled. He didn't even flinch at the loud sound of my cup hitting the granite counter. His gaze remained completely locked on mine.

"I had my head of security do a little investigating. I asked him weeks ago, but then we got a little preoccupied with finding out who was behind the robbery and trying to set-up Townsend Real Estate. That's a mistake I won't make twice. Business comes second to ensuring your safety."

"You were ensuring my safety. The robbery at the condo—"

"Shouldn't have happened in the first place." His face twisted in anger.

I reached across the kitchen island, covering his hand with mine. "Don't blame yourself."

"I do blame myself. I own Townsend Real Estate. I should've been more cautious." He shook his head. "But that's been fixed now. Now, we need to discuss you." His tone brokered no argument.

I yanked at one of my curly ringlets and bit the inside of my cheek. An ugly pit began to form in my stomach, mixed with shame, guilt, anger, and frustration.

"I-I'm not really sure where to begin." Isn't that what everyone says when the truth is they just really don't want to say the thing that needs to be said?

"Start with his name." His voice was hard

"Why his name?"

"So I know exactly who the fuck I need to hurt."

"Josh, you can't—"

He held up his hand. "Don't even try to convince me otherwise. What's. His. Name?"

His tone gave no wiggle room for hesitation.

Inhaling deeply, I prepared myself to say the name of the man I'd worked long and hard to forget. "Michael Stephens."

"Go on." He leaned in farther.

I closed my eyes and just started talking without another thought. "I met him one night while I was out with a few friends from med school. I'd just completed my residency and was out celebrating. He was at the club we'd gone to. We danced and he was a little touchy feely, but I didn't think much of it at first. He asked what I did and I told him. Next thing I knew, we were laughing and having a good time. He told me he was a cop, showed me his badge and everything, so I felt safe. The rest of the night is mostly a blur but I remember his hands..." I trailed off, feeling disgusted. The memory of being on my back, him over top of me, and feeling powerless to move or push him off still haunted me. But I held back from saying that out loud to Joshua.

I shook my head, trying to shake off the memory.

"The next morning I woke up and knew something was wrong. I was at his place. My mouth was dry, I was dizzy and my stomach hurt. I knew I hadn't drank that much. I'd barely had a half a beer. I was disgusted when I stood up from an unfamiliar bed and found him staring at me from across the room. My clothes were … disheveled and awkwardly thrown back on me. The look in his eye was cold and vacant, almost. Like he had no soul." I shivered. "I asked him what happened the night before and all he said was '*You wanted it.*' I picked up my purse and attempted to leave, but he grabbed me by my arm and reminded me that he was a cop and no one would believe a cop was capable of such a crime. I broke free and left, catching an Uber home. I knew I'd been drugged … and worse."

I paused, looking up at Joshua. My mouth dropped open at what I saw. His eyes were the color of coal. His jaw was rigid. He wasn't pissed. He was livid. The steam was practically rolling off of him. I hesitated in continuing but his silent stare urged me to continue.

"I went to the nearest health clinic. I had a blood sample taken as well as a, um … a rape kit."

I inhaled and forced myself to finish the rest of the story to get it over with.

"It came back positive for spermicide, meaning he'd used a condom. I felt disgusted with myself for allowing it to happen. I'm a doctor. I should've been smarter than that. Those are all of the things I told myself. But I was pissed at him. Something deep inside of me told me it wasn't all my fault. I wasn't going to let him get away with it. So, I went to the police station to file a report. As soon as I said his name, the officer that was taking my statement lost interest. He said he'd get back to me but the next day, an officer showed up at my door, threatening me. He was Michael's partner. He made it very clear that I wasn't to press charges and I was to drop the whole thing. I refused and my life became a living hell. I'd come home to messages slipped under my door. Phone calls all day and night. One night after a late night shift, I was driving home and was pulled over by a patrol car. It was Michael Stephens. He claimed some bogus reason for pulling me over, made me get out of my car ..." I paused.

I couldn't choke out the rest.

"He forced himself on you again." It wasn't a question.

I lifted my head to see that Josh had opened the envelope and read through it.

"Th-that's in there?" I hadn't reported the second assault. I hadn't told anyone.

Joshua shook his head, staring down at the papers in front of him. "He did it to someone else."

I covered my mouth.

"Another woman came forward a few months ago. Said the same thing happened to her."

I squeezed my eyes shut.

"I knew he'd done this before. He was too calm about it all. Too skilled in terrifying me. I moved two different times trying to get away from his threats. I changed jobs because I was getting hang up calls at work. But the harassment never stopped."

"That's why you came back to Williamsport."

I swallowed and nodded, avoiding Josh's gaze.

Joshua inhaled deeply, standing from his stool. I watched him warily, wondering what his next move was going to be.

"You know he can't go on living."

I frowned. "What?"

"He can't continue to live and breathe and walk around this earth. Not after what he's done to you. He's the reason you were so different

252

when you came back. He stole your spark. He has to die for that alone. Don't even fucking mention the other women he's done this to. Fuck, Kay! Why'd you wait so long to tell me? You couldn't trust me with this?"

I moved off the stool to stand in front of Josh. Placing my hand against his chest, I gripped the T-shirt he wore. "Of course I trusted you."

He shook his head. "No. You couldn't have."

"Josh, we hadn't spoken in so many years. How—"

"I wouldn't have given a shit. One phone call. That's all that was needed for me to hop my ass on a plane to murder any motherfucker who thought he could do this shit to you!" He pointed angrily at the file on the counter.

Lowering my head, I squeezed my eyes shut to prevent the tears from spilling. I regained control of my breathing and said, "I couldn't tell you. I couldn't tell *anyone*. As angry as I was at him for what he'd done to me, a part of me felt like I deserved it."

Josh stared at me in horror—his eyes wide, mouth set in a hard line.

"I can't fully explain it in a way that will make sense. I just ... I thought ... that maybe what happened to me was payback for betraying Chelsea the way I had, and for being so carefree, and dressing the way I had. When he said I'd wanted it, it reminded me of the way I'd flirted with him the previous night. The other guys I'd danced with, the low-cut tops and tight jeans I often wore around town. Everything. I enjoyed the attention I got from men. Maybe he was right."

"Which is why you started wearing different types of clothing, straightening your hair, less makeup."

I nodded.

"He doesn't have the right to any of you. You are not responsible for his—"

"I know," I interrupted. "I know that now. I knew it all along, I just forgot. I'm not responsible for a grown man's inability to hear the word no, especially when he steals my ability to say no by drugging me. He made me doubt that for a while, but you made me believe in myself again. You reminded me of who I was and why no one gets to steal that from me."

"Then you agree. He needs to die."

If this situation hadn't had been so serious, I would've laughed at how stern his face was when he said that.

"No."

Josh snorted.

"I'm serious, Josh. He does need to face what he's done. And go to jail for it. I felt deeply he had to be doing this to other women. But I'd gotten so scared, and lost who I was, I just wanted to leave and get away from him. However, I found myself again, here, with you. You make me strong. *And* we have proof." I pointed at the papers from the envelope. "That he's done this to others is just further confirmation that I need to help end this. I'm done running."

"What does that mean, Kay?"

"It means I'm going to seek charges. I want him prosecuted."

There was a war going on behind Joshua's eyes. I could see it. He was grappling with whether or not to let me handle this my way or to take matters into his own hands.

He pulled me into his arms, holding me tightly and sighing. "You need this. I can see it but you won't face that piece of shit alone."

I smiled against his shoulder, resting on him. "Thank you." I held onto him as if he were the air that I breathed, because he was. Despite the confidence when I said it out oud, I wasn't entirely sure I could go back to Portland and face the man who'd tried to destroy me, but I did know with Joshua by my side, I could do anything. That was enough for me.

* * *

JOSHUA

"This is them?" I questioned Brutus, staring down at the file on my desk as we stood in my home office. It'd been three weeks since Kay had confessed everything about that shithead Michael Stephens. Since then, we'd spoken with a lawyer about how to proceed. We were going to Portland the following day because Kay had decided she was going to do an interview, to expose the bastard for what he was.

It ate me alive that he had the damn audacity to still be walking around, breathing as if he deserved to live. It took everything in me to hold back from going this alone and taking care of him myself. I had more than enough reach to hide his body so no one ever found him, nor trace his disappearance back to me. But I couldn't do that to Kay. She needed to be able to confront the son of a bitch to get back what he stole from her. I knew that in my soul and it was the only thing keeping me from stepping over the line to becoming a murderer. The only thing. But that didn't mean I would do nothing.

"That's them. Ramirez and Waltz."

I stared down at the three pictures of Stephens and two other officers. The two men in the picture had helped Stephens get away with his crimes. Ronaldo Ramirez was his partner. Jason Waltz had gone through the police academy with the both of them, though he was assigned to a different station. All three were on my hit list, but since I'd promised Kay I'd leave Stephens to her and the prosecutors, I went to work, getting Brutus to find out everything I needed to know about Ramirez and Waltz. I read over the file Brutus had given me. It told of where the two men hung out.

"Ramirez is getting married in a month."

I snorted. "Too bad he won't be making his own wedding," I gritted out through clenched teeth. As far as I was concerned these pieces of filth were just as culpable for what happened to Kay as Stephens was. But the lawyer had already told us our case was against Stephens alone. She was sure she could get a prosecutor to bring charges against Stephens, and the hope was that Kay's interview would encourage other victims to come forward.

But Ramirez and Waltz weren't on the hook for anything, according to the lawyer. As far as proving the threats Ramirez made against Kay when he showed up at her door, it was her word against his. Waltz was the officer who'd taken her initial statement, and "accidentally" lost it. These two shitheads were mine.

"I've already got a guy on both Waltz and Ramirez. When we arrive in Portland, Kay will do her interview and meet with the prosecutors. I'll make sure you are able to get away to rendezvous with these two, beforehand." Brutus nodded at the pictures.

"See that you do." I cracked my knuckles. I could hardly wait for that encounter.

"Hey."

I looked from Brutus to my office door where Kay had just knocked and entered.

"I'll see you in the morning," Brutus stated as he quickly gathered the pictures and moved from my desk.

"You don't have to leave because of me. I just wanted—"

"Yes, he does," I interrupted, pulling her by the hand to me. I jerked my head for Brutus to shut the door on his way out.

"I wanted to see what you wanted for lunch. You skipped breakfast."

"I did, didn't I?"

"Yes."

I lowered my head and kissed her neck, causing a shiver. I grinned as I pressed her back against my desk.

"And it's imperative that I eat, right?" I kissed the other side of her neck, then lifted her up to sit on my desk, legs splayed.

"Umhm."

"Lunch *is* the most important meal of the day." I bent lower, glad that Kay had on one of her flowy skirts, granting me easy access.

"I think the saying is actually that *breakfast* is the most important meal of the day." Her voice was breathless as I pushed her by the shoulder to lean back against my desk.

I had little concern for the few papers on my desk or whether it was breakfast or lunch.

"Either way, sweetheart, I'm about to eat until my heart's content." I gave her a crooked grin before latching my hand around the sides of the lace panties she wore and tugging them off of her.

"Josh!" she screamed and threw her head back when the first swipe of my tongue against her labia occurred. *Damn.* She tasted like fresh strawberries. My favorite fruit. I hiked her legs so they were in my favorite position—over my shoulders—and forced her to lay completely on her back, so that I could take my fill. And I did just that. Licking and suckling wherever I could. In no time, her juices began flowing, coating my tongue with her delicious essence. Her moans sounded around the room.

"Right there. Don't stop!" she pleaded.

I thought to tell her she needn't have worried about my stopping anytime soon, but my mouth was otherwise occupied. I poured every ounce of love and protection I felt for her into ensuring she was satisfied. Within minutes her thighs were trembling around my shoulders and her back spasmed, arching off the desk. She was coming and I kept my eyes trained on the sight before me, as much as I could. Such a beauty to watch.

"Fuck!" she gasped when she finally came back to herself. Her eyes were slits and glossed over but the glow of her cinnamon skin spoke to her satisfaction. "That mouth deserves to be in the hall of fame," she panted.

I chuckled deep in the back of my throat. "I'd prefer it be on your body."

She blinked. "Good point." Kayla sat up, pulling me by the shoulders to her and kissing me deeply.

I loved the way she kissed me after I ate her out, it was almost as if she needed to taste herself on my lips, which I gladly allowed.

Needless to say, lunch was eaten a little later than usual that day.

CHAPTER 25

*J*oshua

They showed up together. Parking now.

I stared at Brutus' text as I waited in the locker room of one of my Portland underground gyms. I quickly typed a response before stuffing my phone back into my bag.

"You ready for this?"

I lifted my gaze to see Connor peering down on me. He'd helped me set up this little venture with the two police officers, having his own Portland connections.

"Am I supposed to be nervous?" I stood, staring at him in the eye.

He gave a one shoulder shrug. "You are planning on taking out two cops."

I lifted an eyebrow. "Who said anything about taking them out?"

His blond eyebrows raised.

"There're more ways to take someone out. These bastards will make it out of here alive but their lives won't ever be the same." That, I could promise.

Connor whistled approvingly before clapping me on the shoulder. "I see I've taught you something."

258

I shrugged him off. "Get the fuck off of me. You didn't teach me shit. This is in my bloodline. Just like kicking ass is in yours. Ask Mark," I commented. Connor was still a little peeved to have learned about Mark's fighting at our clubs when he wasn't around, but I suspected his little brother had finally put him in his place.

"That little shit," Connor grumbled.

I grunted. "Let's go. I'm about to teach you a few lessons on taking someone out while also leaving them breathing."

Stepping around Connor, I made my way through the heavy metal doors that led to the makeshift fighting ring that'd been set up in the building. I grinned when the first two faces I saw were the two officers staring at one another, wearing skeptical expressions. Brutus had conveniently sent these two assholes an invite to an underground fighting ring. They were given specific instructions on how to get to the location, and not to tell anyone besides each other. I had Brutus make sure that they had not been followed or told anyone else about the fight. I knew they would show up. I felt it in my gut that these guys believed they were tougher than they actually were, and they obviously weren't opposed to doing things that crossed the line into illegal territory.

"Gentlemen," Connor shouted at the two, clapping his hands. The smacking sound echoed around the near silent room.

There were others in the crowd who were regulars of the Portland underground fighting scene. I knew most of them, and who I didn't know, Connor did. They weren't talking about any of this to anyone.

"You must be Ramirez and Waltz. Welcome. We can't tell you what an honor it is to have two of Portland's finest bestow us with their company," Connor greeted.

Both men's expressions changed from skeptical to cocky instantly. As if they'd been expecting to have been met with such high regard.

"You know we could shut this place down if we wanted to, right? One phone call would be all it took," Ramirez spoke up, glancing around at the other men.

"Where would the fun in that be, gentlemen?" I finally spoke up, moving forward. The building was dimly lit, and it wasn't until I got within a few feet of Ramirez that he saw me.

His eyes widened a smidgen. "And you are?"

"My name isn't important right now. What is important is that you two came here for a reason. Every man steps through those doors with a reason to fight. What's the matter? Job no longer interesting?" I taunted.

Ramirez' dark eyes narrowed just as Waltz took a turn at speaking.

"Job's a bitch. All of these so called activists shaking shit up. We can no longer do our job the way it needs to be done."

I narrowed my eyes on Waltz. I remembered from his file that he'd had at least two citations for aggressively handling suspects. One had ended up in the hospital with a broken leg, but no serious investigation was ever conducted on the incident. I was going to have fun taking these fuckers down.

"Then why don't we help spice up your life a little bit. How about you first?" I gave Waltz my most endearing smile.

"Against you?" He looked me up and down, sizing me up.

"Only if you promise to take it easy on me. I'm a little rusty. The old suit and tie act prevents me from making fights like I used to," I lied.

Waltz shrugged. "I can't make any promises."

Instead of a verbal response, I tilted my head, cracking my neck one way and then the other. That adrenaline rush I always felt before fighting started to occur, only it was magnified by my growing bloodthirst. I wouldn't be able to take Stephens out the way I wanted because I was leaving him to Kay and the legal system to handle, but these two? They were wall mine.

I pivoted on my heels and went over to where the fighting cage had been set up. I removed my sneakers before stepping inside, leaving me dressed in only a pair of fighting shorts. In my peripheral I saw the other men in the room, including Connor, encircle the cage to get a good view of what was about to ensue. I looked at my opponent as he stepped into the ring. He stood at about five-foot-nine inches, but he was broad, stocky. He worked out. I knew the gym he held a membership at as well as his workout schedule. Brutus had gotten all of the details. This punk fancied himself a tough guy, and he liked exercising his power over so-called thugs out on the street. While there was never any evidence of him raping women like his friend, Stephens, he used his badge to bully people in other ways. Little did he know as soon as he stepped in the ring all of that was about to be stripped from him.

I didn't give him any time. As soon as he entered the ring, I clocked him with a right jab, just to stun him.

"Shit!" he growled. "That was a fucking sucker punch!" he yelled and swung wildly, missing my face by almost a foot.

Easily dodging his second fist, I stepped back and grinned in his direction, shuffling on my toes. "We're just getting warmed up. Don't bitch out now," I challenged, knowing it would get under his skin to be called a bitch.

"Fuck you!" He charged me, attempting to grab me by the waist for a takedown.

Fucking slacker. I easily spun out of the way and landed an elbow to the back of his head, sending him staggering into the chain linked fence. I could hear cheers from the crowd around us, as well a yell from his buddy, Ramirez. Usually the sound of the crowd would spur me on, but I didn't need it that night. All I needed was the memory of Kay's face and the sound of her voice as she recounted what these officers did to her. Not only Stephens but these two fuckers who shut down any investigation into their friend, but then spent nearly a year stalking and harassing her.

"Ahh!" Waltz bellowed.

I hadn't even realized I'd hit him again. Next thing I knew I was landing another blow to Waltz's face and then to his left ribs.

"You son of a bitch!" he yelled.

"More fighting less talking!" I growled back. Words weren't needed in that moment. A swift ass kicking was, before I completed this fight and went to take on his buddy Ramirez effectively ending both of their careers.

"Ugh!" I grunted when one of his elbows landed in my ribs. The blow stung but it only served to piss me off more. I began wailing on him, blow after blow until he was knocked unconscious. Seeing him on the floor, eyes closed, snapped me back to reality and I stepped back, remembering that my aim wasn't to kill the bastard, even though everything in me was screaming to do just that.

"You fucking killed him! I'll shut this shit down!" Ramirez screamed from the sidelines.

That reminded me that I still had more work to do. I pinned Ramirez with my gaze, and for a split second his bravado slipped and a look of panic passed over his dark face. Less than a second later my feet were moving to the opening of the fence and I hopped down off the ring, landing a swift elbow to Ramirez' jaw.

"Aw, fuck! I'm gonna ki—" His threat was cut off by a right hook to his jaw.

"Like I told your friend, less talking more fighting, you fucking bitch!" I growled, taking another swing but missing. Ramirez was quicker than Waltz. My adrenaline spiked again, grateful for a little more competition. I felt a searing pain at my side when a punch to my ribs landed, but I didn't let that deter me. My rage propelled me forward even as Ramirez bellowed about being set-up and how he was going to ensure all of us would end up behind bars.

"Shut him the fuck up already!" Connor yelled from somewhere in the room and a number of guys cheered.

Ramirez went to respond but a cracking sound let out, when my knuckles made contact with his jaw. I vividly recalled the sight of his tooth flying from his mouth, blood spurting out from my vicious blow. My knuckles began to ache, as I hadn't even bothered wrapping them for the fight. I'd feel the pain in the morning something serious, but I wanted to feel my flesh against theirs as I took all of my anger out on them.

By the time I came to, Ramirez was on the ground as well. He was still conscious but barely.

"Everybody out!" Connor yelled behind me. "Show's over for now. Be back here tomorrow."

I kept my eyes on the pile of shit in front of me. My chest was heaving and my arms felt too heavy to lift above my chest but I felt good.

"Don't fucking touch me!" I growled, shaking off whoever had just placed a hand on my shoulder. I spun around to see Connor backing up, hands in the air.

"Hey," he stated cautiously, "just making sure you're still with us. We got shit to do."

I nodded and saw Brutus approach. "Wake them up." I motioned to Ramirez and Waltz, still in the ring, with my head.

Brutus walked over and waved some smelling salts under Ramirez's nose, resurrecting him. He picked him up and carried him to the ring before waving the smelling salt under Waltz's nose, also awakening him.

I pulled one of the metal folding chairs that rested along one of the columns and brought it to the ring, sitting down in front of the two shitheads.

"Who the fuck are you?" Waltz spat.

"Fucking idiots. Don't even know not to walk into a situation where they don't know all of the players." I shook my head. "I'm Joshua Townsend and you two dickheads fucked with what's mine."

"Townsend, as in—"

"Don't interrupt me while I'm speaking. Like I said, you fucked with someone very near and dear to me. My woman. My future wife. The *only* reason you two are still breathing is because I won't have any of my actions come down on her head. But trust me, when I say that doesn't mean you won't pay for what you've done."

"We didn't do shit!"

"Shut the fuck up! My patience only runs but so long. I told you once not to interrupt while I'm speaking. And I'm only willing to give either of you fucks a few more minutes of my time. So here's what's going to happen. You're both going to turn in your resignation letters to the Portland PD, stating exactly why you're unfit for duty. You will specifically detail how you coerced victims of Michael Stephens not to come forward. How you threatened and manipulated them. When you're arrested for your confessions, you will plead guilty. Chances are you'll get minimal if any time behind bars. I'll let the judicial system run its course on that matter, but you will never work in law enforcement again. You'll be lucky to get a job as a security guard at the fucking mall. And that's just for starters." I had more plans for these two. Plans that included running them out of Portland for good.

"You can eat shit! I'm not doing a goddamn thing!"

I chuckled and looked over at Connor and Brutus who both wore amused expressions as well.

"Fucking tough guy," Connor mumbled.

"You will. You know why?" I held my hand out and Brutus tossed me my cell phone. I scrolled through until the pictures I wanted were up, then turned my phone toward the two shitheads.

"That's my fiancée!" Ramirez yelled.

I turned the phone back to me. "So it is. Oh, and who is this?" I scrolled to the next picture, turning it to face Waltz.

He didn't say anything but his eyes widened. It was a picture of his parents as they slept in their own bed.

"You don't want to know how I got these images. But let's just say, pictures are the last thing you need to be fearful of when it comes to me. You messed with mine, I will mess with yours. Ask about me, gentlemen. I don't make idle threats. Your friend, Stephens, is going down, and you two are going with him. And anyone else who helped that motherfucker get away with the shit he's been doing."

I stood, cracking my neck, and stared down at the two now silent officers.

"Not so cocky anymore? I figured. It's late, and I've got a big day ahead of me tomorrow and so do you. It's time to go. Don't worry about your vehicle, Ramirez, my security will escort you back to your homes and help you type up your letters of resignation and confessions. They're helpful that way." I tossed both men a wink before turning and exiting the ring. I still wasn't completely satisfied but it was a start. It was time I got back to my woman, anyway.

Thirty minutes later, I entered the private apartment that I'd rented for Kay's and my stay while in Portland. I nodded at the security I'd had stationed outside of the door before slipping in and discreetly heading in the opposite direction of the master bedroom. I opted to shower in one of the guest bathrooms so I wouldn't wake Kay.

Fifteen minutes after I arrived, I eased my way into the master bedroom, a sense of ease enveloping me when I saw her sleeping form in the bed. I stared down at her, again, mesmerized by the way her auburn hair rested wildly across her face and pillow. I lifted the comforter and eased into bed, letting her body heat warm my naked frame.

She moaned a little when I wrapped an arm around her waist as I scooted closer to her. Her body instinctively melded to mine, allowing me to spoon her comfortably.

"Work ran late?" she mumbled, half-sleep.

I'd told her I had a few work meetings that I needed to get in that evening.

"Yeah."

"Everything okay?"

I lifted my head and planted a kiss to her temple. "Everything's fine. Go back to sleep." I inched in impossibly closer, not allowing for any space in between our bodies, and held her until her breathing steadied again. Soon after I fell asleep knowing that she was safe as long as she was in my arms.

* * *

Kayla

I hated the feeling of nervous anticipation that coursed through my entire body as I paced back and forth in front of the floor-to-ceiling windows in the high profile attorney's office. We were waiting for a journalist from Portland's number one news station to show up. Joshua and I arrived early at my insistence.

"Hey," Joshua called as he grabbed my hand, halting my pacing. "You can do this, all right?"

I inhaled, letting his assurances fill be up and replace my self-doubt. "I know. I just want to get it over with. I hate that this feels like so long in the making. And I hate even more the thought that every second we wait is another second he is out there, on the street, possibly …" I couldn't finish the thought.

"He's not."

I lifted my gaze to meet Joshua's. His eyes were darkened with anger.

"He's been put on unpaid leave since last week when the report was first filed."

I angled my head. "Really?"

Josh nodded.

I knew he had something to do with that. It was almost impossible to get that kind of swift reaction against police officers. It was another thing I opted not to question that morning. I'd noted the time he'd come in the night before along with his bruised knuckles and bruising on his ribs that morning. He'd been fighting and I knew in my heart it wasn't a random fight either. I'd ask about it later, but right then I was just glad that he was with me, assuring me that I could take this next step.

"Thank you for being here for me."

He pulled me into his arms so tightly all of the air was forced from my lungs. In my ear he whispered, "There's nowhere on this Earth I'd rather be. I love you more than I ever thought I could love again. I'm so proud of you." He held onto me until the lawyer re-entered the room, informing us that it was time.

Pulling back, I blinked away tears. "I love you more," I whispered back.

I followed Josh, my hand in his, as he led us out the door and toward the conference room where the interview was to take place.

I sat and looked around, swallowing the nervousness I felt. Joshua stood behind the news anchor, despite the protests from her camera crew. With one glare he'd assured them he wasn't going anywhere and they'd have to find a way to work around him. His position gave me the security I needed, as I could see him directly over the news anchor's head.

"Ms. Reyes, thank you for agreeing to this interview," Tracy, the news anchor, began in her professional tone.

Inhaling, I lifted my eyes to Joshua, who nodded at me.

"Please, call me Kayla. And thank you for being here. This has been a long time coming," I replied.

"Let's start at the beginning."

Over the next hour I recounted the sexual assaults I endured at the hands of Michael Stephens and the months of harassment and stalking from his fellow officers after my attempts to file charges.

"To my understanding, the prosecutor has already proceeded to move forward with filing charges."

I nodded, having heard the same thing just that morning.

"You know, most sexual assault victims do not have their names and faces made public. Can you tell me why you chose to make such a public statement?"

I lifted my gaze to meet those emerald greens of Joshua's. I could see the anger in his eyes as he'd listened to me explain my assault all over again, but there was a softness there, as well. It was meant just for me. It was a reassurance that I wasn't alone and whatever came of this, I wouldn't endure by myself as I had when it first happened. I didn't need to cower and change my appearance or style of dress or my address because Joshua wouldn't let anything or anyone touch me again. That gave me the security to answer her question.

"Because this needs to stop. Sexual assault is the second most reported act of police brutality and it's rarely discussed out in the open. I am not the only victim of Michael Stephens. I am one of at least five that we know about. I'm sure in the coming months we will learn of more. He's one officer but there are others out there just like him. And they overshadow the good officers that go out day after day to stop the very crimes officers like Stephens are committing. Most rape victims do not come forward because of cases like mine. When we do tell, we are treated worse than the perpetrator. It's that much worse when it's an officer whose job it is to serve and protect. This needs to end."

Finishing my speech, I sat up straighter in my chair and pushed out a breath, feeling lighter by having just shared my story.

"Thank you, Kayla. There is power in speaking out."

I nodded. "There certainly is."

CHAPTER 26

*J*oshua

I got out of my car and stared at the ranch-style, one story home. I'd promised Kay I would do the proposal the *right* way, by seeking her father's permission. Though, either way, Kayla Reyes was going to become Kayla Townsend. I was doing this for her.

I stepped back from my car and made my way to the front door of Kayla's parents' home. I'd been to their home a few times with Kayla in the last three months. It'd been that long since we'd returned from Portland. In that time, a lot had happened. Stephens was arrested. His shithead friends had resigned and subsequently were charged with the serious crime of tampering with a police investigation. The charges could land them six months to a year in jail. It wasn't much time but it was something. However, my reign on their payback wouldn't end.

As a result of Kay's interview six more women had come forward to report their stories of assault by Michael Stephens. He was being charged with every single one. The kicker was the dumb fuck had video evidence in his home of all of the assaults. That knowledge had nearly sent me over the edge. Thinking of how many times he'd watched how he assaulted those women. My woman. I knew after that, he couldn't go on living on this earth. I'd given Kay what she wanted. She'd had an opportunity to face him in a courtroom and he was sentenced to spend the rest of his life in prison. She'd gotten the satisfaction she needed of seeing him sentenced. But I wasn't going to let Stephens live much longer on this planet. Not after those videos.

But I wasn't on Kay's parents' doorstep to think about Stephens. With the ghosts of our past out of the way, it was time that Kay and I started focusing on our future. This was the first step.

"Joshua." Mr. Reyes pulled the door open before I even got a chance to knock.

Our eyes clashed. His mouth fell flat as he looked around, as if searching for someone.

"Kayla is at work."

He nodded. "I assume you're not here to bang on my windows and threaten me again, are you?" The twinkle in his eyes revealed his humor.

I grinned. "Not this time."

He nodded. "Come in."

I entered behind him over the threshold of his home.

"Mi esposa is still at work with one of the after school committees she's on." He waved his hand in the air, rolling his eyes. "I can't keep up with all of the activities and committees she runs for that school."

"I know. Kay told me Mrs. Reyes works late on Thursdays."

He nodded. "You want coffee or something to drink?"

I shook my head.

"Sit."

We both sat; he on the love seat, and me across from him in one of the arm chairs. "I figure you know why I'm here."

"You want to marry mi hija."

I nodded.

"Do you have a ring?"

"It's on Kayla's finger."

Mr. Reyes frowned. "Typically, the man asks the father before proposing."

"I'm far from typical, Mr. Reyes."

"I've always known that."

"I'm here because I promised Kay I would speak with you. She wanted me to ask for your permission."

"I'd meant what I said when you showed up here before. About you two's friendship. It wasn't supposed to be."

I frowned, not liking the sound of his words.

"Mi hija always had a special thing for you. Even as kids. I saw it. I just knew it would blow up in her face. When you began dating Chelsea I thought, good, she'll get over this little crush and find a nice boy to date. Someone more her class level. Less intense. But then Chelsea got sick and I watched my daughter lose her best friend and struggle with her growing attraction to you. It was hard, but I kept quiet. As did her mother. When she left I thought it was for the best ... I still do." He paused, looking me in the eyes.

I couldn't hold my tongue any longer. "Mr. Reyes, I came here because your daughter asked me to. As non-traditional as she can be sometimes, I know she still deeply respects you and her mother's place in her life. But make no mistake, whether you agree or not—" I stopped when Mr. Reyes began chuckling.

"I knew you wouldn't be able to hold out through my entire speech. Mi reina owes me twenty bucks."

I gave him a quizzical look.

"My wife and I knew this was coming. I told her I was going to bust your balls a little. I told her you wouldn't be able to hold back. But mi esposa said how you'd matured since eight years ago. You'd be more respectful and let me finish. Though we both knew you'd still propose to Kayla regardless of what I said. I hadn't even guessed you'd already proposed." He stood, grinning, and widened his arms.

I stood as well, welcoming his embrace.

"Welcome to the family. For what you did for Kayla in Portland alone, I'd be proud to call you my son."

I pulled back and nodded.

"You make sure my daughter remains happy and loved and protected."

"You don't have to worry about that," I assured. Kayla was mine to protect, love, and make sure she never went to bed without a smile on her face. I was happy to do all of the above and so much more.

EPILOGUE

Six Months Later
Joshua

"Where the fuck is Ty? If he makes my wedding one minute late, I'm kicking his ass all over this church!" I growled into the full-length mirror I stood in front of as I fixed the sleeves of my tuxedo shirt.

"I think there's some sort of rule about beating someone's ass in a church," Carter informed over my shoulder.

"God will understand," I quickly retorted and turned to my two brothers and father. Aaron held one of his youngest twins and my father held the other, while Carter held his youngest son. Diego sat to the right playing a video game. He, too, was half-dressed in a tuxedo like the rest of us.

"Just as long as my children or my wife don't get hurt, do what you have to do," Aaron spoke up, not taking his eye off of his feeding son. The twins were identical and I still had trouble telling them apart, so I had no idea which one he held. Though, he knew.

"I do—"

"Fucking bullshit!" Tyler finally came storming into the changing room we were all in.

Since Kayla's parents had insisted she marry in a church, we had chosen one of the oldest churches in the city of Williamsport. It was huge, as were the changing rooms. Perfect to fit a wedding party.

"I need a drink," Tyler grumbled as he passed the four of us, not bothering with any greetings.

We all watched as he stomped over to the aged scotch I'd brought to make a toast with my brothers and father before I walked down the aisle. He poured half a glass and swallowed in one gulp.

"You get fucking drunk at my wedding and I'll beat the shit out of you," I warned, calmly folding my arms over my chest.

"I can hold my damn alcohol," he spat over his shoulder, pouring another drink.

"There's only one thing that gets a Townsend man that upset," my father's voice rang out as he moved closer to me.

"A woman," Aaron, Carter, and I all responded in unison.

Tyler slowly lifted his head and gave us all a look, narrowing his eyes.

"My, my, my how the tables have turned," I chuckled.

"Fuck off. Sorry, Father," he apologized, staring at our father. "Anyway, someone wanted me to pass this to you." He pulled an envelope from the inside pocket of his tuxedo jacket.

"Someone?" I questioned, taking the pastel pink colored envelop and looking it over. I froze at the handwriting I saw on the front. It was my name but only one person I knew ever wrote my name with all of the loops in the cursive handwriting. "Who gave this to you?" I demanded.

Tyler gave me a half shrug. "Older lady, said you invited her and her husband. Blue eyes. She reminded me of ..." He snapped his fingers, trying to recall.

"Chelsea," I blurted out. It was her handwriting. I had invited Mr. and Mrs. Armstrong because I'd felt compelled to. Kayla had gone to visit them a few times over the last few months. She'd thought it was the right thing to do to invite them. They happily accepted.

The air suddenly left from the room. "I need a minute," I told my brothers and father, looking up at the four of them. Thankfully, they didn't ask questions; instead leaving me alone to read the letter, taking the children with them.

Slowly, I opened the letter and scanned the words. This was Chelsea's handwriting all right. My heartbeat quickened as I began to read.

Dear Josh,

If you're reading this, it means that I'm gone. I expected that. Something always told me that I was not going to be your forever. I've made peace with it. And if you're reading this on your wedding day, as I've instructed my parents to give this to you, it means you've accepted that as well. It makes me happy to know you've moved on and found love again. We were kids when we first fell in love, and chances are, in time that love would've faded. That is the real reason why I didn't want you to propose to me. What we had was a puppy love. It was real and it was wonderful, but the woman you make your wife will know the grown up love that you have to offer. And she is one lucky lady.

Thank you for loving me the way that you did and as well as you did. You've made my last days on this Earth worth living. I can only hope and pray that my death didn't cause you too much pain. My purpose in writing this letter is to release you from the past so that you can truly move on with your future. Now go get married.

P.S. If it's Kayla you're marrying then my prayers have truly come true. ;)

THE LAST SENTENCE of her letter was what stole my breath. I needed to see Kayla. For what, I didn't know, but I needed to get to her. I threw the door of the changing room open to find my brothers and father all staring at me, startled.

"Where's Kayla?" I didn't bother waiting for anyone to respond. I stormed down the hallway toward the other end of the church where the women's changing room was. I heard my brothers and father call my name behind me but I only had one purpose and that was to get to my wife.

"You can't be in here!" Michelle screeched once she opened the door of the changing room after I'd pounded on it.

"I need to see my wife!" I looked over her head for a glimpse of Kay.

"Michelle's right, Josh. You can't be here. It's bad luck," Patience spoke up.

"Luck has nothing to do with this."

"Son." My mother finally got in the mix, folding her hands in front of her.

Out of the corner of my eye, I saw Kay's mom standing with the three other women. The men in my family would all try to kick my ass if I bum rushed their women to find mine but that was a risk I was willing to take at that moment.

"I just need to speak with her."

"Close your eyes."

I perked up at the sound of Kayla's voice.

"Kay—"

"Do it, Joshua, or I'm not coming out," she insisted.

I growled.

"Ladies, tell me when his eyes are closed."

All four women gave me the stink eye.

"Fine." I closed my eyes.

"They're closed," Patience called out.

"Move him to the bathroom door."

"What the hell?" I groaned.

"Do it, Josh, or I'll call this wedding off."

"Yeah fucking right," I growled.

I was moved until my back hit a wall.

"Okay, he's there. We're leaving now."

I heard footsteps exit and a door close soon after. The room went quiet.

"Hold out your hand."

I did as instructed and was met with Kay's outstretched hand. I wrapped my fingers around hers. We were separated by a door. I couldn't see her but we were touching. In that moment, it was enough.

"You got a letter from Chels, too?" she asked.

I swallowed. "You too, huh?"

"She's reliable like that. Even showing up for our wedding day."

I heard the thickness in Kay's voice.

We were silent for a few moments until I spoke.

"She knew … you and me. Somehow, she knew."

"She wished us luck in my letter. Said she would be looking down on us to make sure we were happy." Kayla got choked up on the last word. "You always say we were meant to be. It took me so long to really believe it."

"I'll spend every day for the rest of our lives making sure you continue to believe it. You and our little one." I tightened my hand around hers.

She let out a small giggle. I knew she was touching her still flat abdomen. We hadn't told a soul just yet but the evidence of our love would be showing soon enough. In about seven months or so.

"I think I've loved you since the first day we met."

"You only *think?*" I chided.

"Jerk," she mumbled, causing me to laugh.

"I've loved you in more ways than one since I was twelve years old. I'd thought I lost you once. I was so angry I couldn't see straight. Thank you for coming back to me."

"Thank you for making me remember how to love. And for being my hero when I needed one."

"You were your own hero."

"I forgot who I was for a little while. You helped me remember again. I will spend the rest of my life loving you for that and for the life you've already given me."

"You won't ever leave me again, right?" I'd move heaven and Earth to keep that from happening, but I still needed to hear her say it.

"Wild horses couldn't drag me away."

"I love you, Kay."

"I love you, Joshua Tobias Townsend."

I grinned, loving when she used my entire name.

"Now, let's go get married before my makeup is completely ruined."

"I'll meet you at the aisle, sweetheart." I gave her hand one last squeeze before releasing it and moving to the door, opening it.

Four very irate women stared at me but I felt like I was on top of the world. I gave them all my most charming grin and kissed my mother on the cheek.

"Make sure my girl gets down that aisle safe and sound," I looked over and told Kay's father who was arriving from down the hallway, before sauntering off.

I clapped as soon as I entered the changing room where my brothers, father, and nephews were. "Let's get me married!"

* * *

Kayla

Perfection. That's exactly what the moment was. Pure and total perfection, as Joshua and I danced under the starlit sky at Townsend Manor. It was still early spring but the weather was warm enough for us to host our reception outside.

"You're going to make me dizzy and cause me to fall," I giggled as Joshua spun me around yet again on the dance floor.

"No chance of your falling when I'm around, Kay." He kissed the tip of my nose.

"You're such a sap."

"For you? I sure the hell am."

Smiling, I lifted on my tiptoes, feeling satisfied when Josh leaned down to press his lips to mine. We continued to dance and I was able to catch a glimpse of the guests who danced and ate at the surrounding tables. Something caught my eye.

"Look." I jutted my head in the direction of Josh's friend, Damon.

Josh looked over his shoulder and narrowed his gaze. "Damon and your friend, huh?"

I shrugged and nodded. Sandra had indeed become a friend over the last few months. So much so that both Monique and our niece, Kennedy, served as our flower girls in the wedding.

I bit my lower lip as I took in the expression on Sandra's face. "He's hovering."

"He's harmless," Josh retorted.

I raised my eyebrows at my obviously crazy husband. "Damon is a lot of things and harmless isn't one of them." I bit my lower lip in worry. The hungry look in his dark eyes as he peered down on Sandra was anything but harmless.

Josh grinned and leaned in, pressing a kiss to my lips. "You're right. He's about as dangerous as they come. But to Sandra? He's harmless. Now back to you and me." He lowered his head again and my breath was stolen by the kiss he landed.

"I love you," he whispered against my lips once he pulled back.

"Forever?"

"And then some, sweetheart."

Closing my eyes, I leaned my head on his shoulder, letting the music and the feeling of safety completely enrapture me. I could stay like this forever.

READY FOR YOUNGEST Townsend brother Tyler? Catch his story in click here to read For Keeps.

INTERESTED IN THE other members of the Underground fighting ring?
Check out Damon and Sandra's book, Just Say the Word here.
Watch Connor fall in love in No Coincidence here.
And what about that mysterious doctor? Meet Jacob in Jacob's Song here.

Thank you for reading!

Looking for updates on future releases? I can be found around the web at the following locations:

FaceBook private group: Tiffany's Passions Between the Pages
Website: TiffanyPattersonWrites.com
FaceBook Page: Author Tiffany Patterson
Email: TiffanyPattersonWrites@gmail.com

More books by Tiffany Patterson

THE BLACK BURLES SERIES

BLACK PEARL

Black Dahlia
Black Butterfly
Forever Series
7 Degrees of Alpha (Collection)
Forever
Safe Space Series
Safe Space (Book 1)
Safe Space (Book 2)

RESCUE FOUR SERIES

ERIC'S INFERNO

Carter's Flame
Non-Series Titles
This is Where I Sleep
My Storm
Aaron's Patience

Printed in Great Britain
by Amazon

10860008R00165